PRAISE FOR EVER

"Harn's entertaining debut uses super powers as a metaphor to delve into class politics in an alternate America."

— *PUBLISHER'S WEEKLY*

"If you want a gritty approach to super heroes with a literary twist that still levels buildings, has aliens, and government conspiracies, don't sleep on this."

— **WAYNE SANTOS**, AUTHOR OF *THE CHIMERA CODE*

"Gorgeous literary writing, sweeping themes about how capitalist gain has replaced empathy in American society, and Darby's usual amazing dialogue."

— **SUNYI DEAN,** AUTHOR OF *THE BOOK EATERS*

"This was a fascinating, fast-paced, yet lyrical read about what commercialized super heroism might look like. Loved it and highly recommend!"

— **SHELLY CAMPBELL,** AUTHOR OF *UNDER THE LESSER MOON*

"★ ★ ★ ★ ★ - *Ever The Hero* is highly recommended for fans of LGBTQ+ fiction, superhero genre readers and sci-fi fans alike."

"*Ever the Hero* gives you complex social class commentary that grapples with the nasty visuals of some superhero stories, and even some ideas about the real-world implications of superpowers that feel like the next logical step after *Watchmen*."

"Superheroes and an alien threat within a dystopian society - all these individually, and seemingly endlessly, fascinating things are combined in Darby Harn's *Ever the Hero*."

A Country Of Eternal Light

Darby Harn

FAIR
PLAY
BOOKS

ISBN: 978-1-7370097-0-2

Fair Play Books

darbyharn.com

Cover art by Al Hess.

www.cultofsasha.com

Please leave your review on Amazon and at Goodreads. Thank you for your support!

Freedom

I will not follow you, my bird,
I will not follow you.
I would not breathe a word, my bird,
To bring thee here anew.
I love the free in thee, my bird,
The lure of freedom drew;
The light you fly toward, my bird,
I fly with thee unto.
And there we yet will meet, my bird,
Though far I go from you
Where in the light outpoured, my bird,
Are love and freedom too.

George William Russell

For Maeve

A Country Of
Eternal Light

CHAPTER ONE

There is success in death.

Fish flop in confusion as the sea peels back to the mainland. Dinner tonight. Breakfast tomorrow, if I'm thinking of tomorrow. I leave them in the goopy, gasping muck. I keep walking. I am far now, farther than I can run when the tide returns. Bereft water jostles in pitted rock. Strands of seaweed coil around my feet. I feel your pull.

Here I am.

This buzz in the air. The tide coming back, surely. I look up, expectant. Meteors rip through the blue, faster than any wish can catch. Broken stalks of rainbows on the horizon. Comets like white lies. Three more today, competing with the big one they call Medusa, with all her snake tails.

I wait for my success.

The sea must have run off to the States with everyone else. That buzz again. Louder. Closer. The turboprop from the mainland comes out of nowhere. The plane hasn't been over in weeks. Most days, high tide swamps the eastern horn of the island, the bit of Inishèan that can accommodate a runway. Right next to the cemetery.

Take offs and landings.

The sea is out. The plane is able to make a landing. He might have medicine, the pilot. Food. He'll have room, for the trip back to Galway. Someone will get delivered today.

I inch back through the green sludge of exposed seabed. Why am I careful? Why am I in a hurry to see someone else get what they want? The envy will keep me warm, I suppose. I run through the beach grass, out to the low road curving with the island. A dozen or so hopeful passengers run toward the landing strip from the village, tufts of clothes puffing out of their luggage.

Buckled tarmac rattles the plane, but she lands. Props still whirring. He's not going to be long on the ground, the pilot. I climb the drumlin cushioning the airstrip from the tides. The stranded tourists all clamor for a spot on the plane, as they've done every time since the ferry quit and stranded them here three months back. Three months.

Feels like three years.

Eight seats. A hundred people. More, like. I'm not envious. A few people pay their way on, and then the plane takes off again. Men and women fall down on the tarmac, heads in their hands. Denied, again.

Colm's little hatchback putts down the road toward the airstrip. What's he out here for? He honks through the tourists, and pulls in to the car park. Someone gets in. A man. Lord God. There's someone.

Someone has come to the island.

○

Someone scratches at the front door downstairs. Like they can't reach the handle. I get this weightlessness in my chest, thinking it's you. The lock turns and she's always opening the door, Ma, letting out the heat, the life of this house.

Away with you, she says.

That dog. Border Collie. I know without moving a muscle. Not that I could move. Legs sore from standing the whole night through beside your cot. Sheets white and unwrinkled from the day you left them. I limp to the window. The dog scratches at the refuse bins, overflowing at their tops. He knocks one over and weeks of empty cans and bottles roll down the low road curving with the island. Inishèan from one end to the other is karst stone, but on the eastern coast it bunches, in earth and grass.

Aoife comes up the road. Morning sun behind her. Every loose, manic strand of her hair a cyclone of fire. Litre bottles under each arm. She picks up a pair of knickers that must have fell out someone's bag yesterday. She pockets them and then she sees me in the window. The statue. She smiles like someone who's been caught stealing.

The smile is gone before I've left the window. Aoife gives a knock on the door, for what I don't know and she's down there, calling for Ma. Pots and pans shift in the sink. The faucet gushes and then sputters. The pipes groan. The house aches. The house has given up all its blood.

"Iris," Aoife says. "You up, love?"

Aoife wads up the brittle, yellowed newspaper carpeting the living room into an ever-expanding ball. The rubbish bin lifts off the floor with the stuffed bag as she pulls it out. A sticky note falls from the cupboard. CLEANING SUPPLIES. I strain my thumb reapplying it. Why bother. All my memos fray and curl and go to the floor, where they pick up fuzz and dust on their adhesives or end up stuck to the newspaper I put down. RINSE YOUR DISHES. TURN OFF THE TAP. KEEP THE DOOR LOCKED.

"Why are you bothering with that, Aoife?"

"You've got gnats in here," she says.

"There's no one going to come by and collect it."

"Still and all. Did you hear?" Aoife says, her voice a whisper as she shadows me through the kitchen. What do we whisper for when we gossip. We're all talking the same shite. "Someone got off the plane. From the States. He's staying in the apartment above the pub."

"Down at the pier?"

"He brought Colm a case of whiskey. The Jameson's."

Of course, he's money. The flight from the mainland had to cost

3

him near as much as it did getting out of the States, with oil being what it is. The whiskey, God only knows. A case of whiskey will keep Colm in customers for weeks. The pub is the only thing still open down there.

I don't know what this man could be here for now. He must be one of those idiots you see on the telly. Going out to the rims of those new volcanoes opening up in the Pacific, or come to surf the giant waves here. Boys chasing their deaths, like. Boys always chase death.

I suppose they think they can catch it.

I look out across the angry bay. "What's he here for?"

"He barely speaks. Barely drinks. If he nurses a tit the way he does a whiskey... I gave it a go. Nothing doing."

"Is he for men?"

She shrugs. "I don't think so. How would you know?"

"Have you never met a gay person, Aoife?"

The hair falls back in her eyes. "I'm not one for minding other people's business."

"She says, fresh from her surveillance of the American."

"I've read all the books in the library, Mairead."

The cupboards are bare. Cargo ship used to come two, three times a week. It's not been since the sea went strange. There's not much beyond fish we catch. The lambs we slaughter. The eggs the chickens yield.

Aoife sets a pot on the burner. We've electricity and little else. She strains the litre bottles she brought with her into a Pyrex bowl she sets in the center of the pot. She turns the burner on low so it's a slow boil and puts the lid over the bowl, upside down. Steam condenses on the surface, and runs down the handle in little drops down into the glass, salt free.

"Look at that," she says. "Bleeding science, that is."

"Why are you boiling water?"

"The reservoir is dry, Mairead. It's been for days now." Did she tell me? Did I care? "I saw this on the telly. I figured it was just more government shite, but it's brilliant."

4

"Is the tide out?"

She brushes the hair out her eyes. "It's in enough I got this without any bother. I've got to refill these again before I head up to the nursing home. Do you want to come along?"

I look out into the empty yard. "I don't think so."

"You could come back to the home, for an hour or so. I can pour a bath for your Ma in the staff loo, yeah?"

Aoife sets the rubbish by the back door. Most of it has just gone out into the fields since the collection stopped.

"Youse are out of the diapers, I take it."

"I don't know, Aoife."

"Come back with us. And then I can pour you one. We can scrub up together, like we did as girls. They just threw us in the sink together, our mothers. Like dishes. What do you say?"

Ma shuffles into the kitchen, coat on like she's going somewhere. She sees the radio and remembers.

"Not today," I say, but she switches it on anyway.

Six past and now time for today's obituaries. Katie Burke, Kilmurvey, Co. Galway, 14th October, suddenly, sadly missed. Iranian quake toll rises. Russian oil fields under water. The Pope condemns American abortion initiative for all remaining pregnancies. Scientists hold vigil over Saturn, her rings scattered like a snowdrift across a country road. All her moons buckshot. Jupiter suffers the most, swollen and bruised like an aging prizefighter, determined to die in the ring.

The government handed out these little LED tickers. Alarm clocks, like, to put on the refrigerator. Counts down the seconds until the rogue black hole intersects the orbit of earth. A year from now. That's all we have left.

If that.

The tides will drown us first. One of the comets will hit us. A planet or a moon will, or comes close enough to yank the earth from its orbit. What difference does it make? What difference is cancer? Parkinson's. A heart attack. A bullet. A car. A black hole. All our deaths are projectiles, hurtling through blood streams or interstellar space or dark coastal roads at targets with no proper sense of the size of the barrel they're swimming in.

I switch the radio off. "I don't want to hear this."

Ma goes behind me and throws it back on. "This is my only getting out, girl."

"You brushed your hair today," Aoife says and Ma sees Aoife in her scrubs and she becomes anxious. Breathless. "Did you brush your teeth? You have to keep your schedule, Iris. Like we said. It helps you remember."

"Don't say it," she says. "You've not put me in the home."

"Not this again, Ma. You are home. Aoife's here to visit."

"Aoife," she says, remembering again. "Aoife's been helping me while you were away in the States, girl."

"I've been home, Ma. Since Da."

"Aren't we meeting you at the pier?"

"Is that what you've got your coat on for?"

She grips the belt, surprised. "Caoimhe... Caoimhe and I are..."

"Who's this Caoimhe you're always on about?"

"We are going to... now I just had it. Do you know? Do you know what I'm saying? Do you know?"

Lord God. She goes on, and on, and on. *Do you know? Do you know? Do you know?* as if the more she says it, the closer she'll be to unlocking whatever riddle it possesses.

Do you know?

"Go and watch telly, Ma. I'll put a pot on."

She shuffles into the living room. TV bristles with static. Water gurgles. I pour a cup. The pill bottles in the cupboard have gone from baby rattles to empty change jars.

"You're doing better than we are at the home," Aoife says.

Ma can't reach the cupboards. She's like a child. I've found pills stuffed down the crevices of her recliner. Under the soles of her shoes. Part of me thinks she's doing this consciously, but so little she does now is conscious. I grind a Selegiline to powder and drop it in the cup with a tea bag. Before her sickness, Ma was clever. She saw the lines in everything, even people, all their cracks and fissures.

"You've been careful with the morphine?" I say.

She nods. "I don't know how much longer I can hold on to it, though. I've been trying to tell you, Mairead. I don't know how much longer we can do this."

"You've been ringing Dublin?"

"Every day. And every day they say the same bleeding thing. They're on repeat, they are. There's no petrol. And so there's no drugs. There's no relief. There's no transporting the residents to the mainland. We're on our own."

"What about the news? Have you tried them?"

"Do you maybe want to come back and make some calls?"

I stir the tea. "I don't know."

"You roped me into this volunteering business. I'm no nurse. I'm no administrator, Mairead."

The spoon rattles around the cup, swirling with its own vortex. "Neither am I."

Even before the black hole was discovered and everyone decided they were relieved of paying their taxes, money for health services was scarce in the islands. For years before all this, we couldn't find a general practitioner to help cover for Da when he was sick, let alone eventually replace him. The order to evacuate came down and our help stopped coming. I went from volunteering the three times a week at the home to shaming any able bodied girl on the island to cover the place full time.

I tried.

I tried to maintain the rotation where I worked a few days a week. The volunteers dwindled to Aoife and one or two others. I slept there. I ate there. I lived there and every half hour I called home to check on him.

He's grand, Ma said, when he was already gone.

Aoife sits at the table. Knackered. "We're nothing without you."

"I should never have started with that place. I should never have left him... I should never have left him."

"Mairead... I know I can't understand..."

No one can understand. No one can know this fear, this exile from you and don't say it's forever. Say there's more. Say there's a God and Heaven and reasons, even if God and Heaven and reasons exist only to hurt me.

"It was an accident," Aoife says.

The dog sniffs around the edge of the stile outside, before trotting down the road. An accident, she says. As if it's no one's fault.

As if no one is to blame.

Ma *tsk tsks* at some impropriety on the telly. Some grievance she holds but can never bring herself to say.

The teaspoon spins around to me. "Do you want any, Aoife?"

All that hair falls over her eyes. She's nodded off, Aoife. I'll let her sleep. One of us should sleep. I take the tea into the living room. More blather on the telly about the end of the world.

This gleam dawns in Ma's eyes. "You spiked this."

"Don't pour it out."

"That's who I raised. A drinksmith." The cup jitters in her hand. "I'm always having to pour you out."

The human puppets on the telly distract her. She slurps at her tea as they hop and skip from one disaster to another.

"Did you hear this, girl? They said there's a wandering black hole. What does that mean? Three years. Three years they've known. It's been three years since your father died."

She lives it all over again. The loss of him. Ma looks around in a daze. This empty house.

"Mairead. Where's Declan?"

The two of them trail me out the front door. The noise they make. Cans tied to a bumper. *Where's Declan? Do you know? It was an accident, Mairead. You have to forgive her. You have to make peace.*

Do you know, do you know, do you know.

Gravestones list in the beach grass.

They make an uneasy pavement to the crumbling eastern shore. Half the cemetery gone to the tides. Bones exposed in the calved earth. The waves leave nothing but stones and boulders. I follow the path I've worn through the grass to the one I made yours.

All I have.

The wind scattered your flowers in the night. Waves loosen the scrim of wire covering the small shrine on the rock I've made for you, holding in place the little toy boats circling around your picture.

Mo leanbh. Mo stór.

Your name painted on the rumpled stone. The ocean rushes in against blunt rock. Spray showers me as the waves recoil. Headstones wash out to sea and then return as torpedoes. The wave barrels in again and this goes on, endlessly, as it will after we have gone. The last sound on earth surely the thunder of waves.

I close my eyes.

Absorb the violence. The unnerving way the stone squeals, like the whine of a bad axle. I wait for a wave to jump the track and take me. My grief like the tides. No rhythm. Only this fierce rush to find the end, but there's no end. It's like that cartoon, isn't it? The Looney Tunes, like. When he falls through the floor, and keeps on going.

Who was it did that?

I don't remember. I forget everything. I feel like I'm forgetting you. I hold to all our moments but they squeeze through my memory and i'm just left holding this empty shape of you.

But you knew all their names, didn't you?

The cartoon characters. You were so smart. So good. You loved coming out here. Chasing the rabbits. You'd disappear in the beach grass and Lord God. The stop you put in me. If you'd wandered off the beach. If you'd fallen in the water. I'd call for you, the wind alive with your laughter and then you'd come out of the grass, every time.

Here I am.

O

Morning now.

The day like a headache. The sea merciful for once. Exposed shells gleam in the sun. Seals bask on a distant promontory. The carpet of Galway Bay rolls out, as if to say, come.

Come, Mairead.

Come to the far country. Mushy seaweed sucks on my shoes. The rock bristles with possibility and this scratching distracts me. That bleeding dog is back on the shore, barking at me like I'm somewhere I'm not supposed to be. I look back and he's standing there, too.

The American.

CHAPTER TWO

The American looks back toward the shore with that pensive look about him some people have, like they feel they're always being watched. Skin so tight you can see the cracks forming.

"Are you ok?" he says.

I can barely see the shore. "Where did you come from?"

"Iowa."

"Where's that?"

He points east. "If you keep walking that way, about 6000 miles."

"Couldn't get a flight out?"

The face on him. He doesn't know where he's come to, The American. What. "I thought I saw someone... I thought I saw you."

Water spills in my shoes. That first lull. That cold, hard tug and you're there. You're just there. Something brushes my arm and I jump. He's got his hand on my elbow, the American. This fear in his eyes. And this want. I know this want. This blind, drunk hunger. What's he out for?

"We should head back," he says.

His hand slips to mine. His hands are freezing. White as snow.

The rising tide chases us back to dry land. Stone teeth stabs my hands as I stumble up the steps of the island to rock wrinkled like brains.

I crawl back to your rock. He sees your pictures, your boats and me clinging to the wire and he wants to run. He wants to scrape himself off the shame of interrupting me but it's like he's landed on another world of greater gravity and now can't move. Is it this place. Is it you. Capturing everyone you touch. You were always touching me, learning, connecting and the pictures hold me. The toy boats. The idea you're going to walk out of the grass.

"I'm sorry," he says.

"Did you come here to die?"

He's like a shit version of a ventriloquist's dummy, his mouth opening and closing. The words out of sync. "I came to scatter my dad's ashes."

"You must have been close, the two of you."

He fishes a fat pill bottle from the inside of his coat. Full up with gray. "This is the closest we've ever been."

"You didn't get on?"

"They got divorced when I was three, and then... he'd come around sometimes, but then disappear. For ages."

"No one gets divorced here," I say. "Even now."

"My mom was Wife Number Two. Two of Four."

"Fuck."

"Well. He had to complete the set."

"And how is she, your ma?"

"She's ok. I don't know. She keeps saying she doesn't understand it, you know. All this. No one understands."

"I don't care," I say.

He starts to say something. What do you say. "Can I get you anything? Coffee or something?"

"Thank you, no."

"I saw you, and... I see you. Every day. I come out here and try to... I don't know. I can't bring myself to do it and you're out here every day in the rain. In the dark."

I look off to the sea, drowning without me.

"I see you, and... you're so strong. You must be very strong."

My arms unbutton. "I don't feel strong."

"You are. You have no idea."

"You have no idea..." My head shakes, my own mouth open to words with no form. "You've no idea."

"I wish I knew what to say."

"Everybody does," I say. "Everyone says you've got to get on. Think of yourself. He was all I ever was. I don't even remember my life before. Isn't that strange?"

"No."

"I called home just five minutes before. You're watching him, I said. Aren't you? *Ah, he's grand.* That's what she said. Ma. And he was already out the yard, probably."

Our house is far enough back on the road to be safe, or so I thought. That day a rogue wave rolled over the eastern end of Inishèan, all the way to the house. Washed away hundreds of years of stone and wood and history.

My future.

"I'm sorry," he says. What else is there to say.

"Why here? For your father's ashes, like?"

"Our family is from here," he says. "That's one of the stories anyway. All anyone knows for sure is we left during the Famine. In one story we were horse thieves. We were chased out of Fermanagh into Connacht and finally America. We changed our name. I always thought it was because Irish couldn't get work back then, but they chiseled the O off the front of O'Flaherty from the tombstones. Like they were erasing themselves."

"They erased the tombstone?"

"I think we're always trying to change the past."

If I could. "I lost my Da, too."

"I'm sorry."

"Cancer. Yeah. The liver. No mercy in it. Ma has Parkinson's.

And then all this. One, two, three. Like that. And then I got pregnant with him, and I thought..."

What did I think? What was I thinking.

His eyes skirt around me. "I'm sorry."

"Is the plane not coming back for you?"

"Yeah, I'll call him. Haven't found the right spot, I guess. I keep coming back here to the cemetery, but..."

"Don't get stuck here."

"There are worse places." Finally, he looks at me. "Sorry to bother you. If I can get you anything at all..."

I take the framed photo of you from under the wire over all your things. I don't know why. "Just two days before, this was."

His hand starts toward mine. I mean for him to take the picture, but he doesn't. He pockets his hands.

"He's beautiful," he says.

"Do you have children?"

"No."

"You're blessed," I say. "To not fear for them. To not have to live with their dying. Do you know what I mean?"

"I can't," he says. He's the first person since you've gone to not hide their ignorance. "You don't sleep out here, do you?"

"The Garda kicked me out after dark. Then the waves became too much and they left me to it. I don't know what I do. Sometimes I'm here, and sometimes I'm in the house."

He just stands at the edge of the rock. He'll fall off.

"Are you money, then?" I say.

"Money?"

"What is it you do you can afford the plane?"

"I worked for a bank," he says.

"Worked?"

"People aren't exactly paying their mortgages anymore."

"Still and all. You didn't fly here on air."

"Mostly it was vodka." Waves punch the rocks. He turns his back to the spray. "What I wanted to be was a writer."

"Did you ever try and get published?"

"I sold a book, actually. About ten years ago or so."

"Doesn't that make you a writer, then?"

"I suppose if you keep writing."

"Haven't you?"

"Actually, I never stopped. I could never finish anything. I just... froze up. Listen to me. Like it matters."

"I used to write songs." I put the picture back. "Would I have heard of your book? Are you famous?"

"Only with my mom."

"Your Ma must worry about you."

"She's wondering when I'm coming home."

"You should," I say. "You should be getting on."

He's caught again, between leaving and going. Days he's been coming out here to the shore, to let go. And he can't. What is it that you're waiting for. What is it you think you'll find.

Do you know.

"Well, I'll get going," he says.

"He loved to come here," I say. "Declan. He thought the tower up there was a boat, like. A shipwreck. You see it?"

The hollowed drum of the round tower lurks in the fog on the cliffs, the center of a universe of orbiting birds.

He nods, the American. "Yeah, ok."

"Ah, it's class. Amazing view. Westernmost monastery in all Europe. He thought it was a boat, stuck up there on the cliffs. He had such an imagination." This pain. This ripping my heart out like a weed, every time it grows back. "The tower would be a proper place for you. Watch your step though. Don't go down a puffing hole."

"Puffing hole?"

"A hole, like. Right through the island. The water will come up *whoosh* you know when there's a big sea. But it's not marked, so. The ground just opens. Don't go falling in."

"I'll be careful," he says.

"Don't fall."

"I won't."

That hunger again in his eyes. That need. He wants to leave, but he doesn't. He wants to scatter the ashes, but he doesn't. He wants it to be over, but he doesn't.

"Yeah, so. Get a start, while there's no rain. What's the rain, anyways. You've a jacket on."

"Maybe you can show me the way."

I haven't been up there since. Something pulls at me. The same force from the sea. "You'll find it. It's a good day for it."

The waves fill in the silence.

"I'm Gavin, by the way."

"Mairead."

"Are you going to be ok?" He flinches, knowing how fierce and stupid that question is the moment it leaves his lips. "I mean... you're not going back out there. Are you?"

"It just came up."

He clenches his smile. "I'll see you around."

"Aren't you leaving?"

He smiles, the American. "I'll see you."

The island is somehow different with a visitor. You see it as they see it. The bubble of our insularity punctured. The myth of our peace. Government notices paper the plywood covering the doors and windows of houses around the pier in Kilbanna.

EVACUATE IMMEDIATELY.

Reed-legged cranes stalk through heaps of seaweed and wounded sandbags, pecking out crabs deserted by the sea. A storm surge left the ferry half on the road. Cut sections of the hull curve over sand-bags like ramparts, the island a castle sinking in its own moat.

Feels so empty now. Inishèan was a popular tourist destination before all this, mostly for weekenders thinking they were completing the circuit of all the Aran Islands. Inishèan is not properly part of the

Arans, trailing dot-dot-dot off the unfinished sentence of Ireland just five miles to our south.

We're more a stray comma.

You hear all sorts of theories on the crescent shape of Inishèan in the pub. The island is the ruin of a great ring fort erected in the sea; it's the remnant of a volcanic crater. Most visitors came for an ancient monastery built on a precipice on the cliffs over the Atlantic. A nameless monk founded the monastery in the 7th century. Monks kept the monastery for over five hundred years, until some of it collapsed into the sea during a violent storm. For the near millennium after, the monastery has been the domain of the birds which supposedly gave the island its name.

Gulls with black cowls perch on irregular fences of piled stone making a patchwork of green-flecked fields rolling up the hump of the island. The cliffs behind them protect the island from waves that have washed away Inverin, Rossaveal and Westport on the mainland, but Inishèan is no sanctuary. The houses clinging to the shallow slopes of the inner crescent will just be the last to go.

I see him up there on the high road. The American. His shape strange. Alien. The dog chases him on his bike, like it used to chase all the boys and girls peddling back to the pier as the evening ferry left. Like he's chased me these last months since you've gone, out in the grass and on the rocks and in the sea looking for you. Wherever I go, the dog follows. He only leaves with the dark.

There is no following him.

Some nights I go down the beach. No light but the stars. The accretion disk of the black hole growing like a tumor in Sagittarius. The branches of craggy trees make electric arcs by the battered moon. I could be the only person on Inishèan. The only person in the world. My only company a dog I can't keep. Stray cats picking through the mounting rubbish festering down at the harbor. Chickens roosting in the ledges of boarded up windows. Horses grazing in the remains of an ancient church. The island a preserve, or a dream of the future where nature has reclaimed the world and man was a memory. Sometimes a plane will pass overhead, before disappearing to the shuttered west. Everything passes through, and over. Nothing and no one can last, but the island, refuge to lost creatures.

O

Fog reduces the world to your grave.

I can't see past the headstone. Your name. Your life, chiseled in the gap between my thumb and forefinger. Two years. A moment. A lifetime. Time slows in fog, like it must as you fall into the black hole. Death drawn out to infinity. A moment that is all moments.

Here I am.

After Da, someone came to the door every day. They stopped me on the road, weeks on, the first I'd seen them since he'd passed. Death is a public thing in Ireland. So much of life here is private. Separate. We all come to this. We all go through this, so you make yourself known, as if the effort will indemnify you somehow.

No one sees me.

No one comes to the house. No one comes to the cemetery. I am this repulsive force. I am this living, breathing vision of the future and we are all going to go through this. We are all going to come to this but no one wants to know now. No one wants to see or to hear or to believe. One, aye. Two's as maybe. Not the lot of us. Not the whole bleeding world, swept out to sea like a helpless child.

O

Stars fall.

Dozens at a time. The sky like wallpaper that won't stick. Comets like scabs of dried glue. Beach grass gives to ground thin and spongy, crunching with the shells emptied of urchins, crabs and snails. The Border Collie trawls across the green, his nose sniffing at the craters of rabbit holes. The lost limbs of crabs. The pearlescent medico of a bird skull. He smells of rain. The salted air. Thorns and twigs stud the matted net of his hair. His paws pink and raw. I expect him to follow me the short walk home, but he runs off through the field. A bike leans against the piled stone fence bordering the road. He's out here, the American. He's out here in the dark somewhere.

○

Days of frustrated sea. Sky full of comets it won't release. The apocalypse is such a tease. Won't you come on, then? All of human history you've been flirting with us.

Won't you just get it over with.

That dog scratches against the rock behind me. The American not far behind. Lord God, the two of them. Strays both.

"Hey," he says. Like we're friends.

"There won't be any runway left for your man."

He looks off west. "I think we're all out of runway."

"It's a long swim."

"I've been working out," he says. He glances me, sideways like. He's joking. He's testing me.

"Do you want to scatter the ashes here? Is that why you come back? You're more than welcome."

He sits on a rock. "I was going to bring you some coffee, but apparently there aren't any lids left."

"There are no lids?"

"They ran out. Boat didn't come. Do you want to go get some coffee? It's terrible, but it's warm."

"Thank you, no."

"Are you hungry? Would you like to get some lunch?"

"I've been chewing on grass," I say.

"Colm is still serving food. Fish, mostly."

"I don't want to do with any people."

"Maybe we could go for a walk, then."

"You should leave."

Up he goes from the rock. "I'm sorry."

19

Waves atomize around us. "Don't get stuck."

The American just stands there. Paralyzed. The words pound on the doors of his lips until they force them open.

"I am stuck. I have been, for... I just stand there, in the apartment. I've got my coat on. My shoes. I'm ready to go, out here or some other beach. And I just stand there and..."

He smiles a bit, like he's telling a joke.

"I stood there at the door, waiting for him. He got the weekends. Friday after school, I'd get my bag together and stand there staring at the door handle. Waiting for it to turn," he says and I see him there, that little boy, waiting. "I saw him. My Dad. In a gas station, a few weeks before he died. I hadn't seen him in years. I didn't say anything."

I picture him in one of those sprawling truck stop gas stations they have in the States. Those temples of petrol built on every interchange. His father in line ahead of him. And he doesn't say anything.

"Why didn't you?"

"I don't know. That's not true. He wasn't part of my life forever and... I ignored him. And then when he died..." He winces. "I was angry. Why was I angry? Why now? The next thing you know it's two years later and you're thinking you need to make it right. As if doing something will make any difference."

"Two years?"

"That's me and my Dad," he says, the shame of it naked on his face. "Long periods of pretending the other doesn't exist interrupted by fierce attempts to prove that they do."

On the ferry back from the OB-GYN in Galway, I wept the whole way. In the span of three months, I had lost both my parents. I learned the world would end. I was pregnant.

I was twenty-five.

Ma held tight to the armrest, flinching with every heave in the sea. There are stones on this island more travelled than my mother. She only first set foot off Inishèan to bear me, and that was at forty-

A COUNTRY OF ETERNAL LIGHT

two and with fierce reluctance. My primal image of her is of a woman worn and battered, like an old ship. Bothered with life. Youth.

"You punished him," I say. "And now you're punishing yourself."

"I don't want to anymore," he says. "I don't want this."

I shake my head. "What else is there?"

"Take a walk with me."

"Why?"

"I don't know. I don't know what I'm doing."

I have to laugh. "You've convinced me."

"Of which part?"

What would I do? Go for a walk with him? Go for a tea? And then what? Go back to the home? Go to the market? What would I put in the cart? It was all for him. Go back to saying hello? *How are you? I'm grand, thanks. Did you hear?*

Do you know?

I crumple back to the lump of fleece I had been and The American stands there, stricken, hands wanting to reach out, take hold of me and pry me back into a shape more human. There's instructions, for the funeral. A style guide, for the obituary. But not for this.

Not for after.

One foot in front of the other, they say. One day at a time. What do you do when you have no more days? When there are no more years? Just this empty, lonely fall.

I take Gavin's hand. "Just a short walk."

CHAPTER THREE

Colm stands next to his car in the drive, holding a catch of fish. Men like shadows on this island. You've got two if you've got one. He scratches that beard of his. Longer every time I see it. More white now than red. A winter fox.

He tips his cap. "*Slan*," he says.

I walk past him to the door. "We've fish yet."

"I'm going around, checking the furnaces. I know it's been a spell since yours has had any maintenance."

"You put it in, didn't you?"

"I did."

"Half the reason you're always fixing things on this island is because it was you installed it in the first place."

Hard to tell if I've wounded him. He has the one expression. A sort of permanent scowl. I've hurt myself. This anger bruises me. Dislocates me. All my bones and organs are displaced for all my hurt trying to get out and all it takes is a person showing up at my door.

"I tried coming by before, Mairead. I thought I'd wait, and then... I thought about going out there. Talking to you. I didn't want to disturb you. I didn't want to interfere."

"You're kind."

He shuffles back to his car, defeated. What does he drive the car for. We don't have the petrol to spare to be wasting it driving the few miles up and down this road.

"Weren't you always going to off to Ibiza or somewhere, Colm? Why haven't you?"

"Nepal." He scratches the gray scruff on his chin. His sleeve sinks down his arm, uncovering the simple lines of dulled tattoos. "You want to die at home, I suppose. Some of us do. Others... well. You've met Gavin, I hear."

Of course he's heard. "You're friends, then?"

"I rented the apartment to him once. This was years back. He was here on a weekend from Dublin. I got to know him a little. I know him. He's been wanting to come back, ever since. He's been wanting to stay. Picked a time for it."

"He's not staying."

"Keeps a man busy," he says. "Going after himself."

"I've noticed. You never told me why Nepal."

"I went hiking there, about twenty years back. I had seen this shirt in a store in Galway. Katmandu, it said on the front. Just like that, I wanted to go to Katmandu. So I went."

"Maybe you can go when the plane comes back."

He smiles, a little. "Or you could."

"You're shite for jokes, Colm."

"I'm shite for a lot of things, it turns out."

"Never seems to stop you."

"You have to keep trying."

I open the door. "*Slan.*"

"You come to places," he says. "You come to places and you think, the wonder. The beauty. You see the sights, the shops, the buildings, whatever it is. You don't see the life. The living. Not unless you really spend time there. You can't know. People tell you, *Oh, you can't go there.* The fighting, or the disease, or what have you. But I could die tomorrow. Any of us, you know. Just crossing the road."

23

He drifts off, somewhere.

"One day there in Katmandu, I went into this store for some bottled water. I headed down the road and the clerk came running after me. I'd dropped twenty cents. This is more than they make in an hour. A day. Three hundred Euros a year they make. Here a Euro goes on the ground and someone's foot goes over it. And here your man was, giving me my twenty cents. Of course, I let him keep it. They had given me so much. There in Katmandu, the Hindus burned their dead on the river. They let me watch. The smell, you know. The pop of the skin as it melts. I was a total stranger. But they let me into their grief."

I slam the door behind me. Ma wakes up from some dream in the recliner. She's forgotten it already. If you could forget life.

If you could wake up, brand new.

O

Dead of night.

Must be. Pins and needles. Soaked to the bone. Why don't I stay. Why don't I just walk out to sea after you. I'm in the bedroom now. How did I get here. The hours like flies. I swat them way.

The door creaks open. *Keep your voice down,* Ma says.

How could I be saying anything, hoarse as I am. I don't remember my own voice, to say nothing of yours.

Lord God.

Why couldn't it be you I'm forgetting, Ma? You forgot him and I trusted you. I trusted you to focus on the only thing that mattered to me and you left him alone to go mop up the drool and the piss and the shit of a dozen people shriveling like old fruit and why didn't you just top up their morphine and be done with it and fill the earth if the earth is so wanting and I'm right here waiting in the dark and the cold and the waves waiting for you please here I am I've been waiting Declan won't you come here I am and *The neighbors,* Ma says.

Black-headed gulls flounder overhead like torn shingles in a summer storm. Gavin and I walk the long, curling sandy beach to its end and then back through the cemetery, as we do most days. Along the way, I peer into the fluttering grass, behind every hillock and into every sunken depression in the soft, wanting sand.

I'm always looking.

"Da would come out here and fish," I say.

"Your dad was the doctor here?"

"Did I tell you?"

"Colm told me."

I claw at the beach grass. Stalks bend and twist in my wake. "What else did he tell you?"

"Colm doesn't say much," Gavin says.

"What do youse talk about, if you don't drink?"

"How do you know I don't?"

I shrug. "Aoife might be a bit of a talker."

He takes a breath. "I'd say so."

"Is she not your type?"

I don't need to ask. If all he wanted out of the island was a shag, he could have got it from her in the pub loo. He wants more. I feel it, strong as I do the pull of the sea.

What more is there?

Stones older than America lie broken. They make a pavement in the thicket to the open grave of a tiny church sunk into the ground. Rusted coins scab the floor inside. He holds my hand as we navigate pools of water the tides left in the cemetery. The church a shipwreck. Stone carved into pinwheels and eroded figures that walked across centuries. The broken remains of an ancient high cross. A horseman cut into its face, engraved there at the last millennium, when people thought the world was ending.

"A good spot," I say.

Gavin nods. That pill bottle like a rock in his pocket.

25

The curtain of grass fringing the dunes flutters with promise. "He'd be proud of you, your Da."

The gulls heckle the futility of the gale. He hardens, Gavin. Shrinks like an old, dried out paintbrush. He seems old now. A deep, wide silence grows between us.

Gavin looks up the cliff climbing behind us, to the monastery. "I haven't been up there yet."

The island becomes steps, none even and none linear. In the shops and cafes and pubs the tourists would all ask the same question. Why did the monks build their monastery in such a difficult place? The answer seemed obvious, even to me as a girl. Any journey to God is meant to be difficult. How the round tower must have loomed, when she stood tall and full. A silhouette against the rising sun, a crack in a door you could just see yourself getting through.

Today, the round tower is no summit and no refuge. The husk of the thing perches on the precipice overlooking the sea, alongside the remains of stone beehives. All of them birdhouses now. Gulls. Puffins. Refugees from other worlds.

Patches of sunlight glitter on the gravel gray sea, marking a path to some distant west. Some say the monastery is much older than is thought and was not founded by Christian monks but the same pagans that erected Dun Aonghasa on Inishmore three thousand years ago or more. Some say Inishèan is in fact Hy-Brasil, or was once Tír na nÓg, the lost Land of the Young, forgotten as the people turned to the new faith. Some say the island is an arrow pointing the way to the land where flowers are always in bloom, forests drip honey and little boys never grow up. One must cross a great stretch of water, and then travel beneath the waves a great distance to find this place.

Cracked and crumbling pavement gives way to untended weeds, as if I'm in the car park of an abandoned shopping mall back in the States. They just build things there and let them go to rot. As if to give themselves history. A slow, steady pounding grows in the distance. Spray rains down in icy pellets, the ejecta of geyser-like eruptions rocketing into the air. I come to the edge of the puffing hole. The ocean moils at the bottom of a cavernous abyss a hundred feet below, thrashing against chiseled limestone walls, spinning around a furious center. Runoff from the constant deluge drains back down into the maw, channeling under scabs of rock, lifting, pulling, coaxing them away into oblivion. I teeter. I waver.

He takes my hand.

Gavin sits on a seat of rock the sea provided, just for him. Us. The dog lies down at his feet.

"This dog," he says. "Follows me everywhere."

I sit with him. "Must be annoying, like."

He smiles, kind of. "Does he belong to anybody?"

"People die, and animals go to wander."

"I wonder if I could take him back with me."

"He'd be better off. He stays here and we'll turn the knife on him once the sheep have gone."

His face shrinks. "Jesus."

"You need to go home, Gavin. You've seen the news?"

He rubs the back of his neck. His eyes red and sore. He doesn't sleep. "I'm trying to avoid it."

Ma turns on the radio and I can't. "This oil thing. With China and Russia. What does it mean, 'tactical nuclear war?'"

"It's slang for 'Jesus fucking Christ.'"

"Fair enough."

"Terrified me as a kid. Nuclear war."

"Was this during the Cuban Missile Crisis?"

He reaches for me like he means to grab me. A game. I don't know if it's me reeling him in, or him me and I don't care.

We're caught.

His thumb brushes my ribs. Guitar string. His heart this mad drum. This music we make. This anxious rhythm.

"I don't feel old," he says.

I clear my throat. "This black hole. It's like getting all our apocalypses together at once."

"Greatest hits. Farewell tour or something."

"I don't know why now."

"Well. The Cubs won the Series, so."

"Inconsiderate of them," I say.

"When I left Chicago... there were all these people. " His chin lists against my shoulder. "Jumping off the buildings. Lighting themselves on fire. There were all these scorch marks on the street."

"Do you think we'll do ourselves in first?"

"I think there's some part of us that wants it to be over," he says. "And there's another part that never quits."

The puffing hole gurgles like an old man coughing up spit, routine and we are routine. We are creatures inhabiting the spaces of our lives unable to press the borders. I think Gavin is a fool to stay here for one day, let alone one hour and yet he's living. He's dying. He's caught somewhere between. He's caught me up in his string, the yo-yo and I look back over my shoulder to the crest of the island. Ireland beyond. Inishmore at war with the sea. You're here. Somewhere. I know you are. I know someday you'll come out the grass.

Here I am.

○

Rabbits scatter back to their burrows, paralyzing the dog with choice. The house glows like a paper lantern beyond the field. No rain to drive Gavin back to the pier tonight. No excuse. No reason to be here at all. What will he do. Sit there, alone at the bar. Thinking of me.

"There's a party here soon," he says. "Colm was telling me. For Halloween or something."

"*Samhain,*" I say. "That's weeks away."

"I've got time."

"Are you the only one?"

He winces. "I've got time I want to make good on. Let's put it that way. Come with me to the party."

I'm never going to the party. He'll be gone by then. But it doesn't sting, the idea of it. Us. He tastes like a cigarette, Gavin. A hard drink. He burns. He makes me hurt in ways I've forgotten, better pangs than those I live with now.

"You'll be asking me to marry you next," I say.

That shrug is just barely an act. "Everybody is going to Vegas."

"You came here."

He smiles. "I did. Let's go to the party."

"But you're ancient."

"I'm only forty."

"Ancient, yeah."

"Seems like I can keep up with you."

"We'll see."

"Is that a yes?"

My head shakes. "Gavin..."

"Or maybe we can just go for another walk tomorrow."

Wave after wave explodes against the dunes. Ghosts of rainbows in the spray.

"Walk with me for this bit," I say and we turn back through the grass. I stumble in a crumbling burrow; he grabs my hand.

I keep it to the road.

CHAPTER FOUR

The bedroom door creaks open. Aoife leans against the frame, this shit eating grin on her face.

"Dear Penthouse... I never thought this could happen to me..."

"What are you on about?" I say.

Aoife stretches out on the bed. Hair snarled. There's no comb in creation to tackle all that.

"Your gentleman caller. The American."

"What's he been saying?"

"Doesn't say a word. Just sits at the end of the bar and sips his whiskey. Every night. He's a man of routine, Gavs. Goes for long walks, so I'm told. Down the shore."

"He's leaving," I say, as I pull on my coats.

"He's been leaving for a week now."

He has, so. Every day I think he's leaving the next and then there he is, with that bleeding dog.

"What do you do with him?"

I turn away. "We just talk."

"Why do you talk to him? But not me?"

The words just come. He just comes, and Lord God. I want to

tear his heart out. I want to drag him into the sea with me. I want to drown us both in our sorrow.

"I don't know," I say.

Aoife lies back on the bed. "Well. It's good you're getting out, anyways."

"I'm not getting out."

"There's no shame in it. You're not the only single woman on this island, Mairead."

"Have at him."

She clicks her thumb, like she's flicking some lighter. "He's no interest in me. Or anyone else. There's American girls stuck up the bed and breakfast. College girls. Big bouncy tits. They're dying for a hammer, let me tell you."

I go to the door. "Are you finished?"

"They come in the pub and snake up to him. It's so obvious. He's no time for them, either. The one is bleeding gorgeous. The blonde. End of the world and all. She'd do in a pinch."

That's all she thinks about, Aoife. Getting her oats off. The woman has done nothing else her entire life. She's never been anywhere and why should she. Until all this, the entire world walked off the ferry twice a day in the summer. Spanish boys, Italian boys, French boys. Bleeding Omaha Beach it was. They never stood a chance. She's like fly tape, Aoife. Still and all. She probably sleeps fine. She worries for nothing, not even the end of the world. She'll be pissed and naked when it comes.

"I have to get on," I say.

Downstairs, Ma stands at the front door, her coat half on. Lost in the fog of her confusion. She sees me, in my coat. The two of us going some place. Neither of us knows where.

○

There's a little plastic sack waiting for me on the rock in the morning. Some granola bars. A little note taped to them.

In case you get hungry. – Gavin.

This isn't what I'm hungry for. What do I want. Why should I want for anything. You're waiting on me and here I am wanting. My whole life. Never enough. Not the island. A liquor store full of booze. I always need more. This hunger always inside. This space I have to fill. Fuck you. You fucking piece of shit. What were you thinking? That he'd keep? That the light of him would somehow spoil the darkness? You could hold on? There's nothing left to hold on to. You're alone in a cemetery and not even good enough for the dirt.

Fuck you.

Fuck you fuck you fuck you fuck you fuck you fuck you God fuck you Ma fuck you Colm fuck you Aoife fuck you Gavin fuck you dog scratching against the stone why won't you just break and I'm in the water and Gavin grabs my fists and I'm no weight and I fly through the grass no no no no no no no no let me go let me go let me go leave me in my grave with my boy leave me alone why won't you leave me alone why are you here I didn't ask for this I don't want anymore in my life you'll just get taken away everything gets taken away and this is what I want so let me go let me go let me go let me go let me go just

"*Let me go!*"

He can't. He won't. "What are you doing?"

My hands curl around an empty space in the air between us. No words. I grab those granola bars he left and they could be gold to someone these bleeding bars and I mash them inside their wrappers. I throw what's left at him.

He turns his cheek, sore, afraid and knowing his folly but he stays and I punch, scratch and thrash in his arms but he never lets go. I pile all the weight of my anger and my sorrow on him, but he never lets go. I exhaust myself. I list into him and we make this heap against the stone. His arms close around me.

We find our shape.

○

We huddle under the awning over the front door. The rain mad yet. He wants to say something, to keep me from going back out there and he knows there's no stopping me. There's no stopping any of this. The sea creeping up the road. The sky falling on our heads. The rumble in our bellies shaking down the houses. The two of us.

I should have him in, Gavin. Give him a go and then when he's asleep I'll go back out and he kisses me.

I slap him.

He steps back. "I'm sorry."

"You're leaving," I say.

His shame slicks off him. "I'm leaving."

I grab his hand. "Wait until the rain stops, at least."

O

The newspaper on the floor sticks to our shoes as I lead him quick through the squalor up the stairs. The only mess in my room is the piles of books along the floor and wall. They encase a squat, full bookcase like a stone mound. I close the door and I pull his jacket off.

"Do you need help with anything?" he says.

Do I need help. I peel his shirt away. My neglected nails claw at his damp skin. I kiss him. Blood runs down my chin. He stops. His fingers at his lips. He tastes my copper. The salt air. The grit of beach sand. The earth begging for its dead.

He holds me close. "Mairead..."

I kiss his cheek, still red. "Be quiet."

His hands slow. "Are you..."

"Don't be talking now."

His arms lock around me. He wants me. He wants this. But he doesn't want this quickness. This adhesive of a moment we put on our trouble and then I toss him back out in the rain. I know the fierceness in the way he clutches me now. The desperation to hold on to anything, or anyone, to keep from drowning.

The dog scratches at the door.

I closed the front door downstairs. Didn't I? This house always open. Every dead house is open to the world.

Gavin's hands roam free. "I'll put him out."

"Strays, the two of you. It's embarrassing."

He kisses me. "He's my people."

"You're an Irishman alright," I say. "The only thing you ever forget is the way home."

He winces. "What do you mean?"

Lord God. What am I saying. What are we even doing. "You could both do with a bath," I say. "I'll boil some water. Scrub up. Warm up. Then this dog goes outside."

He sits on the bed. "You've lived here your whole life?"

"I have."

"We moved around a lot. We never had money for the rent and three months went by and we moved somewhere else. There were times... she never gave up though. She never quit."

"I'll boil the water, then," I say.

I pick up the mess downstairs quick while the water boils. What would it be if not for Aoife? I bullied her into helping me at the home and then I left her with it. Lord God. Gnats swirl about me as I stand at the sink crying a fit over hanging her with all the responsibility. I was ready to leave it all a few hours ago. I don't even think I've shaved my pits. Lord God. I haven't done. The fuck am I going to do. I'll take off my shirt and he'll think I'm some French girl, like. Why should I care. He'll take me as I am. He'll be taking me where I tell him.

I come back in the bedroom and he's stretched out on the covers. The bleeding dog curled up beside him.

"Your water will go cold," I say.

"I'm good right here."

"You'll be getting that dog out of my bed."

○

I shave my pits quick like in the downstairs sink. My legs. I was never much down there. He should be so lucky. Ma stands in the door of the loo when I go back with the towels, a bashful smile on her face like a child too shy to say hello.

"Ma, I told you to stay downstairs – for fuck's sake, Gavin. You do not have the dog in the bath with you."

He draws his knees up to his chin, as if he has any shame. "Yeah, just stand there with the door open."

"Let's go Ma. You've seen enough."

"He's in the nip," Ma says.

"So he is." The dog barks at me. "Don't you be getting thick with me. You'll be in the street. The two of you."

"I'll work it out with her," I hear him say as I lead her out. "She's like the weather here. Just wait five minutes."

I come back in the room. "Five minutes, is it?"

"Huh?"

"Don't start with me."

"I think I'm finished."

I bite my lip. "This is how you repay my kindness?"

"I see how it is. *Quid pro quo.* I guess I'll be expected to do, you know, favors and stuff."

"We'll see who's doing anyone any favors."

"Clearly I'm the bigger person in all this."

"I'll be the judge of what's bigger," I say.

"Come here," he says. "Judge."

I button my arms. "I've got a fire going downstairs."

"I'll bet you do."

"Let's see it then," I say, and come to the tub. Gavin curls up all bashful like and I try to uncurl him. The dog stands on the curved edge and growls at me.

"Be careful now," Gavin says. "You don't want to get bit." I poke him in the shoulder. The dog snaps. "Better watch it."

"Watch what?" I flick him in the same spot.

The dog lunges at me but slips off back in the tub. He laughs at me squirming in the spray and I lean in to let him have it and he grabs the wet sleeve dangling off my arm.

"Don't – "

The fresh, dry sweater I just fucking put on falls heavy off me as I crawl out of the tub onto the tile. The dog barks at me and with a look I send him running into the hall. Gavin laughs and I throw my soaked shoes back at him.

"Uh oh. She's mad now."

"You want to see mad?"

"What? You're going to poke me again?"

"I'll give you a poke, like. You've no idea the pain you're due," I say. "None. Deirdre Gogarty. Right fucking here."

He shakes his head. "Deidre who? What?"

"You're fucked is what I'm saying."

"I feel like I can take you."

I come back to the tub. I stab my finger into his shoulder. "Are you starting with me?"

He reaches out, waiting; waiting for me to stop this. His hands brush against my hips. My panties bunch in his fingers. He pulls them down, dropping the curtain on the scar channeling beneath my belly. He kisses me there and I go to my knees, hand over my mouth to muzzle sobs so deep they can't surface. Some sense of modesty keeps him in the tub. Shame.

"Come here," he says.

"You'll prune," I say, and leave. I come back for my shoes, floating in the water with him. My sweater. My knickers.

He hands me back in pieces.

CHAPTER FIVE

Little blinky lights pass high overhead, back to America.

Their sound a soft rumble indistinct from the waves. I'll never be on a plane again. I'll never leave this island again. The sea goes out and I could just walk through the mucky land of the dying but I drown. I drown every hour of every day but I can't die. Wave after wave after wave and I choke, I crush, I survive, like the cracked rocks, the rumpled shore, the island stuck in the sea.

Gavin risked his life to let go of this man he didn't know. How do you do it. Book a flight. Fill a pill bottle with ashes. Build this map in your head. X marks the spot. This is where. This is when.

Do you know?

Rain pelts my cheeks. The morning's far. Or somewhere yet I can't reach. It's nothing compared to all the pithy years passed here in the cemetery, years like Irish rain showers.

○

I lose Gavin for a day.

When he comes back to the shore, he has some shit flowers he bought up the Spar. The poor sod.

The paper wrap crinkles in my hand. "Did they fleece you?"

He shrugs. "It's ok if you like them."

"Who did you say you were buying them for?"

"I just bought them."

I rest the flowers on your stone. "You're kind."

"I'm awful," he says. "I was awful, Mairead. I'm sorry."

I look away. "It's nothing to be sorry for."

"I think about you all the time."

"Go on with yourself."

"I worry about you."

Waves punish the shore. Spray beads on the wrap holding the flowers that have been sitting up there at the Spar long enough for them to become hard. Dull. Brittle.

"Do you know there are wild flowers you could have picked?" I say. "Primrose. I would have done with primrose."

He nods, like someone in a movie who's acknowledging some secret sign or code. "I'll do better next time."

I pull a dead petal free. "I like talking to you."

"I like talking to you, Mairead."

"If we could just talk... that'd be grand."

Gavin sits on a flat rock across from me. Red with the wind already. An hour goes in our talking, but he doesn't move, red as he is, sore as he is, cold and soaked as the spray leaves him.

○

A fishing boat makes a go of it out into Galway Bay. Every angry wave I think she'll go under. I surprise myself with my stake in their success. Someone should be so lucky.

Gavin watches with as much anxiety as I do. This is the only sport on the island now. Watching each other die. Cold today. The mood of the weather as mixed up as the spray and rain.

"My dad fished, too," Gavin says, and we wind on through the beach grass fringing the edge of the island.

I trail after him, letting him lead. "Do you?"

"Not really. As in, not at all."

"You're more an indoors type."

"For a while my mom and I lived in this duplex close to the river, over by the meat packing plant. I was twelve, thirteen. He was always down at the river, under the railroad bridge. Saturday or Sunday mornings. I'd see him sometimes, when I'd take pop bottles back to the cigar store downtown to turn into money for comic books."

"Comic books?"

"Most of the kids I knew went down there to sneak into the nudey section. I wasn't a normal kid."

"Clearly."

"Every time I open a comic book, I smell cigars."

"You still read comics, like?"

"I wrote them for a while. I tried to, anyway. So. What kind of music were you doing in the city?"

New York. Feels like a movie I watched half asleep on a plane. "Do you know The Sundays?"

"Oh, yeah. Harriet Wheeler."

"Of course."

"Well, I was the right age."

"You were," I say. "It was a bit Sundays, the music. Smiths."

"Do you have any tapes or anything?"

"Tapes, he says. Maybe I had some records pressed."

"Vinyl is making a comeback."

"Is it now?"

"Things come back," he says. "Eventually."

"I don't know. Could be one or two lying about."

"I'd love to hear them."

"You didn't happen to bring a copy of this book of yours with you, did you?"

"Why, did your heating go out?"

"Will soon enough," I say, biting my lip to kill my smile. He brushes my chin. I step back. "We're just talking."

"You're bleeding," he says.

"Oh."

He unzips his jacket and takes a cloth out of his pocket you use to wipe your glasses, like. My lower lip curls under the top and he has nothing to treat.

He hands the cloth off to me. "I can bring you some lip balm. I don't have it with me."

"I'm grand."

Gavin looks for that fishing boat. I don't see it, either.

"They probably made it over," I say.

"Right."

I lick the copper off my lips. "Why didn't you come back before now? You said you loved it here."

"I tried making it as a writer. Didn't work, so I got a job. Made good money. Got comfy. And then I'm 40 and…"

"It just goes, time."

You laugh, you cry, you say your first word and those two years are as quick and gone as a dream. I fight to remember every last thing, sitting out here, standing in the room, walking out to the naked sea after you. I don't remember anything before you. I wasn't alive. I was just a dream that didn't take on any meaning until you woke up.

Gavin touches my hand. "Do you miss the States?"

"I miss the anonymity." My head shakes, like some bobble thing. How did we get out here? How long have we been out here? "Everyone knows who you are. Everyone thinks they know."

"Would you go back, if you could?"

"I might have stayed past my welcome. By several years. I wasn't there properly, like."

"Fucking Irish. Taking our jobs. Our women."

"Well, the women. I cannot be blamed. And you, then? How is it you don't have a wife?"

We wind back into the beach grass, littered with tide thrown rocks. Crooked crosses.

"Haven't found her, I guess," he says.

"Best get a move on."

"Where did you meet women in New York?"

I roll my eyes a bit. It had been a joke. "You're looking for tips, is it?"

"Research. For the book I'm working on. Did I tell you? Dating tips during the apocalypse. Do's and Don'ts."

"More in the Don't section now, I suppose."

"What are some ideal places?"

"The gym. The showers, like."

"You're sort of right there."

"Opportunity, yeah."

"Probably not a good strategy for me," he says.

"You've some sense at least."

"Is it true? Women are better lovers?"

"You've never been with a woman?"

"I left myself open for that."

"You were doing so well," I say.

He laughs. "Was I?"

"You were."

I want to talk to Gavin. I want to tell him everything but even now, after being half naked with him in the loo, there's this fight in me. Do with him. Don't. No good starting something now. No sense digging your heart out to for someone. My heart is gone, besides. Does he hear, Gavin. This empty rattle.

The wind pushes us out of the grass. I look back for the fishing boat. Nothing but spray out there in sea.

The good fortune of some men.

○

Aoife raises the bottle of whiskey in toast. "It was Eamon, tonight. *Slan abhaile,* Eamon."

She sits at the kitchen table, pissed. Scrubs faded to a wine stain. She drinks the Jameson's straight from the bottle and I want it. I want it so bad I can taste it. I'll fuck that bottle I get it out her hands, but what I want for I am denied and so long as I sit here, wet for it, I remain dry.

"What was it?" I say.

"Heart attack. We've no aspirin left."

I look in on Ma in the living room. Somehow watching telly and not watching at the same time.

"The son's in Dublin, I think. Or he was." Aoife swipes the wet paste of hair from her eyes. "I couldn't find the contacts. Could you come back and help me with it?"

"Were you looking before or after the whiskey?"

"You make these distinctions, Mairead."

"You bought that off Colm?"

She shrugs. "I traded him for it."

"Even you have standards."

"I traded him an IOU." She snorts. "It says – listen to this now – on the note, like – it says: *'To be paid in full and with interest in one year's time.'* A year, Mairead."

"You're clever."

Aoife blubbers her lips. "How's your man?"

I cross my arms. "He's not my man."

"Is Gavs not stealing you back to America, then?"

"God, you're a shite drunk."

"You're literally in line to be one of the last ever members of the Mile High Club and you're going to pass it down?"

"This is why I don't talk to you."

"*This* is why?"

I glance at the bottle and then look away. Look away. "We're just... we're just keeping each other company. That's all. And that's fine. I appreciate him."

"You 'appreciate' him?"

"If he'd come before... who's to say."

"He did come once before."

"I would have been all of twelve, Aoife."

"You can't let little details like that get in the way," she says. "Mairead. If he wants to take you for a ride, let him. Youse can pretend like you're not shagging every night down the pier and we'll all pretend like we don't know you are."

"We are not shagging. And you'll be keeping your gob shut."

She laughs. "He's seen you naked. He's got that glint in his eyes. Been touched by God, him."

This bleeding woman.

"If youse get on, we've got a solid year, they say. That's plenty of time to work up to a threesome, like."

"Don't you have rounds?"

"What do you even bother with him for then?"

I don't know. I don't know why I bother with anything. There's no point to anything but waiting now.

Wanting.

"Can you imagine it, Mairead? The three of us? *Ménage à trois.* I've got whiskey for him, too. Call him down."

"Aoife."

"When in Rome. Or Greece. We'll do it Greek like. Do you remember? Patsy? That night at the pub? Absolutely banjaxed she was. Asking for it, Mairead. The lube. Going around the bar. *Do you not have any?* The state of her."

She almost vomits laughing. She runs to the sink to wait for it. Nothing comes.

I brush her hair back. "Just take it easy, Aoife."

She grips my hand. "Can I sleep here? Do you mind? Or would you come back to the home with me?"

"Who's up there now?"

"Saidbh."

"For Christ's sake, Aoife."

"She's some worker, Mairead. She's no equal."

"She's sixteen, like."

"She doesn't know that – "

All that whiskey brown and sweet comes out her mouth. Chunks of something she ate. What has she been eating. Tears and spit hang off her and I hold her hair back, like I've been doing since we were girls. All that hair, Aoife. Like beach grass. You get lost in it. I brush her cheek. Red and warm. She's gagging now but it's not the drink. She slumps against the counter, weak and tired, sore from watching us die, one by one. I left her there at the home, like I left you here. It's all I do is leave.

And still, here I am.

○

Her scrubs need washing. I'll do it down the shore later. I stuff them in a plastic grocery sack I've been keeping and I don't know what for. Years all these sacks drifted across the road and spoiled this harsh beauty and now there are no more. You hold on to things.

She curls her leg around me. Damp heat against my thigh. She's sweating out but I pull the covers over us. I'll wait for her to fall asleep, and then I'll go. I owe her sleep. Her heart skips with all the drink she's taken. He'll be furious, Colm. Let him be angry for something. Her hands jitter. Words mumble on her lips. She whimpers and whines, Aoife. I kiss her cheek. Her fingers brush my lips.

I'm sorry, I think she says.

○

In the morning, I go down to the water with a litre bottle. No sense making Aoife come all this way. Though doing this a bottle at a time is shite. I should see if Colm still has any kegs still at the pub. Forget it. I'll walk the mile for every bottle. The sea rolls out like a carpet. I think I hear the dog. Pebbles of hail bounce off the naked rock. Off me. The weather is turning now. It's so cold. Ma will be cold.

I ought to get home.

Loads of birds this morning. Black-headed gulls. Pintails. An Eastern Kingbird. He is far, far from where he should be. Birds from far away as Africa are known to find their way to the island. Will he go back, I wonder. Does he have anywhere to go back to. Sanderlings skirt across the exposed beach, pecking for food. The tide rolls in and they sweep up the shore, each one a cursor speeding across a blank page. The tide goes back out, they sweep after it.

Back and forth.

The tide in, the birds up, the tide out, the birds down and on it goes like nothing's happened. Once I loved these hurried birds. Their dogged gonzo for life. Now they offend me, the Sanderlings. Their blind devotion to routine. To instinct. Their ignorance of you.

Their shadows grow. The birds scatter, in every direction. The sky catches fire.

Lord God. A meteor.

The blanket of gray evaporates around the meteor and it's coming straight down at the sea and I rise from the rock in anticipation and then it flares out atomically.

There and gone.

I take my place back on the stone, stranded somewhere between relief and disappointment. Why am I stranded? What is it I'm holding on to? The manic waves carry on. The birds. This slow erosion. And then the loudest sound I've ever heard sends me off my arse. The shockwave ricochets off the hills and dales of the island and windows shatter miles away.

I take off running for home.

CHAPTER SIX

Every window in the house is gone. The front door off its hinges. Lord God. Ma. I run in screaming.

"Ma!"

She's sitting in front of the telly, flipping through her channels. Broken glass in her lap. Ma looks at me, confused.

"Mairead... when did you get back from the States?"

I brush the glass off her. She bats my hands away. I grab hers and I could just throttle her. I could, just. Stupid woman. Where's your head at? Where are you? WHERE ARE YOU?

Her head shakes. "What are you crying for, girl?"

"Ma..."

I fall in her lap, sobbing like a child. She pats my shoulder. The best she could ever do.

○

Outside the nursing home, the car park is empty save for a horse and cart at the main entrance. Wandering the hall I find Domnhall Walsh, hat in hand. Years this man waited at the pier for the ferry to unload all the tourists so he could scoop them up, ten a head. Domnhall goes sour soon as he puts eyes on me. People don't want to talk to me. Deal with me. Everyone says hello on the island. Everyone greets you with a smile, until you're grieved.

"I came by with Tilly Ni Laighin," he says with a shrug, and then follows with one of his characteristic pauses.

"If she's in for her hair, take her back."

"Is there no hairdresser today?"

"There aren't any windows today."

Aoife zombie walks through her rounds right past me. Doesn't notice me at all. I follow her room to room, waving at the residents bright with their smiles but quiet with their secret and I hang just behind until Aoife turns around, forgetting something, right into me.

She wipes her nose. "Am I off me face?"

"Are you not always?"

She scoops me up in this great big hug. "You're back?"

"I just came in to check on you. Did anyone get hurt?"

"Didn't notice, most of them," she says. "Not that I did. Anyways. Your man is out there now boarding up the windows. Or he was. Is it still today? Or are we still tomorrow?"

"You ok?"

"I'm tired, is all. Yeah. Just tired."

I take the charts from her. "Go get some kip."

"You're back?"

"Go on," I say. "You're knackered."

She hugs me. "I missed you. I miss you."

Aoife goes down the hall, into an empty room she's been sleeping in overnight. Lord God. Has she even been home. One thing at a time. I go into the supply room. The girls here have been rationing pills, bandages, needles and the like for weeks. I go through the counts again in the medicine depot. Edna Malloy gets a whole for her dementia. Eamon Ní Dhuibhne gets a half for his arthritis. Eamon is passed. A line through his name. I do the count again. The home has six days supply at best of essential drugs. Say a week if we're creative.

Colm's voice rolls down the hall like a cloud of gravel after a pickup truck. "Anything else needs nailing?"

I come out the depot. He's mortified to see me, Colm. Gavin just surprised. The state of him. Covered in mud and sawdust.

"I thought you were someone else," Colm says.

"I imagine St. Peter will say something similar."

"We've finished covering the windows."

"*Go raibh maith agat.*"

He scratches his chin. "I had a look at the generator as well."

"We've power."

"For now."

Cables run power under Galway Bay from the mainland. We've had little to fear even in the fiercest storms but to hear it from the news, there have been outages on the mainland.

"What's wrong with it?" I say.

His fingers work overtime. "Fuel lines are corroded. It's been sitting there dog's years without any proper use."

"I have people on ventilators here."

"I'll dig around and see if there are any replacements. Unlikely. We've no diesel, besides."

"I suppose you'll tell me next there's no Santy Claus."

His brows arch. "As it happens. How are you down the house?"

"We'll manage."

"We've got plenty of wood left," Gavin says, trying to make eye contact with me. I stare into the charts.

"That's kind."

Colm claws his chin. "You'll let me know, if there's anything more I can do."

"Aoife will ring you, if there is."

"*Slan,*" he says.

"Yourself," I say and go back in the depot.

Gavin steps in the door. "Are you ok? Your mom?"

"I'm fine."

"I was worried about you."

I give him a quick look. Doesn't seem to be hurt any, except for the mess on him. "You'll get left."

"I'll come by. After we're done."

"I'm thinking I'll be here a while."

He nods, I think. I try not to look at him. I try not to give him anything to hold on to. What we are we holding on to?

He turns, Gavin. He goes.

O

I try to catch up on the dishes. Ma goes behind me and dirties them again. She laughs like it's a game. As if she's a girl. I suppose she is now. It's all a game. Flip over a card. Try and remember its match.

Nothing matches.

Some birds got in through the broken windows. The cold or the confusion killed them. I set them on the table to take them out to the sea when I go but there's so much work here.

She sighs, Ma. "Not another dead bird."

When I was a girl, I'd go out to the shore. The wind becomes confused around the island. These vortices form and on certain days you stand there atop the rim and your hat will leave your head up into a funnel high in the sky. The wind sends birds into the cliffs and I'd bring them home, thinking myself some type veterinarian. *Don't say it,* she said. *You didn't bring home another dead bird.* I loved birds once. What I wanted to be was a bird.

To just fly away.

Every day the same shape but none of them match. Who am I. Where have I gone. Ma confuses me for her mother, for this woman Caoimhe I've never heard of and she argues with me. *Mairead's gone to the States. Where's Declan? Not another dead bird* and I am a dead bird on the kitchen table, wings fluttering with the breath of a little girl trying to blow life back into me.

Do you know.

○

Mornings I go down to the shore for water. The Sanderlings sweep back and forth, back and forth. Nursing home by 9. Rounds. Pills. Vitals. On the phone by 9:30. I ring the head office for Health Service Executive on the mainland. As per usual the HSE refers me to the pharmaceutical suppliers, as the 'entire nation is experiencing critical shortages' which originate with them.

I go down the list.

In every case, some poor soul unequipped as I am tells me all outstanding orders will be fulfilled, in the order they were received, once supplies arrive. Supplies arriving then from China or India, where 80% of the world's pills are made, and where currently there is an ongoing experiment in the practical limits of tactical nuclear war.

The man at Pizer is in India, in a call center in some office tower in some city so far unmolested. In the background I hear the chatter of other voices, the nonsensical rhythm of tapping keys. They sound like they're in an arcade, like.

"What do people do for medicine in India?" I say.

"I can only address inquiries as they relate to Pizer."

"I'm sure they're listening."

There's a sliver of a pause. "Our calls may be recorded for training and quality control purposes, yes."

"At least tell me it's warm. Is it warm where you are?"

"We are catching fire," he says.

Rounds. Pills. Vitals. Try to eat something, anything for lunch. Scrap of toast. Maybe some shut eye. If I get ten minutes before Edna Malloy sets off the larm going out the fire door I am blessed. Roisin Ni Shealbhaigh resists death in her respite bed. Not even her family holds their vigil. The son asks me where the plug is. There's no plug on her. Though if you would kindly pull mine. He does not oblige. I keep my charge. End of shift I go to the cemetery until dark.

Where's the plug.

Down to the beach. Rounds. Pills. Vitals. The nursing home beds only twelve, but all are full. The residents need as much attention as Ma. More, like. Truly she should be there, but there's no room. Twelve hours I would spend there when I started, and it wouldn't be enough. Eighteen. The old devour the young. Ring the HSE. Sit with you until the mercy of dark and then don't sleep. No sleeping. In the fog of the same dream I have every time I close my eyes. I'm in a boat. Lost at sea. Ghosts in the fog. This scratching sound. There is no sleep. Up all night searching through chat rooms and forums for the grief stricken, searching for scraps of hope, tools for dealing with this how do we deal with this I don't want to deal with this.

No way under or around, you just have to go through.

I lost my husband nine years ago you never get past it.

Life evolves. Grief evolves.

The evolution of life is death and I'm not evolving.

O

It just goes on.

There's so much work at the home. Across the island. A week after the meteor there's a meeting at the Halla Fáinne. I don't want to go, but Colm says people need to hear it from me, the state of things at the home.

I try not to be heard.

This is the first time I've been out in any proper way since. This is the first time I've seen any of these people and I don't look. I try not to look. I try not to see them, strung together in the hall with their children like strands of people cut out of construction paper.

I try not to be seen.

Colm says his bit. He reads off this little piece of note paper he's got up at the end of his nose. Wood stocks. Fuel stocks. Whiskey stocks. He calls me to the microphone. It's a wonder the world doesn't crumble now. There's a black hole right here in this room.

We're after talking and now onto tea and what little cake someone scrounged together flour for. I try to go but everyone has some ailment. Some pain. Pale we are now. Hollow. The islanders tiptoe around their bother.

Can you take a look? What do you have for it?

Really they just want to gather some intel on me to take back to the rest. *She's out, then. Tragedy, the boy. Who was the father, anyways?* I may as well be on stage.

Colm shoos them off. Gavin sticks to his corner on the other side of the hall, but he's got his own line forming. Other Americans, mostly. The college girls Aoife talked about. Each of them with a pitch. A promise, in their girly laughter. Aoife falls on the grenade for me. She chats him up and carts him over to me in the corner.

Have youse met, she says, her cheek poked out.

After a few diligent minutes of relating something she saw on the telly about the mating habits of seals in the Arctic, she excuses herself to go top up her tea.

"Hi," he says, like we've just met.

I remember his lips stuck on mine. "Hi."

Old Brendan keeps coming over to us. Spittle flecks his red jumper as he talks, his words a mash of Irish and English. There's no telling what they were to begin with. Each time he sees Gavin, it's like for the first time. His jaw drops on his toothless mouth and he holds out his hands as if to say, you've left me? For him? Are you with him? What's happening? I don't understand what's happening.

"On your way, Brendan," I say.

He wanders off somewhere.

"He likes you," Gavin says.

"That's me," I say. "Always attracting old men."

Brendan comes back. He stands there a moment, in faux shock. I try to imagine his trouble. All the women on the island seem to be with older men. The young leave if they can. If they can't, their youth and beauty is spent in service to the old and I left but I am the broken blade of rock carried out to sea on a wave and then washed back in.

There's no leaving.

We stand there a long time, Gavin and I. The music of other

voices the only sound between us. Brendan returns, on schedule. He wags his finger at us. I humor him.

You're humoring him. Aren't you?

I hold the cup to my mouth. "Can't be very cozy for you, living in an apartment with no windows."

"This is all going in my review on Trip Advisor," Gavin says.

I look for Aoife in the crowd. Eyes ricochet off mine. Everybody talking. Where did she get off to.

"There's music tomorrow night," he says.

"Some trad, isn't it?"

"Maybe they take requests."

"You'll want to hear something ancient, anyways."

"I'd love to hear you sing."

I finish off my tea. "They've heard enough from me."

His smile comes and goes, like rain.

"The weather's grand," I say. "The whole week, you know."

He squints, Gavin. Trying to figure me out. "I'll be here."

"There's no one in after you?"

"I think it's just me."

"You must be lonely," I say.

He wears all his years now. "I don't want to trespass on anyone."

"They'd tell you. If you were."

"We could go for a walk. Or something."

"Something."

So much relief in his voice. "Do you want some more tea?"

"I can't taste it."

Brendan swings back on his orbit through the hall. The shock of us less this time.

O

Coal fragments into the clusters of tiny orange stars in the fireplace of the apartment he rents over the pub. It was easier coming here on the way back from the home and there's no one down the pier besides.

He puts on another log. He doesn't say much, Gavin. He seems tired. He seems far from me.

"I read your book," I say.

I didn't know a person's eyes could get so big. "You what?"

"I downloaded it. On the tablet, like."

"You read my book?"

"You're a good writer. You are."

"But?"

Get down off this one, Mairead. "It just felt like... you had something you wanted to say, but you didn't know how."

"Well. I can start anything," he says and sits in the chair before the hearth. Shadows of flames flicker on his face. "I can't finish anything to save my life."

"Did it do well for you?"

"It got some good reviews. That's what people say, when it doesn't happen. *It got good reviews.* I thought it was the start, you know? But then... nothing happened."

"One thing I didn't understand was... it's obviously the island. The geography. But you changed the name. Why?"

He shakes his head. "I thought I had to create this distance. To be able to write about what happened."

"If it's true, then say it."

"Not all of it is for me to say," he says.

He looks into the fire. This age in him now. This fatigue. I sit in his lap. His hands like coiled springs.

"I liked the idea of it, though," I say. "This world beyond ours. This gate, up at the monastery. You just walk through, and..."

"I was always wanting to live a different life as a kid. Some other life. We were poor. I was... awkward."

"No."

"Oh, yeah. I suppose it was a children's story. My book. But, like you said. I didn't know what I wanted to say."

"What do you want to say?"

He pulls the blanket over us. "Stay."

"I need to get on, Gavin."

My hand closes around his wrist and he pulls and I push and we struggle for the blanket. I poke him. He lets go. The softie. He's not so soft right now. He's all this tension. He's warm with the friction of it. He's so warm.

"Colm said I should leave you alone," he says.

"He did what? Why?"

"I know I'm trespassing on you. I am. I know. I just..."

"You're not trespassing," I say.

"I know you're going through a lot and you're kind of... I'm not trying to take advantage of anything."

I can hear them all now. *Has it even been six months?* It is strange, this want. But it's not strange, to put ice to a bruise. To bandage a wound. You're meant to wait, with grief. You're meant to postpone everything, even your own suffering and we don't have time. What if we did. How would we act then.

Do you know.

"When I got pregnant... Ma told me to go to the UK. To get an abortion. *Don't*, she said. *Don't bring a child into this hell.* But I lost Da and I was losing her and I was so alone."

He holds me close. "You don't have to explain."

"I thought... it won't happen. It can't. God wouldn't give him to me to take him away. The black hole will miss us. We'll be saved. I'll be saved and I'm being punished for my hope."

"You didn't do anything wrong, Mairead."

"I should never have left him..."

He holds me, Gavin. The embrace of the condemned.

"They all talk. They all whisper. '*Serves her right.*'"

"Mairead... I don't think people say things like that. I think everyone feels terrible for what happened. So many people depended on you and I think they feel like they let you down. Life let you down. You didn't deserve this."

"Then why did it happen?"

"I don't know." He holds me tight. "I don't know."

We rest a long while in front of the fire. Me wanting to get back down the road. Him wanting me to stay. This tug of war between us and neither of us moves a muscle. I feel this weight on me. This soreness inside. I have to get rid of it. I want to.

I poke him.

He grabs at my hand.

"Don't start," I say, and poke him again. He pinches me so hard I squeal and I don't know. I take off running. The dog chases after the two of us on our lunatic parade through the apartment and before the bedroom door is closed behind us my knickers tear away in his hand. My exhaustion stolen by surprise. We fall into bed, his lips dancing from mine to the nape of my neck, my breasts, sore for him. I hold him close and only let him go to smooth down between my legs. His tongue slicks its way up my back, slow to my lips. I taste myself on him. My youth and my fear and the salt kiss of the island. I never left. I want to leave. Inishèan, this world, this life. I want to be more than this body can contain. I climb on top of him. I press against his chest, my fingers gripping, sinking into his skin and I am open. Unleashed. His salt mixes with mine. His sweat. His blood.

○

I only want.

My grief a deep yearning. I suppose I have to fill it with something. I take to him like some famished castaway. My hunger insatiable. Frightening. This isn't me. This isn't a woman whose son has just died. Yet the thought of him triggers this flood of appetite strange as the pangs when I was pregnant and we devour each other, Gavin and I. All night long. Our kisses volley from soft dabs to hungry grabs. My lips hurt. My legs. My skin, taut from the residue of dried sweat. From him. We're like virgins, discovering our bodies and potential for the first time. What begins as cautious and slow, soft and delicate becomes competitive. A race. A dash to get our fill, before.

Years we have to make up for.

The room falls away. The island, the world and its suffering to only our naked living. The exhaustion of love. I ache, and not just from us. It's this tension. What now? Come morning I'll go out to the shore, and then what?

And then what.

In the morning, he's gone. I hurry up and dress. In he comes with a bundle of fish. This light in him.

"Hey," he says.

"Hey."

"I actually caught this myself. Somehow."

"I should get out to the shore," I say.

The light goes out in him. "Eat something first."

"It's half nine already. I usually don't sleep this late."

"Do you... do you want me to..."

"Maybe I'll not have you come out today."

"Oh."

"I'll come by yours," I say. "After dark, like."

"Ok."

"I've got to get her some tea before I go. Her pills."

"Right," he says, and sets down the fish on the counter. "Absolutely. I'll see you tonight."

"Tonight," I say, and I'm gone.

CHAPTER SEVEN

There's a line out the door when I get to the nursing home. A dozen or more huddle in the car park, or sit patient in Domnhall's buggy. Given it's full up, a fair number must have walked here. The island is seven miles one end to the other. Old or infirm or both, that's no Sunday stroll. They're all big, empty sacks of jittering bone and teeth.

"Where have you been?" Domnhall says as I walk up.

I push through the crowd. "What's all this?"

"For the daycare."

"I don't have staff for these people."

"You said at the meeting things were back to normal."

"I did no such thing."

"You're back, though."

"Nothing is normal," I say, sharp enough this gets through his age. "And nothing is coming back. Daycare is for folks I don't have beds for. I'm not running a clinic. What did you do, go round knocking on doors?"

He shrugs, Domnhall. "I offered to take them."

"For a Euro?"

"Two's as easy."

"Take them back."

Moira Twombly grabs hold of my hands. "I need me heart pills. Mairead, you've got to have them today."

"I'm sorry. Nothing has changed."

They go off like rockets, like. Fuck's sake. What are youse complaining for now. You had your chance to go. You knew what it was staying. We all did. Those rocks the waves leave in the road will soon be left in our kitchens. Our kitchens will soon be left in Rossaveal. Doolin. Outer space.

"Listen," I say, and their voices go up. "You'll be hearing me now. The mainland can no longer support us. There are no supplies. There will be no supplies. That's it. It's done."

The lot of them looks at me in shock. Gasps. Whispers. This fear dawns in Moria's eyes. Her grip on my hand tightens.

"I'm sorry," I say.

Aoife cracks open the lobby door and pulls me in. She locks it behind me. They're banging on the plywood covering the broken window. Lord God. This isn't happening.

"Fuck off you zombies," Aoife says. "Go and die with dignity, or at least with the telly turned up."

"We're entitled," I hear Angus say.

The crowd echoes Angus. It would be genuinely terrifying if they all weren't about to keel over from a heart attack. The plywood cracks. They force their hands through and pull open the tear. Christ. It's like *Alien* or something, but in slow motion. I'll have to have Gavin fix this now.

Angus reaches in for the door lock. I slap his hand. "Did you leave your hearing aids at home?"

He wags his bony little wizard wand of a finger in my face, Angus. "You'll see me today, Mairead."

"You're a referral, Angus."

"You'll not refer me!"

"You're all fucking referrals, like."

"I demand medical attention. My heart's going."

"On account of your screaming and shouting. Go home and sit in your recliner and drink a glass of water."

"The tap's gone dry," Angus said, pulling off his hat again, twisted up in the misery of it all. "The reservoir's low. When are they going to come back with the tankers?"

"They're not..."

I lean against the door. There's no energy for all this. It only gets worse. "Go boil some sea water like the rest of us. Let me do my part while the phone still works."

"You can't turn us away."

"I'm not even the proper nurse," I say. "By rights I shouldn't be here. They'll sack me when they find out."

"Who will sack you?"

"The HSE, like."

"I'll paste them on the wall, they lay a hand on you." Now he's bleeding. The *eejit*. He cut himself. "I'm making color."

"Look what you've done... when I open this door, you'll behave yourself or it won't open again. Do you hear me, Angus?"

"I'll be civil."

"The same goes for your mob, like. We're going to open and I will only see non-referrals. You got something I can bandage, set or stitch I'll see you but everyone else gets a referral to the mainland and you've got to follow up with them. If you don't let me do my work, I'm no good for finding any more medicine. I have to do rounds. You have to understand, I can't help you."

Angus turns round to the clustered faces in the window behind me. "You'll be civil, or I'll paste youse on the wall."

I turn to Aoife. "You be civil, too."

Her smirk can barely contain itself. "What laws do you want me to break?"

"Keep two lists. One for referrals. Another for in-patients we treat today. The referrals, you'll enter their information in the system like always. That's all."

"We're referring them to..?"

"Proper physicians and specialists on the mainland."

"Which they can't get to."

"What else can we do, Aoife?"

She hurries behind the visitor's station and takes up position in the chair. "We should have done this before."

"We'll be doing it tomorrow," I say, and open the door.

○

The telly in the nurses' station crackles with news of millions of starving Indians flooding into China, gone to dust in earthquakes and I've no strength to stand for this. I've no strength to walk home after twelve hours nursing the dying through another night but I pull on my coat, like someone else is pulling it on. This isn't me, drafting a schedule. This isn't me, penciling my vanishing mother into the renewed rotation for the daycare, and this isn't me walking down the road in the pissing rain into Kilbanna, round the bend of the harbor to the pub. This isn't me walking up the stairs on the side of the building, through his door, into his bed and into his arms.

This isn't me, sleeping sound and easy.

○

He wakes me with his lips. I pretend to still be asleep. Dawn comes, as if it's lost the plot.

Days of this.

○

Someone knocks at the door.

I don't know if I should answer. Who would it be, anyways. Who would be looking for him besides Colm and he's out with Colm boarding up the entire bleeding island dawn to dusk. I won't answer.

I've been waiting on someone at my door since you've gone and I open the door. My disappointment must be obvious.

The Italian kids on the stairs have this look on their faces, like they've disturbed the dead. A boy and a girl. Not even ten. Swimming in their clothes.

"*Scusami*," the girl says, and looks past me, confused, into the apartment. "*È signore qui?*"

"He's not," I say.

The stairs clang as they ran down to the courtyard. I keep to the landing, waiting. Wanting. Across the empty harbor, the sun flattens into the sea. Waves wash over the eastern curl of the island, over the runway and the far, crumbling shore beyond.

○

Friday comes due. I renew him. Another week. The two of us a good story. A distraction, and yet I can't quite get through it. I'm out nothing if I get to the end of this or not.

It isn't something you keep.

○

Rainwater spills down the steep pass to Dún Nead, pooling in reservoirs created by stone fencing graze land on the terraced cliffs of the island rim. A dead cow floats in uretic slime. Black headed gulls circle above, diving and then sinking with the cow into the rank water. A steep climb over loose rock becomes steeper, until the island plateaus into uneven ground. Gavin holds my hand the entire way and I don't know I could have made it without him. I made the same climb a dozen times as a girl. Now it seems positively treacherous.

I squeeze his hand. "Here?"

His hand touches the bulge in his coat pocket the way it does any time we come to some place. This moment. Scattering the ashes. Releasing his obligation.

His guilt.

"Maybe," he says.

A ring fort makes a loose horseshoe on the edge of sheer cliffs three hundred feet over the Atlantic. The distance less all the time. People think the monastery is the oldest settlement on the island, but this isn't true. Dún Nead has not survived as well as others, like Dún Aonghasa over on Inishmore so it doesn't attract as much attention but for centuries, the fort was the site of the most brilliant observation of *Samhain* in all of Ireland.

Lines of piled stone curve and bend near the outer wall of the fort and we are inside the dun without knowing it. I've only been here once before. I got the sense as a kid the fort was like the rusted old tractors in the fields, or the old buildings caving in on themselves no one buys, not even for the land; it's no use. Let it go. Gavin found use for it in his book. He changed the name, but otherwise the fort is the fort, down to even the placement of the stones. The ground like the jawbone of some impossible creature.

In his book, he goes back to an ancient night thousands of years ago. The day our ancestors marked the turn of the year from light to dark. Summer to winter. Life to death.

I can see them. People press together in concentric rings around the altar. The night alive with anticipation. A nervous heat. A bonfire rages from a basin atop the altar, making a shadow of the woman standing before it. Nude except for the paint of mud. The echo of the old tongue swirls around the compressed space of the fort.

The woman calls home the spirits of the dead, free to roam the hills and roads this one night of the year when the veil between the world of the living and dead is lifted. Now the veil must be dropped again, and the two worlds separated.

Ach ní anocht, she says. But not tonight.

The crowd stunned. This is not the way. This is not the script. All the living and dead forever and all time are here, in this limbo, wondering what she's up to.

Tonight, we douse the fire. As the dead disguise themselves among us, we disguise ourselves among them and we will not know each other, nor death, nor despair.

The woman sinks her hands into the smoldering ash and smears the dead soot on the faces of the gathered. Warm and cool at once. Everyone gets their dark and a more bountiful darkness replaces the light she consumed, one candle at a time.

Gavin takes my hand. "What are you thinking about?"

You take my hand. Palm my ashen cheeks. Kiss the inherent fire. Your life the flare of an ember, cooling forever, a mote of dust on the cheek of God.

"Nothing," I say.

The sky swirls with the ejecta of constant waves. Comets in the mist. Up here, as high as you can go, you see the bend in the island. The strain of such a long war with the sea. Only a few inches of packed seaweed separates you from stone that has denied an ocean for ages. The landscape all around us is emaciated, the skin of the island sunk to veins of piled stone. Its endurance impresses.

Mystifies.

The same passion that spurred men to search for the fountain of youth draws people here like honey. On the surface they think they've come for the language; the antiquity; the remove from the civilized world you both love and hate. Yet all those things represent the one thing, the unnamed thing, the primal desire to connect to the beginning. To Eden. Xanadu. Tír na nÓg.

Life as it was then and always is. The Irish soul is eternal and gentle, and never more so than in Aran. But here you discover the true nature of eternity: haggard, scarred, and existing. To live forever is to do so at the expense of life.

An tús.

We cuddle up on what had been altar. I know he's not giving the ashes to the sea. This wandering of his is as much for me as it is him. Or maybe this is how he's letting go. Sewing up the space his Da left with me, a stitch at a time. A day at a time.

"There was an Italian girl looking for you today," I say.

He makes this face. "Busted."

"She was young for you. Just."

"They come up to me in the pub. I don't mind, but... their parents send them, I think. They want to know when the plane is coming back. How much money it will take."

"How much?"

"It was twenty-five hundred for me."

"Lord God. Round trip?"

He rubs his neck. "Not exactly."

I say nothing. What is there to say.

He sits forward, his arms on his knees. How far America must seem now. How hopeless.

"I talked to my mom this morning," he says.

"Wasn't it the middle of the night for her?"

"She's always up late. I told her I was still here, and... she started talking about my dad. She never does. He came back from Vietnam, and he was... he had a really bad time of it over there. They met at a bar. She said she thought she could sort him out. She thought she could help him."

"Some people can't be helped," I say.

He tries a smile. "I guess that's all of us now."

"She wants you home, your Ma."

"She never really says what she wants."

"Maybe she's trying to tell you something, but she's too polite to come out and say it."

He takes a long look at me. "I think she should just tell me."

What does she do, his Ma, up all night? Watch television? Reruns, I imagine. Infomercials. The bleeding news. She sits and she watches the same shows over and I don't know why he needs to make some peace with this man he barely knew. Men invest so much in reaching some understanding with their fathers. Mothers an afterthought. They are all just boys, off on their own journeys, looking for the same thing but rarely intersecting. And the mothers. The mothers sit on the shore, and wait.

"The party is next week," I say. "*Samhain*."

He goes tense, as he does any time this comes up. Now I think about it, he played a bit dumb talking about *Samhain* with me before. He had to have known about it, to write his book.

"You've been here to the fort before."

"When I first came to the island," he says.

"And the monastery."

He nods.

"You acted like you didn't know what it was."

"I just wanted to talk to you."

"Did you know who I was?"

"I'd seen you. I asked Colm about you. He didn't really say, you know. He acted like he didn't want to talk about it."

No wonder they get on. Two men sitting at the bar pretending not to know what they know. Don't we all pretend. Here we are acting like a couple teenagers, and the world is ending. The sea closing in. The future washing away.

I look out to sea. "There'll be no landing here at all soon."

He lets go of me. "Yeah."

My fingers caress the back of his neck. "Long swim."

"Doable."

"But you're ancient."

He rests an arm inside my leg. "I don't feel old. I don't feel ready to... I feel like I can do anything."

Almost. "You could build a plane from scrap."

"If you've got one lying around, I could fly it."

"You could not."

"I took flying lessons a while back. It's been years, but I remember most of it. I never got my license. It was one of those things that seemed important for a minute."

"What else can you do?"

He shrugs. "There's like, some sexual stuff."

"Hmm."

"Plus – don't tell anyone, but – I'm CIA."

"Are you now?"

"I'm developing you," he says, leaning into me.

"For what?"

"I can't say. Triple Double Top Secret."

"Have I been selected? For the rocket, like? There's a rocket, isn't there? You're picking one girl out of all the countries in the world to go and repopulate humanity somewhere else in the universe."

"You figured me out."

"Are there men from all over as well?"

"Nah, it's just me."

I pinch his ear. "Lucky you."

He rests his head in my lap. "It's my burden."

"I'll have to learn to share you, then."

He brushes my cheek. "You'll be my wife, though."

"The others are just your concubine?"

"Everybody has their place."

I kiss his hand. "You have one seat. On the rocket now. Who do you send? Me or your Ma?"

"Um. Bono."

"I'll throw you off the cliff."

"Is this like Bono anger, or..."

I give him a little push. "I'll do it."

"Why do you hate Bono?"

"And I was going to let you do your sexual stuff tonight."

He sits up. "I'd pick you."

"Too late."

"You know I would. You'd be queen of the new order."

I shrug. "I can't be bothered, really."

"Are you negotiating a better position? You're queen."

"You had it. You lost it."

"I would," he says. "Marry you."

"Don't be daft."

"I love you, Mairead."

"Listen to you."

He kisses me. "I do."

I squirm out of his arms. Some black leech thing stuck to my pant leg. It comes away in this string of mucus, like. I throw it to the sea. Gavin sits there, a lump of defeat. I tell myself it's going to be like this. These dead ends. These potholes. He doesn't mean anything by it. No one does.

But then I know it's not going to be like this.

It isn't going to be anything at all, because he's leaving. This is just us walking together for this bit of our lives. This is just the mercy we allow ourselves.

For now.

CHAPTER EIGHT

Birds peep out the slats of the old post box Colm converted to a feeder out the front of his house. Always tinkering, him. Trying to take something broken and make something better of it. I find him in the garage, as you do. The boot up on the car.

I must be a ghost, the way he stares. "How's herself?"

"Do you know I checked the furnace?"

"And?"

"Probably does need some care."

"I'll have a look at it today, if you like."

I start down the drive, but then I stop. "And don't be bringing Gavin with you when you do. Don't be bringing me up with him again. It's none of your business."

Pipits orbit the feeder, each waiting their turn. Colm built that for me. He meant it for me.

Grease streaks Colm's chin. "I meant nothing by it."

"I don't need any looking after."

"Could be I was thinking of the both of you." Colm scrapes the grime off his hands with a cloth looking like he's been using it all my life. "Could be I was thinking of myself."

"What's it to you, anyways?"

"He's a bit like I was, Gavin. In my younger days. Or my more recent days, but when I had his legs. Men search, you know. You understand. We have to have some purpose. Some mission."

"I'm no one's mission."

"Which is why I told him. You're not Superman, come down from on high. And she's not your salvation."

How could I be anybody's salvation? Why would Gavin ever think so? "He's leaving, so. He's going back."

Colm scratches his chin. "Is he?"

"What does he tell you?"

"He doesn't tell me anything. He doesn't need to. He loves you. That's plain. And you seem... better, Mairead. You seem like you're doing better."

I claw the hair out my eyes. "I'm not doing anything."

"You've gone back to work, haven't you?"

"They need me."

"We all have needs. None of this changes that. You deserve love in your life. You deserve happiness."

What do I deserve. Do you know.

"Do you love him?" Colm says.

My heart doesn't flutter at the thought of him. My heart chews through my rib cage to get its teeth in him. I want the fire between us to consume us both. I want love to be what destroys me. Not God. A dead star. I want there to be love enough left in me to kindle fire. We don't have any time. There's no other way it could have happened.

This is our time, and that's that.

"He's leaving," I say.

"Your Da came here on a weekend. He stayed the rest of his life. So many have. Terrence. The German woman. There's something here, we don't see. It's born in us. You have to leave to know it. This bounty. This privilege."

"We live on a rock in the bleeding ocean."

"That's all the world is. An island lost at sea. Anyways. Your Da found what he was looking for here. Didn't keep him from drinking, but it kept him from walking out into the bloody water. So we got on, Gerry and me. Your man was a master in the art of the drink. Your man was Yoda. I was but Luke Skywalker. He trained me, that man. And I learned well. He got where he couldn't keep up with me. I couldn't keep up with myself."

Colm puts the hatch down on the car.

"You were his joy in life. If he had any idea of your suffering now... he asked me. Gerry. There at the end. 'You'll be looking after her for me, Colm.' You'll forgive me."

Tiny puffs of gray clouds race across the veil of others, like pilot fish. "You're assuming."

"I'm asking."

"You're talking about bleeding *Star Wars*."

"I was thinking of you, earlier. It was a day like today, the day you were born. The sea was excited that day. The sky was anxious. They dragged your Ma kicking and screaming onto the helicopter down the airstrip. You could hear her across the island. Your man called me from the hospital in Galway and said she'd delivered you on the way over. In mid-air."

"In limbo, from the start."

"You were too good for the world, even then."

The birds twist around the feeder in confusion. "I just came here for the furnace, like."

His hand touches my elbow. "You did nothing wrong, Mairead."

I step back. "I have to go."

"You're angry. You're hurt. You're punishing those you love to punish yourself. I understand."

"I have to."

I walk back to the road. The air clings with rain. A haggard, hungry pant funnels down the stone sluice of the high road. The dog scampers out of the mist. I look ahead, expecting Gavin. For once, it's just the dog. It's just me.

"Go on now," I say. "Away with you."

He trots to the mouth of a boreen off the high road, leading down to the eastern shore. The vanishing headstones. Ireland, ghosting in and out of fleeting clouds.

There is something here we don't see.

○

Rain scours the roof. Wind nips at the flimsy plywood covering the windows. The apartment erodes around us, and the night, down to the soft recoil of our hearts in the mattress.

"You do this thing when you're not sure," Gavin says. "Your nose goes one way and your lips the other."

He chases my lips with his. My nose. He kisses my eyes. *I love your eyes.* What does he see in them. A shrinking universe. The tiny, rocky world of the girl who grew up on the island, too small for her. The glittering giant of New York, ringed with light, its surface covered in an ocean of alcohol and I've never experienced this with anyone, this existing, naked of thought or fear. We shed our inhibition, our clothes as we are drawn into the slow, inevitable dance of two bodies caught in their respective gravity, colliding, drifting apart and then back, always falling back into impact.

○

On the way back from the home, I find Ma half naked in the road. She weaves circles around me, the sleeves of her sweater flapping in the breeze like little penguin wings.

"Inside," I say.

"Caoimhe," Ma says. "My father's not home."

"I said inside."

"Not home. Not home. Not home."

I pull her along with me into the yard. The front door half open again. Lord God. This anger. I'm going to scream. I can't scream. She dances around me, like a bleeding loon.

"You'll catch your death."

"Not home."

"Lord God, I can't do this. I can't. Not home not home not home and nobody's fucking home."

"Caoimhe!"

"There's no Caoimhe, Ma."

She twirls back out into the road.

"Go on, then. Go on and leave me."

I slam the door behind me. Ma corkscrews back through the yard, singing this song about some woman I don't know.

I want to scream.

I hear this scratching. I go to the door. The dog outside.

I find her in the yard. "Ma."

"Caoimhe."

"Ma, come inside."

I sit her down in front of the telly. A snowstorm of fear. I place a blanket over her and start to go make some tea and she grabs my hand. *Shh*, she says, her finger hooking at her lips. She pulls me into the recliner with her. *Shh.* I'm on top of her and there's nothing to her but she holds on to me like I'm the last bit of dry land in the ocean. I wiggle in a bit so we're both kind of in the chair together and we're holding each other, Ma and I, watching the news as the day dies in the west. The night goes on. Gavin comes after dark, but I don't want to move so I let him knock. I let the dog scratch and we sit there all night, laughing at fucking reruns and shite commercials.

Tomorrow will be different.

For a long stretch, his mother wrote bad cheques to get them by. Gavin tells me this in bed as rain falls mad on the island. The two of us comparing scars. War stories. This was back in the 80s, when people still wrote cheques. They never had money. Something called food stamps came at the first of the month, but if it fell on a Saturday

DARBY HARN

or Sunday or worse yet a holiday and you missed the postman, it was days, he says; days of piecing together meals from boxes of stale cereal from the food bank. Expired Mars bars. Powdered milk.

"But you have everything in America," I say.

"Including poor people."

We were comfortable. No real money, but Da did fine and Ma has his pension. Or she did, until they closed the banks. She wouldn't notice, even if she were well. When the lights go, she'll not be bothered. There was no electricity in the house until 1981 and to hear her tell it, the lights are an inconvenience. There was no bloody phone until the 90s. The world beyond and all its convenience couldn't reach us until it came all at once in the new millennium and I think she thinks I was swept away by it. How could I not be.

I am not my mother. I am not made of harshness and determination. My father was a wandering soul, fitful and wanting and there is something here I do not see. The island was relentless in its wonder, he told me so. The snowflake sunrises. The reed of a single flower growing in the shelter of a deep crack in limestone. The salt fringed hair of a young girl with a pocketful of birds. Life flourishes here, despite all its inhibitions. Ma was the island to him. The remoteness. The desolation. The beauty. The strength.

What does he see here, Gavin. What does he want for.

He goes on with his tale of woe. Finally, the stores got smart about flagrant cheque bouncers and one day the sheriff came for his ma. It was summer. Sticky. The electricity wasn't on. It was sweltering inside the house, the two of them clustered around a portable television/radio combination box that ran on batteries. Johnny Carson by candlelight. The world still black and white. His ma stood in the door and argued with the police.

I won't leave him.

The sheriff took her away. Gavin sat there, for hours, in front of the TV, looking back at the door, expecting her to come through. Sometime near dusk his father came over.

It's two hundred dollars for bail, he said. *Get your shoes on.*

The two of them went out to some place called K-Mart out on the old highway. Father and son, on an adventure. Each of them picked out a pair of tight jeans and went into the dressing room, one after the other. They pulled the jeans they came in wearing over those and walked out. They did this five or six times and then because the store took returns back without receipts then, they returned each pair of jeans that same night, one after the other.

My laughter escalates with each pair of jeans. "Did your man not wonder where all the fucking jeans were coming from?"

The two hundred dollars came quick and they got her out of jail. With the little extra left over they all went to the truck stop, the three of them for the first time in years, for the last time in their lives, 1987.

"I still steal things," he says. "Sometimes."

"Don't start."

"Ink pens. Batteries. Gum. I don't know why."

"But you're money, now."

"I just fix on things."

"You've stolen things here on the island?"

He brushes my lip with his thumb. "Feels like it."

Everything feels stolen: your life. This moment. His being here at all. Mine. We are thieves all of us, and our punishment is for our lives to be stolen back. There were nights growing up for him trying to fall asleep in a house without power, belly rumbling, as railcars full of grain rumbled down the tracks a few blocks away from his house. Oceans of corn stretched into Iowa infinite. Inishèan yields little beyond some of the most staggering sights on Earth. That is the magic of the island. Beyond is at your doorstep. Our bellies may rumble, but our souls never do. I am starved. I am mad with hunger. The monster in me devouring all my living so quickly the force of the feast sets my entire life in motion, spinning about an empty center. Everything I know and love swirling down the drain, crashing and colliding into each other, reducing down to nothing until *poof*.

All gone.

○

"Here?" I say.

Gavin and I inch down grass carpeted limestone steps from the buckled road to a strand the sea exposed. This is foolish of us but then this is our fashion so we go on, being fools, further out into the moonscape the retreating sea exposed. Crabs skulk through the seaweed. The rock slick. The seals beach hundreds of yards off shore and we just keep going, skipping from one pink stained stone to the next, like playing hopscotch with no end.

Do I want it to end?

A rogue wave could come in. I could slip on a rock and brain myself. He could. Could I? Could I slip, right now, and pull him with me? I squeeze his hand. He squeezes back. He's got me. I pull and then he's done; he guides me to a flat bit of rock and we sit, where people have not sat or stood since there was ice covering the world.

His hand touches his coat pocket. "Maybe."

For a long time we watch the seals sleep. They rest their hairy chins just over the water. How tired they must be, spending all night in the turbulent sea. How sad they must be, to fight this war with the water every single day. How angry they must be. Who do they blame.

Do they know.

Gavin holds the pill bottle in his hands. The current surging through him to twist off the cap. The strain on his face. The trap he's set for himself. It's like giving up the drink. You want to. You just can't. It's nothing to do with wanting. You've no control over it.

He can't let go.

He never had any handle on his father to begin with if I understand him, and this pilgrimage he's taken to Inishèan is not so much about his father as it is him. He never knew his father. There will never be an answer as to why; why his father disappeared and reappeared in his life like a comet. No one could tell him why his father ignored him, his brothers, his sisters from other women, his own health until that gave up on him the same as the rest.

76

There is no letting go.

There is only the loosening of your dead fingers as the current rips you away from the thing you've held most dear. Why does he want me to be here for this. Why do we go through this. I wouldn't tolerate someone sitting over me, watching me, tapping their watch and I brush his cheek. The dust of a beard on him now. The gray in it gives him this quality. How to describe it. He seems his age. Himself. He buttons me up in his coat. Heavy with the weight and smell of days of rain. Of the sea. In his frayed sweater and tattered jeans and wrinkled shoes he seems one of the men of the boats. A man of Aran. He could be a man. I could be a woman. We could just be, fighting over our bit of earth every day, for as long as we can.

We kiss long and sweet. He holds me close. So close. The pill bottle like a rock between us. Would you have wondered over your father. Would you have known anything was missing.

Would I have ever told you.

You can see the black hole in the day now. Properly it's all the mess of planets the black hole is gobbling up so fast it can't get to it. I don't know a thing about the planets. You would have liked them. Frontiers. Possibilities.

"At least there's no one suffering out there," I say.

Gavin rubs my back. "What?"

"On those planets. Saturn. Whichever one it is."

"There might have been life on Titan once," Gavin says. "There's probably life on Europa. We'll never know."

"Europa?"

"One of Jupiter's moons."

"How could there be life?"

"Europa's covered in ice, but under the ice there's this ocean. Europa gets pulled back and forth between Jupiter and the other moons, so it has an active core like we do, which heats the ice and creates the ocean. There's no sunlight at all, but there's none on the bottom of the ocean here, so there could be little guys down there."

"Little guys?"

"Like anglerfish or something. Lanternfish."

"And they're going to be killed, just like us."

"Maybe the black hole yanks it loose, like it did Pluto."

"So... say Europa got spit out, like. This ocean would still be there? The little guys would?"

"So long as the core remained active," he says.

"Say it happens. It will happen. The little guys survive."

"The little guys survive."

The cold of the water settles in me. The sober clarity of the air. Gavin's eyes linger heavy on the shadowed mainland.

"You know... there's this theory, in quantum physics. Information can't be destroyed. Anything that goes into a black hole, it comes out somewhere. So it's not the end. Stephen Hawking said this thing once... he said if you ever find yourself in a black hole, don't give up. There's a way out."

"Joke's on him."

Gavin brushes my cheek. "There's always a way out."

The seals bark in confusion. The tides answer in the quickening rhythm of distant thunder. We scramble back to a ledge. Tangled in the seaweed we find a dead dolphin. Blood caked at its nose. I've never seen a dolphin before. We climb the steps back to the road. A boy stands on the shoulder.

"Declan?"

Eithne draws him back. The color goes right her face when she sees me. She looks back down the road, like she's afraid of what I might see but I hear them. The lash of their laughter. The punch of their joy. The raw scrape of their boredom. Lord God. She's brought the entire school out here. The children that still bother going, at least. Eight of them. Her smile is the smile of a stroke victim. She can't look me in the eye, Eithne.

"*Slan,*" she says.

The fuck do I say. The fuck do I go. There's nowhere to go. Gavin takes my hand. He's taking my hand and she's looking at us queer like and I snatch it back.

He clears his throat. "Field trip?"

"The school's all boarded up, you know," she says.

"Right, right."

"It felt closed down. It felt like we weren't to be there and I thought, the sun's out. What's reading books? Especially now. So. We'll take a walk, then. I'll teach them the seals."

"Cool. I think you've just missed them, though."

The boy stares at me. His hand gripping hers. Nose red and crusted in snot. His jumper streaked with it.

"You can kind of see one," Gavin says. "See?"

"Oh, yes," Eithne says. "Do you see him, Colin?"

The boy shakes his head. Gavin leans down and helps him out by pointing. The other kids cluster around him, their awe and indifference scattered on the breeze like buckshot. He points out the bobbing heads of the seals in the swelling sea and his enthusiasm bleeds into theirs. His boyishness becomes nauseous and Eithne tries her smile again. The rigor won't come out her face. She's stricken with the same paralysis everyone has been since you left me. Everything frozen here except the days. The tides. The erosion of the roads and the island and the soul.

Her hair is the end of a flamethrower in the wind off the sea. "Youse are on a field trip as well?"

"What?"

"Showing him around, are you?"

I step back. "I am."

"That's grand."

"You shouldn't be on the road with them, Eithne."

The words grind in her teeth. "There's no traffic."

"But the tides."

"They seem polite, today."

The tide crashes into the rocks below. Children squeal under the splash of spray. The most washing their clothes have seen in a while. Giggles rupture with the breaking of the waves. Their little teeth like fences of irregular stone.

"It's not safe," I say.

She nods. "Every day, I ask myself... what do I bother for? What point is there teaching them any of this that they'll never get to use and... I can't send them home. There's nothing for them to do there. There's nothing to eat." Her fingers pinch my jacket. "Isn't it awful?"

Another year. Another year and you would have been in the preschool. I would have dressed you in a red jumper and taken your picture in it and put it on the fridge, like and your schooling would have been brief but you would have been.

"Awful," I say.

"I can't think of it," Eithne says. The numbness loosening in her tongue. "Their parents. The hell they must be going through, knowing. I think myself lucky, I suppose. All the doctors and the money, but now... I don't know. Maybe it's better this way. Do you know what I mean?"

"Better?"

"Oh. No. Mairead."

I start down the road home. The confusion of the children stabbing me in the back. Their quick indifference. Gavin runs after me. That dog. I cut off the low road up a boreen snaking up into the hills and he doesn't know why I'm going or why. I leave him there stranded, like a rock. A dead dolphin. Every single one of us, shrouded in seaweed soon enough.

CHAPTER NINE

Back at the house I dig that bottle of Jameson's Aoife left out of the cupboard. My hands shake as I pour a deep, quick glass. Ma smacks her lips as she passes through the kitchen like a gray meteor and I dump the glass down the sink. The rest of the bottle.

Bleeding coward.

Aoife made me out to be some hero, going to the States. Maybe I made myself out so, back then. Anything to get my blood up. Truth is I was scared to death. Lord God. That first year. I shared a one bedroom on the ass end of Bergen St. with Delphine. Delphine the talker. Everything excited her about the city. So it did me, but fuck's sake, there was no need to yammer about it all night and day. She couldn't be blamed, I suppose. Delphine was a Dub, so she was keen for a proper city. It didn't matter we lived on top of each other, or that hot water was a theory more than a practice. My theory of New York disproven in lonely nights trying to ignore the kids making games out of running up and down the stairs, the industrial music of the street outside, the moaning and wet snap of lips from her room.

I wanted the city. I hated the city.

I hated myself more for not liking New York the way Delphine did. The way everyone did. I took my guitar and sang at open mic nights. I pulled tabs on bills for WANTED: SINGER. Answered online ads. I'd sing a while in this band or that one. The Piss Jitters. Ghost Jail. Back Issue Diver. Nothing ever clicked. I wanted to play in an Irish band; I didn't. I wanted to write my own songs; I couldn't. There was something wrong with me. This cavity opened in me. This monster. Hungry. Thirsty. Always. I was in this drain, funneling down with all my doubt. It was my fault I wasn't getting on. My fault I was spending my nights alone in a city of 8 million people, sick for home. Ma's voice in the back of my head: *It's like I told you.*

Every time I rang home, Da gushed down the line. *My American girl.* He understood the dreams of a distant country. He tired of Belfast, past its troubles but stubborn in the memory of its hurt. He fell in love with the idea of some rustic peace in the foggy moors with his doting, country wife and his quiet, respectable daughter. He imagined me weaving a life of promise. I never had the heart to disappoint him. That wasn't me, pouring my fear of failing, of fulfilling her prophecy of me into the drink. Drowning out her nagging with the hum of the bell I rung myself with. That wasn't me who disappeared Wednesday nights when I got paid at the bar and returned, unscathed like, for the weekend. No one noticed. *She's quiet, that one. Steady.* I never touched the drink at work. A person must have rules. Temptation is a fact of life. A rule of physics, like gravity. Gravity can be escaped. You first must understand it. And did I ever achieve escape velocity; I got lost in the void. I became separate from her, the drunk. She became a completely different person.

That wasn't me, chewed up and spit out on the rooftop of a building down on the waterfront in Brooklyn with not a fucking clue how I got there or how long I had been. My knickers gone. I thought that was the bottom. I went to a meeting and I turned to God. Deliver me, Lord. Please. That wasn't me, let off the hook by Da getting sick. In the market in Kilbanna just back, everyone fawned on me. The prodigal daughter returned.

Here I am.

○

"My name is Mairead and I'm an alcoholic," I say and my name comes back at me. We are four, gathered in a circle on the dance floor at the Halla Fáinne. "I am three years sober. I saw a boy today."

Angus twists out of his chair for the coffee stand. Trevor McDonagh stays put. He is one of the few men my age still on the island. Other men went to London or Sydney. New York, like I did. His parents own one of the hostels. He works there as a cook. Or he did. I've had no talking to him for months now. Most people here think he's your father. He's no woman. He's never had one, not even Aoife. Not that she could tell his interest.

"I saw them all," I say. "Down the seal colony. They're all going to be buried in those uniforms of theirs."

The hall creaks with men shifting in their chairs. I hear this scratching somewhere outside.

"If they're buried. We'll all be washed away, won't we? Like Declan was. Swept away. We should bury ourselves. We should anchor our bodies. Scar the earth."

The Earth should bear the scars of its living. Her grief should be ours. Her children gone before her. We'll be the first to go. The last living things to die on earth will be the little urchins on the bottom of the deepest sea. The telly said so. The old things. First ones in. Last ones out. The sea vacuumed off of them. Their deaths this achievement. Sea urchin to astronaut in a single move. Better than we've ever done. Fuck evolution. All you have to do is wait.

Thank you, Mairead. Glad you came.

Colm scratches his chin. "I'm Colm. I'm an alcoholic."

He had a drink today. He had a drink yesterday. He drinks and is a drunk and so it is. Thank you, Colm. Thank you for your ensuring that we drunks would have whiskey yet at the end of the world. A desert, always, the end of the world. In films. The truth is we're all going to drown. May as well be a pint as the ocean deep.

The door creaks open. The dog nudges through. He scampers across the hall and spreads out at my feet.

Angus mashes his gums. "You'll let anyone in here now."

Colm grunts. "You knew that coming in, Angus."

I expect Gavin to be behind him, but he's not. He's not cursed with the drink as I am. His father was. And yet he told me how his father was sober over twenty years. A sponsor, at AA. He met them all the first time at the funeral. Gavin had no idea. He didn't understand how his father could ignore his family and then at the same time, be there for strangers. I don't understand.

The door opens again. Aoife comes in out of the rain. Hair drizzled like amber all over her face.

"Singles night is Saturday," I say.

"Ha ha ha." She kisses my cheek and sits beside me. "Hiya. I'm Aoife. I'm an alcoholic. A drug addict. Sex addict."

"This here is just for the drink, Aoife."

"It's the same hole, no matter what we fill it with."

Trevor sighs. "I'm Trevor. I'm an alcoholic."

She rests her chin on her hand. Lord God. She's dripping wet with the drink. "Spill it. Ha."

"I'm three days sober. I'm doing my best. It's hard."

"And any sexual issues?"

He shakes his head. "None."

"No frustrations."

"I'm developing one."

"I'll help you sort it out," she says.

"I'm grand, thanks."

"You are." She leans over to him. Her hand on his knee. Christ. "Be honest, Trevor. What is it with me?"

Colm scratches his chin. "This is a legitimate question."

Trevor scoots away. "Have we all gone?"

Aoife leans back so far she nearly tips over. "Oh, c'mon. Have some fun. We're all for the grave, like. Tell me. How many women you been with, Trevor?"

Angus grunts at the coffee stand. "You let in one..."

"Shut your hole, you old git. You only wish." Aoife nudges Trevor's arm. "So? How many?"

"I don't know. Not a lot."

"Doesn't matter for men, does it? Four."

"That's a good guess."

"I'm talking about me now."

"You've been with four women?"

Her smile is slow in coming. She holds up four fingers. "What do you say? You want to be a thumb?"

Trevor laughs. "I bet that works."

Aoife is bewildered. "Why shouldn't it?"

I pull at her sleeve. "Catch yourself on, woman."

She turns to me. "How many women you been with?"

"You've soured me on the lot."

She sticks her tongue out.

Colm sighs. "Anything else anyone wants to add?"

Angus Dolan clears his throat. "I'll tell you my trouble," and the faces of the others sink. We were done. "I'm supposed to have this higher power. And I have these prayers, written out for me. These aren't my words. Someone else wrote these. You can't talk to God with someone else's words. It must be why He doesn't answer. None of these words are His. None of these words are ours. We had words. We had our own faith. Our own way of living and then we took on the idols of others and now we are ignored. Now we are judged. We're fucked."

Aoife snorts. "Except for Trevor here."

I pinch her arm. "Come on to fuck, Aoife."

She sours. "Can I sleep at yours again?"

"Are you not at the home tonight?"

"Why, are you down the pier?"

"Shut your gob."

She covers her mouth. "I didn't say anything."

"It's a very difficult time," Colm says, his voice cutting through the hall. "You and I have discussed this before Angus. Every day is a contest. Every day a battle. I guess I'm trying to say keep talking to God, Angus. Don't give up."

Thank you, Colm.

Angus shrugs. "What answer can there be?"

Colm sighs. "There won't be one."

"Then what am I talking to him for?"

"You're asking the question. The question is all that matters. God gave you one thing above all other creatures and that's the ability to question your existence. But there's no understanding. Not in this life. And no sense carrying around questions for answers that'll be waiting for you at the end."

"Practical," I say.

"Christ was a practical man. Same as Yoda. You take with you only what you need. Nothing more."

I roll my eyes. No wonder he and Gavin get on.

Trevor spins a straw around his cup of coffee. "We're all fucked, aren't we? We've heard the answer. The answer is I'm tired of youse. Youse are yesterday's news."

"What was Christ's answer on the cross?" Colm says.

"Christ was resurrected," Trevor says.

"We may yet be."

Trevor shakes his head. "As what? To where? In the Bible it says God was to make the world his Kingdom in the end. There's not going to be any world, is there?"

"Angus gets no answer because there's no answer," I say. "We all create our own higher powers but it's us talking to ourselves. There's nothing else for us."

"There's grace," Colm says.

"The fuck do I care about grace?"

Colm opens his mouth to say something, then thinks different. He has plenty on his mind. He doesn't say it. He doesn't know how. He's never had the words for me.

"Say your peace," I tell him.

Colm scratches his chin. "Finding grace is us finding our better selves. Asking the question. Accepting the silence."

"I don't want my better self. I want my life back."

"We can never go back. Only forward. You pray each step is better than the last. Each step is true."

"Did you get that out of a fortune cookie?"

"You've road ahead of you, Mairead."

"What's the rest of my life, Colm? Watching Ma go to pieces? Everyone here on the bloody island?"

He grimaces. "We all face that."

"I won't," I say. The air goes out of the room. "I won't be some dog wandering the hills knocking over refuse bins. I won't be sleeping in ditches and pleading for mercy at the end. I'll be going to my death. I'll be going to my son. He's waiting."

The room creaks.

"We've all thought about it," Trevor says. "It's a decision we all face. Mairead is being very honest. She's told us a lot tonight. Thank you, Mairead. For your courage."

I shake my head. "I'm a coward."

"There's no cowards allowed in here," Colm says.

Thank you, Colm.

I listen to them debate and argue, like I'm not even there. I've been so deep in my own pain it never occurred to me what anyone else thought about the end. They go back and forth now as if they've had this conversation a hundred times, and so they have, in their heads. Their hearts. For each, it's different. Angus has his wife, her sister, her children, their children. Colm has only himself now. Aoife has no one. Her parents are both passed. Her brothers and sisters gone to the mainland. She leans on her hand. Drunk. Exhausted. Alone.

I pinch her again. "Come on, then."

She picks up her coat and stumbles after me. The men go on arguing their deaths. The dog stays put. He seems confused. Like he doesn't know if he's coming or going. I hold the door open.

I'm always holding the door open.

Curled claws patter across the hall. We go out into the piss. Gavin is closer. Ma is waiting. You're waiting, I know. This pain. I can't live with this pain. My chest open. My heart gone.

Mo leanbh. Mo stór.

She leans on me, Aoife. "Can I... can I sleep?"

"Let's just go to the home. You can rest. I'll take the night shift, yeah? You get some sleep tonight."

"What about him?"

We trudge up the hill, toward the home. He can manage without me for one night. It's not as if I'm going anywhere.

○

Rain syrups the roof of the sunroom adjacent the oratory in the home. Paintings of the island adorn the walls, along with wicker baskets and ceramic crockery. A pictorial tells the story of the bright red dresser at the center of the room, tracing its crafting on the island in the 1950s through its recent restoration by the residents.

The last one is of some stranger, an unbridled smile on her face as her son palms paint all over her cheeks. The caption reads: *Making a mess.* The Mairead in the photo doesn't seem as alien as she might have a few weeks before. I can still smile. He makes me smile; he makes me laugh. We are childish, almost. We are young.

I feel young.

Aoife plops into a sofa "Telly said the storm is going to be the biggest on record."

I haven't seen any news. Rain skitters and skats against the boards of the home and I can't tell it from the drumming of idle fingers and rattle of near empty pill bottles. I haven't been away from here, out in the dark, for days.

"Are you fine here, Aoife?"

She blows away the hair that's fallen across her eyes. "Have an orgasm for me, will you? Be a love."

○

Spray flicks my cheek and I flinch. Fog gone. Dark left. The moon like a piece of paper someone set on fire to watch it burn. Tides wash over the broken lighthouse on a knot of an island between Inishèan and Inishmore. The peaks of Connemara like the shadows of sleeping giants across the bay on the mainland. Another land. Another world. Are you there.

Are you waiting for me.

I haven't been to the cemetery in days. The home absorbs all my time and attention. Gavin. For months I've been out here on the shore, wrinkled in a damp, cold fugue, laced up, sewn up and ready for earth. Now I shy from the spray. The wind. The sea shies away, as if to tempt me into chasing it and I've got to get on. They're waiting for me back at the home. They need me.

Don't you need me.

The sea swipes at my heels. The tides jealous. Spiteful. This going back and forth. This tearing me apart, day and night.

I've got to get on.

○

"This is going to be a proper storm," I say.

The dog sits on the floor in a permanent state of alarm, head darting after every sound the gale produces as it blunts against Gavin's apartment. The boards over the broken windows bow and stretch. All this and the worst of it is still days away. On the telly, the weatherman tracks the progress of Storm Asterisk out in the Atlantic. Headed right for us. *Storm of the century,* he says, without any trace of irony. The mannequin at the anchor desk asks him what he's calling it 'Asterisk' for.

The century being truncated so, the weatherman says.

Gavin puts some of the shredded plywood on the fire. "Come over here," he says. "You have to be freezing."

I keep to the window. "When I was a girl... a big storm would come up like this and I'd go up to the monastery. Into the tower. The sound the wind would make. I'd sit in there with all the birds and just listen. I suppose it was a bit mental."

"Your mom had to have been scared to death."

"She didn't notice," I say. "I should get back to her."

"You'll get soaked."

"Shall I call a taxi?"

"Colm will probably take you. He has gas."

"I'm fine walking."

"Let me walk back with you, at least."

I shake my head. "They say the storm surge will be deadly. Could wash out the road, tides being what they are. I suppose the airstrip will be washed out as well."

He sighs. Why do I bother. If he lets go of that pill bottle, it will be as the waves wash over the rim of the island.

"I don't want to... push," Gavin says. "I don't want to get too far ahead, but then I think there's really not that much runway left. Mairead. This feels like home to me. You feel like home."

The boards groan off their nails over the window.

"The party for *Samhain* is tomorrow," I say. I wait for him to say *Yes. And as we agreed, I'll be leaving.* He says nothing. "I'll probably fall asleep before midnight, anyways. Usually I watch the *Voyager* at 11 and nod off a bit."

"*Voyager?*"

"The *Star Trek*. Idiots."

"You watch *Star Trek?*"

I leave the window, and sit in his lap. "Did my stock just go up with you?"

"Well, yeah. By a lot."

"It's terrible, though. I only watch it because... I don't know why. They're always losing shuttles. The ship is always getting torn to pieces. The only thing Janeway ever runs out of is the fucks she has to give. And anything ever goes wrong, they just re-route the whatever to the whatever and on they go. They're stranded on the other side of the galaxy with no way to get home and no food or supplies and they just keep on going, one week after the other. Do you know what I mean?"

"I may have written some angry fan mail," he says.

"You could go to the party, like. As an alien. I could boil up some mashed potatoes and stick it to your forehead."

He pinches me. "I remember this *Star Wars* thing. I don't know. I was in grade school yet. I just had the mask. The little slit for the mouth was so sharp, I cut my tongue on it."

"Why do you men pretend? 'I dunno. Some *Star Wars* thing.' You know full well what it is. You know all the names. The serial numbers on the little robot things, like. You saw it in the theaters, didn't you? The *Star Wars*."

"I saw it at the drive-in."

"Ahhhh, you're *ancient*."

"Too old for you?"

My lips dab at his, once, twice, three times until he catches me. "I'll dress you up. What's his face. Your man with the laser sword, like. Obi-Wan Kenobi."

"It's a lightsaber, just FYI. You'll go?"

"If I go... I'll go with Aoife. I'll meet you there."

He kisses me. "Ok."

"Don't... don't be kissing on me. Don't be hanging on me."

"People tend to expect spectacular displays of public affection from me, so I don't know. I'll do my best."

"Do you know what I mean?"

"It's no one's business. It's just us."

I rest my head against his. "It's just us."

"Mairead. I want you to know... you opened your heart to me. You don't know... I was vanishing. Just like he did. I just went cold. I stand here and stare at the phone. The door. I just close off. Turn and walk out. Drop into the vault. I don't want to do that anymore. I want to live. I want us to live."

"Gavin…"

He chases my lips again. "What if I stayed?"

Lord God. "You can't stay."

"You don't want me to."

"All I want is my son."

He can say nothing. He can do nothing. What is he doing.

What are we doing.

I kick the last of the blanket off and leave the chair. "I need to get on. Ma's waiting on me."

It's all he does is think about this. I know it. How to say it. How to convince me. "Mairead, I love you."

Love. That word lands like the wind against the plywood covering the window. The board strains, bending far as it will go. He's not in love with me. This is just our fear.

Our desperation.

CHAPTER TEN

From up the dark road, the ends of cigarettes seem like fireflies on the front patio of the pub. For a moment it's like it used to be, walking down the lane back home late on a Friday night after some trad. It was never like this, though. Ma was never with me. We've never been anywhere together except funerals and wakes. Tonight she's a dog going down the road, drifting toward every person she comes on.

Ma charges right in to the pub. I keep outside. That German bloke stuck here with the others mixes his accordion whine with all the percussion of the sea, in a chair outside the patio area of the pub.

I nod to the German. *"Tráthnóna maith duit."*

He doesn't look at me. *"Diese contemptable sprache."*

"There's a lull in the storm. The plane will come back."

"Es gibt keine hoffen."

Doesn't sound optimistic. I straighten the cat ears I cut out of some old felt, flopping down on my hair band. The patio fills up. A black-eyed moon plays hide and seek behind some low clouds.

"Cat Sidhe," an Arabic man says. A French glaze to his voice. He sits alone at one of the little tables with a bottle of wine and a deflated pack of cigarettes. I don't know the age of men. They all seem boys to

me now, whether they're gray or not. "I've no milk. Now I will have bad luck."

"I'm bad luck in any case," I say.

"Some wine?"

"Thank you, no."

"Cigarette?"

"They make me gag."

"You must have some vice."

"I keep bringing home things that don't belong to me."

"You are more cat burglar, then? What do you steal?"

"Hope."

He nods, sanguine. "*Oui.*"

"I keep doing it. I just won't be told."

"You cannot steal hope," he says. "Only give it."

"I don't mean to trouble you."

"You are no trouble. *As-salamu alaykum.*"

"*Céad míle fáilte.*"

"*An bhfuil tú ó anseo?*" His Irish is perfect.

"*Tá mé ó Kilbanna.*"

"Ah, the seals. I love the seals. Zaim. My name is Zaim."

I sit with him. "Mairead."

"The nurse?"

There's no disguising it. "I am, so."

"You are not stealing hope from anyone. Let me tell you. There is no hope among we who are stranded here. But when one of us goes to you, they come back with it."

"I don't see how."

"There is hope in strength. And purpose. And order. Order? *Comment dites-vous?* Normalcy. They are sick, you fix them, things are normal. Things continue. Continuity. You have so many words."

"It's just putting bandages on wounds I can't heal."

"There is a lot of hope in bandages."

"That won't go on a card, Zaim."

Zaim waves the cigarette curtly: no. "Perhaps that is why I'm still a poor man. *Tant pis.* Are you sure you will not share some with me? It's the last bottle on the island, so I'm told."

I want to lick the inside of the glass. "Better not."

We sit in the silence, Zaim and I, broken a bit by the intermittent call of the German's accordion.

"You got stranded here, then?"

"I came here with purpose," Zaim says, and tells me what they all do. He came on holiday to the island many summers ago. He had gone up to the monastery with his friends, and on the way back he saw a woman coming out of the water from a swim down the beach. His friends went back on the evening boat. He stayed with her.

"She's not here with you?"

"No," he says, and stabs out the last of the cigarette.

"I'm sorry."

"I have been sorry. A sorry man, without her. But tonight... I am thankful. When I came back here a few months ago, it was to honor our memory of this place. To find something of her again. I meant to go back to France. Now I understand, I began and I end, here."

I should be out there, at the cemetery. In my ending. Why did I come. You know why. I have a start in me yet. I have love yet. So much love. A drowning love. An apocalyptic, fierce love. I'd find those birds on the rocks and I'd bring home to Da to fix. *Fix 'em, Da.* And he couldn't and I'd weep, like I did when it was him there dying and I'd pour myself into the drink just to find a container for all this feeling. I poured all my love into you. Bottomless you were. A reservoir for oceans of love. And I've still love in me yet.

Hope.

"I've upset you," he says.

"It's nothing you've done."

He lights another cigarette, Zaim. "Are you sure you don't want one? It will give you something to do with your hands."

"Hand it over."

He lights a new one on the end of his. *"Besseha."*

I cough a bit. *"Sláinte.* She was from here? Your wife?"

"Italy, in fact. We each knew only a little English. I knew no Italian. Here we were in a place beyond language. This is a place only of heart. Love. You are blessed to have been born of this place. You are born into a love most will never know." He takes a long drag off his smoke. "We hold on, so hard, to their memory. Their sound. Their smell. And the more we remember... the farther away we get from the truth of them. Who they were in truth is gone and dies with every memory. I came back to remember, but now I must forget."

"Forget?"

"It's only when we truly let them go that we may find them. I struggled with this for a long time. I found her. I want to be found. I want to go out to the beach, and be found again."

Mo leanbh. Mo stór.

"I sit and I wait... do you know?"

"*Oui.*"

"I've been waiting, for so long... and he doesn't come."

Zaim nods, like he understands. "May I tell you something?"

"You're drunk, anyways."

"*Oui*, yes." He looks around the patio. "This is life. Here. And this is death. Together. Connected. We look at the world, and we see lines on a map. But there are no lines. Life and death are countries, but there are no lines. We live in hope. We also live in grief. In death. They are here. We don't see them because we think we are some place else, but there is no other place but where you are."

The waitress floats from one table to another like a bee, *bzzz, bzzz, bzzz.* So young. Martin Garret's girl.

"They're serving bacon," Zaim says. "The last bacon."

"I'm not hungry."

He looks up, Zaim, in consideration. "What was the line, in Synge? Early on, when talks about the flour and bacon."

"'*If anything happened to America.*'"

"'*If anything happened to America...*' *Oui.* Have you heard the latest? They passed the law, outlawing pregnancies. Millions of women marched in protest all over the United States. There were riots. Fighting. It was surreal, to see women die for the right to bear children who are doomed to die themselves."

Ash rains on my pants. "Women died?"

"Many."

Da said there were always two Americas. The America of the world, and the world of America. The former opened its arms to the tired and poor. It liberated Europe from its own madness. The latter chased land to the ocean, and swept away an entire race of people in the process. Here at the end, in the twilight of humanity, everyone lives in the world of America, gone from a shining city on a hill to the fiery cap of a waking volcano.

"Mothers should die for their children," I say.

"'*If anything happened to America.*'" He smiles, and gestures to his cheeks. "Back to fish, and poor skin."

"*An tús,*" I say.

"*Oui.* Back to the beginning."

I never read Sygne's book until I had gone to New York and was sore for home, though it has always been around. A constant signifier of our existence. Same with *The Man of Aran*, playing non-stop in the museum in Kilbanna. So many accounts of the lives we live. So many souls come here to discover a way back to something they themselves have lost and in doing so exiled us.

The waitress buzzes through the patio again. I can taste that bacon. The salt. The tongue of flesh it forms in my mouth as it curls under the roof of my mouth. The suckle of fat, soft, pliant, wonderful like the brim of Gavin's lip.

A woman walks past our table. Her eyes linger on Zaim, and then on me, trying to figure us. She goes inside but she must be in the window because Zaim does this little waive.

"I think you've an admirer," I say.

"I have several."

"Go on with yourself."

He laughs. "They flatter me."

"You may as well enjoy yourself. Everyone else is."

Zaim shrugs. "I come here to end."

"I thought the end was the beginning."

"Here I rediscover her. Us. The shape of my life."

These bleeding cat ears won't stay up. "You don't think... you don't think you could meet someone else? And be happy with them, for a little while, at least?"

"Perhaps," he says.

"Maybe they can make the hard parts easier."

"Perhaps, yes."

"It's not what you want."

"This is my story," he says. "This is my choice. I forget my life and perhaps I will be remembered, on the shore."

The accordion fills in the gap in conversation again. Waves break across the island, against the cliffs. This blunt punch, knocking the wind out of the island with every breath.

Zaim clears his throat. "What do you want, Mairead?"

My only start was you. I ended with you, but here I am. There is nowhere for me to go to rediscover you. I go to the shore, as I've done since I was a girl, and you're not there. I can't close the circle.

Aoife stumbles up on the deck. Lord God. Tits bulging out her halter. "Meow," she says, and kisses my cheek.

"You'll ruin my make-up."

She snorts and kisses me on the lips.

"Don't start, Aoife."

Aoife thumbs the lipstick off me. "Oops."

"You out on the piss already?"

"We're going to show these old gits how it's done. One last time, yeah? You and me. Like it was. Who's this?"

"Zaim," I say, leaving the table. "*Slán*."

He nods to me. "*Slán go fóill*."

Aoife hooks my arm with hers. "Picking up another man, Mairead. You've got yours. Leave some for the rest of us."

"Don't be daft. And I'm not drinking. You hear me? I've got to get Ma back, besides. Have you seen Gavin?"

"Your man said he'd be a little behind."

"What have you been talking to him for?"

"He took a fall down the pier. I patched him up."

The bottom goes out of my chest, and my head reels back to that moment Colm sat me down in the living room and told me what I already knew. "He fell?"

"Not very handy, if I had to say. Or... *is he?*"

This woman. She never left puberty. She dangles in front of me like she's on strings, this dopey grin on her face.

"Ah, it's good to see you out. It's good seeing you well."

I don't know what I'm doing here. I told him I'd come and I shouldn't have come. Everyone on the island will be here.

The children.

My cat ears droop down. She straightens them out. "There you are. Look at you. Absolutely fucking state of the art."

"I'm not staying long," I say.

She pulls me along. "C'mon."

"Wait, who's looking after the home?"

"Saidbh."

We both laugh.

○

Vampire nuns lurk next to zombie fisherman, straw men and a robot like, made up of cardboard boxes and cut up litre bottles. No one says a word. Dozens sit at the candle lit tables throughout the pub, silent in their society. At the bar, they pass their drink requests in scraps of paper. The only sound the flutter of the curtains.

Iris falls into line at the bar with the other old timers, their cheer in seeing her not diminished in silence and her joy – this joy, where has it been – is not either. I don't think she ever came out for one of these my entire life, and here she is the life of the party.

Such as it is.

People cluster in front of the fireplace, hogging the heat. An empty table forms the axis of the room, frosted cake and grilled fish and steamed cabbage heaped in its center. A feast like I've not seen in ages. How long has it been since I've had a proper meal. Plates and silverware set out for four, but no one sits at this table.

This is the table for the dead.

In France, during the Reign of Terror, they would have these macabre balls. *Bals des victimes.* You had to be a relative of someone who died at the guillotine. The women would tie these red ribbons around their necks. And Ring a-ring o' roses. *'A-tishoo!, a-tishoo!'* That started during the Black Death. People would walk around with posies in their pockets, because of the smell. People make light of darkness. Death a game. A show. A lullaby. If children can laugh at death, then what fear is death? We all fall down.

The candle on our table struggles. The wick short. The people across from us play a pulse-racing game of hearts. A father, a daughter and a son, in a baby seat.

Aoife drinks. And drinks. And drinks. I do not.

Gavin comes in. He does a ruddy job going to the bar first, and then just naturally arriving to my table.

"Hi –"

I put my finger to my lips. He squints in confusion as I pass him the pen and notepad they left on each of the tables.

???

I take the pen. *No one can talk. Until midnight.*

He pokes me in the shoulder.

Don't start.

He flicks my hand. I make little cat paws and it's so quick with him. Instinctual. Lord God. They're gawking at us.

He takes the pen. *It's hard not being able to talk.*

You'll talk to anyone.

?

Were you going to tell me you fell?

Gavin looks at me, confused. Everyone is confused. The curl in their noses. Their pens scribing like mad. What must they be writing. *I see she's over it, then. Moving on, her.*

Gavin writes again. *What's wrong?*

I write nothing in reply. We sit a long time. The silence like pressure in my ears. Aoife stews, like she'd rather it was just us girls and Gavin sips at his whiskey. I don't know what I thought coming here. I felt this stir in me for something else and I won't even look at him. Everyone is looking at us. When they find my eyes they've something on their mobile. No one is talking and we've been talking for days, Gavin and I. His voice like a breakwater against all these thoughts and you're out there alone and

They should have set out a highchair.

I hunt through the pub for one. They all look as I do. What's she going to do, the woman out there on the rocks? The statue. The gargoyle. Mad with grief, her. In the back by the toilets I find a high chair. Like they hid it from me. I stab it down at the table for the dead. I go back to the table. The clink of glass the only sound. Aoife slinks away to the loo. We're showing them now, aren't we, Aoife? Ma doesn't notice any of it, lost in the company of the silent chorus at the bar. Gavin acts like he doesn't recognize me. How can he.

He takes the notebook. *Let's go.*

There's no leaving.

Gavin drifts over to the bar. The men he bagged sand with the other morning down the pier. Pats on the back. Incomprehensible gestures and muffled laughter. They hang on each other and he is linked in arms going around the bar. He finishes his whiskey and he puts it back and it's full again and the air is full in here. I track down Ma. Let's go. Come on, woman. She makes this noise in complaint and everyone is looking now. Gavin comes over. He puts his arm around me, pulling me in close like he does in the dark or out in our anonymity and he whispers drunk.

Stay.

O

Someone's got trouble with the latch to the stall in the loo. Aoife teeters out to the mirror, thumbing her nose.

"Christ, Aoife."

She stuffs the bag of coke away in her bra. "Want some?"

"You'll be keeping your nose clean when you're on duty."

She snorts. "It is just like old times. I'm still telling you to loosen up, and you're still telling me what to do."

"Lord God, woman. If you were any more loose I'd be carrying around a wrench."

She touches up her lipstick. Fuck's sake, Irish girls and make-up. We slather loads of it on without any sense of its application. She looks like a bleeding drag queen.

Look at me.

My makeup running away. I've gone dark. I brush away what's left of my whiskers with the back of my sleeve and I make it worse. Ash Wednesday all over my face. And still. I don't know who this is, looking back at me. Naked with power. Confidence. Vitality. And yet wasted to bone. Bruised with rain. Pale as the day.

She snorts again. "You even told me what to wear. Do you know? You just made me yours. And then you left."

"There's no talking to you."

Aoife saunters up behind me. Bloodshot eyes staring into mine in the mirror. Her breath hot on my neck.

"Even with all that shit on your face, you've a bit of a glow about you, Mairead. I'd say you look flushed."

"I don't know what you're sore about," I say.

Her voice hushes to a whisper. "I'm always sore for you."

"Don't start."

"What is it, then? Are you worried they'll see youse together, or that they'll see you're happy?"

I dig that bag of snow out her bra. We fight over it into the stall and the bag tears apart between us. Aoife goes to her her knees, trying to catch the falling snow with her tongue.

"You happy now, Aoife?"

Aoife grabs at me. She pulls at my pants and her hands are under my blouse and her tongue is my mouth and she's kissing me. Her damp, quivering palms cradle my face. Her lips linger on mine, as they did when we were girls, practicing.

"Aoife..."

Someone else comes in. A scarecrow, like. She goes right back out. Aoife peels off me. Checks herself in the mirror. Straightens her tits. Wipes the coke off her nose, and she's as ever.

"Someone should be happy," she says, and leaves me.

○

The wind dials me southwards on the crate. I scratch the grit out of my eyes. Domnhall Walsh's horse and cart rests at the stile. No mourners on the road. Just a few men in the mist, carrying a body through the beach grass. The ground they shovel becomes shrapnel. The rain and waves make mud of their work. The dog jitters bashfully in place as I come up to them. Colm plants his eyes in the ground with his shovel.

"Who is it?" I say.

"We found him on the beach," Gavin says, and I pull back the tarp. The blue canvas curls back over Zaim's face.

I stagger back through confused grass. Gavin my shadow to the grave. I go back to your photos and shells and little boats. Gavin reduces to a human sliver in the turmoil of rain, sand and spray in the cemetery. The men lower the body into the grave, welling quick with water.

○

Pebbles of hail skitter across the rock. Bullet my skin. Beach grass tenses with the cold, as if frozen with memory. The angry wind snaps them clean, and makes arrows of the blades.

Here I am.

The ground crunches beneath his feet. He brushes away the snow melting in my ear. Kisses my red, numb lobes. He palms the snow into a ball he mashes against my cheek.

"This is perfect snow for a fight..."

"He never saw snow."

Gavin dusts his hands. Red. Calloused. "I don't know if it's safe out here right now, Mairead."

"When is it ever?"

The snow piles on our silence.

He sinks to his knees next to me. Head bowed, like he's waiting for the chop. "You should come in."

"I'll just sit on my own a while."

"I'll leave the door unlocked."

"I'll be at the home tonight," I say.

He shoots up. "Yeah, ok. Um... are you here tomorrow?"

"I'm here everyday."

○

The day goes without him and then at dusk he comes. The air heavy between us on the way home, filling the grikes, the pits in the road, the crack in the front door.

A cloudy, bloodshot iris floats in the gap. "Don't say it."

"Ma, go inside."

"Like a cat you are, always bringing home dead birds."

"Get yourself indoors, woman."

The door creeps shut. Gavin laughs, a little. "You ok?"

I stand in the door. "You'll be leaving now."

"I'll see you tomorrow?"

"You'll be leaving."

He doesn't know what to say. What could he say, without sounding selfish.

"I've done something wrong, I know, but..."

"You've been gentle," I say. "You've been kind. It's a good thing you're doing for your Da. Now do it, and go home."

"Don't. Don't do this."

"I don't want anything more in my life."

"I do." That shame in him again. "I'm sorry. I'm sorry. I'm being clumsy, I know... I just don't know what to do."

"Go home, while you can."

"This is my place."

"I don't love you."

He reduces in front of my eyes. "Mairead..."

"I don't want you. Don't come around anymore."

He just stands there. Man of stone. All his words dying for breath. Go on. Go and live. There's no living here. He leaves down the road. The dog runs off to his wander, the opposite way.

CHAPTER ELEVEN

I give Ma some shite tea. The sun room of the home drumming with rain. She sees me in my scrubs and her eyes brim with recognition. She slams her fist against the arm of her chair.

"Don't say it," she says.

"It's just until the storm passes, Ma."

"I said don't put me in the home."

"It's not safe at the house."

The steam goes out of her. There's only so much. The tea cup rattles in her hand. "Who are all these people?"

The cafeteria clots with some of the tourists, put out of their hostels. They play cards, or read books in their sleeping bags. The Italian boy and girl look at me from the corner, expectant. As if I hold the key to their getting home. A few months from now, whoever is left on the island will be pressed into this room, chased up the island from the rising tides. This is the future, here. The moaning, dying future.

"It's just for now," I say.

"Are you still here?"

"What do you mean, am I still here?"

"I thought you left, girl."

I brush her cheek. "Drink your tea."

I go over the checklist with Saidbh at the nurses' station. What to do if the power goes. What to do if the generator fails. What to do if people fail. She nods through it. She already knows all this. Sixteen years old. Nothing surprises her now. I go room to room, checking on the residents. Roisin Ni Shealbhaigh persists on the ventilator. Months now. This idea she'll come out of this coma. For what. All the residents cling to some expectation of health. Recovery. Life. All of them expectant. Even now. Their flame down to a flicker. Drowning in the rain and the sea. Even now, they expect to live.

I find Aoife sleeping in the room Eamon left vacant. "Hey."

She snorts awake. "My dreams have come true."

"I'm going for a walk."

"Are you mad?"

"I'll be back later," I say.

She grabs my wrist. "You can't go down to the shore tonight. The storm is right over us, Mairead."

This is the most we've said since the party. We've had rows and spells where we got bored of each other, but not like this. I'm not talking to anyone now, save for Ma. What do I say.

What's the point.

"I'm not going down to the shore," I say.

"The pier, then? I thought you broke it off with him."

"I did."

"Then where you going to, Mairead?"

"For a walk, like."

"A walk, she says. You walk one end of the home to the other you've walked the island."

"You've got things handled here," I say.

"Go down the pier, then. Talk him up here. He's not going anywhere until this blows over, Mairead. If he's going anywhere at all. Colm says the surge may take the airstrip."

I look out of the room. "Ma thinks I've left."

"Mairead... you can't do this."

"I'll be back," I say, and go.

○

The wind demands submission but I keep my place.

I bend against the gale, no longer a gale but a physical obstruction in the air. An invisible steam roller pushing on the sea, on the island, on me, on the cataclysmic waves disintegrating into spray that never quite lands but clouds the air like a murmuration of starlings. Every drop a bullet. The bruises deep. Nothing between skin and bone but weak blood. The wind distorting me, peeling at me, skinning me but I move only to replace the flowers and candles and pictures the wind disturbs and I am knocked down. I am pushed and bullied and hurried and harried but I will not give in. I will not be moved.

Here I am.

○

Every wave a car crash.

The echo thunder. Rocks shrapnel. The ground takes on a strange gelatin quality. Headstones topple and are swept out to sea. Even the night lost to lightning. I'll not leave you. I'll never leave you.

Mo leanbh. Mo stór.

○

Spray drenches me.

Sand pits my cheek. The wet deep and heavy through all my layers and I feel my heart *thud, thud, thud* inside the drum of my chest like I felt yours curled up in the chair with me. Sleepy eyed baby boy. Curls all a mess. Where did you get those curls? Go back to sleep. Ma has to go. They're waiting on me at the home. Sit and watch telly with Nana. She pats her lap and up in her arms you go. Ma saved all her love of children for you.

You'll be watching him, I tell her. *You'll be watching him close.*

The horizon fuses into a sear of igneous light, a smoke masked furnace of the lightning and the dawn and the comets like little sperm eager to fertilize their death. The apocalypse of the black hole seemed inevitable to me. Rote. It was just the one I got, after dropping a quarter in a dispenser full of plastic bubbles containing any one of dozens of catastrophes. Sometimes you get the one you wanted. Sometimes you already had it. The apocalypse a regular occurrence: drowning in the drink. Cancer. Parkinson's.

A baby boy, here and gone, like a dream.

○

This hydraulic sound in the sky like the brakes of a city bus pumping. Inching through constant traffic, crawling through the day grinding out its passage on your skin, red and raw and numb. My lips dry and taut. Taste of copper on my tongue when I wet them. Skin of my face so pressed and stretched and pressed again I can't move to wince at the pain, to mouth the pain, to show the pain of the storm.

I feel nothing.

I am the marble of the headstones. The karst stone of the island, cracked and broken in some places clean through, yet the life; the color; the flowers, ribald and unrepentant, Japanese knotweed, Mediterranean wild flowers and the nests of African birds, the bugs, the slugs, the snails, the seals, the men come here seeking refuge.

The fools.

○

Loose stones teeter, the oldest and least secure going over with gusts. The wind whistles through gaps in the stone fences bisecting the island, the eastern cliffs a flute playing a mad melody. The moans of exposed cattle up on the cliffs carry down over the cemetery, on out to the bay and smashing against the heavy concrete wall of cloud cutting off my view of the mainland and the world beyond. My nerve in staying out here. My sanity.

○

Buckets of rain now.

The sky a nail gun. The ground puddles and loosens and little urchins crawl through the grass left by the waves, as stunned and shocked to be deposited here as I am. They crawl on your shoals and I throw them to sea.

They come flying back.

The wind punishes me for standing up. I huddle low against the rock. Rain burns like cold metal and I sink with the stone. I feel your cold. I'm cold through. Just a few feet between us now and you can sleep easy because Ma's here.

Mo leanbh. Mo stór.

The morning's not far. I'm ready now. I'm tired now. So tired. The storm won't let me rest. Is that the dog scratching against the stile? Just the rain. The island going to pieces.

The rock moves.

The next wave will take it. Me. Will I drown with it. Be crushed by it. I want both. I want to be trapped beneath it, the water burning in my lungs, the pressure crushing my chest one second for every day I spent out here a coward and the manic flutter of the beach grass becomes a trample. A rush. I peel off the stone just enough to look.

Declan. Come to Ma.

I see it in his face.

The hope that dies in my eyes. Gavin knows, as soon as he sees me. He made a mistake coming out here. His life a series of mistakes trying to make up for another and this was hopeless, the two of us both waiting for someone who would never come.

But he stays, Gavin. That's what he does.

He stays beside me, shivering and if I tell him to leave, he won't leave. He'll die out here with me, just to prove himself wrong. I could have been anybody, he would have stopped that day at the shore. He would have asked if they needed anything. He would have said he was sorry for their loss.

He came back for me.

The life he found with me, strange and unlikely, like the stone of the island, blooming flowers from its scars.

O

I won't leave.

He begs me, with the claw of his fingers. The ferocity of his heart. The waves pull at us. I won't leave. He won't let go. I pull at him. Back through the grass, to the rabbit fields. Up the cliff, sheer, slick, unforgiving; into the round tower.

O

He doesn't say a word, Gavin.

He just holds me inside his coat against the chaos swirling around the tower. Any second the bloody thing will come down on us. Waves smash against the cliffs crumbling just beneath us. A ripple goes through us with every impact. Will this be the one. His heart thunders against mine. His hands shake. He could have died coming out here. Him and that dog. The two strays.

"What is it with you and that dog, anyhow?" I say.

"He won't leave me alone," Gavin says.

"Must be annoying, like."

"Do you want me to go?"

"You'd just come back."

"Probably."

"A yo-yo, you are..." I'm all tangled up in his string.

His lips twist up in all he wants to say. Quiet this whole time with me but the words always there, bubbling under the surface. His mind this engine running on the steam jetting up out of the caldera of his heart. All that fire and passion and wanting under a mountain of doubt and regret and fear.

"I was dead before. You've given me my life, Mairead."

"We've just gone for a walk, you and me."

"Walk with me for this bit."

I'm so tired. All this back and forth. All this waiting. For the storm to end, for you to come, for deliverance. I think of Da, near the end in the hospice room at the home. All his hair and his weight gone. A blow-up skeleton. I sat with him hours, watching soaps, football, anything. His hand like a piece of wax fruit in mine. Ma came and went. Always some errand. She made me angry, so. *Will you not stay, for an hour?* He tolerated it, like he did everything else. He asked me to be good to Ma. Fair. She had suffered a lot in life, and suffered more in silence. *So be fair.* He told me about my grandmother, Nora.

My grandmother suffered no one, not even herself. She produced four girls, three stillborn. Family myth has it she died of a broken heart soon after Pegeen, born after Ma, but Da told me how Ma had confessed to him in a singular bit of openness early in their marriage that Nora had drown herself after Pegeen. My grandfather took it out on Ma. Those days, a son was still the most valuable possession a man could own. Without a wife or hope of sons, Ma became a liability.

"Don't be sad," Da said. His voice hollow. Carved out. "Be happy. Make happiness. Go back to New York. Don't worry about your mother, she'll be fine. She might even be looking forward to some time alone. I keep thinking I interrupted her."

"She loves you," I said, regardless.

"And she loves you. So go back. Find someone. Make someone happy. You'll never do something more worth your time here than making another person happy. There's nothing else. This is it, Mairead. We're all just here. So make happiness."

Those last few days, I kept afloat on his mission for me. Go back. Be strong. Find someone. Then he died. The days just vanished. I don't know. Life. Ma got sick. The world found its end. I had you. I made you. You were my happiness.

And then.

○

Dawn comes in spite of itself.

The morning sun makes a honeypot of the Atlantic. The cliffs dripping with gold. Little pellets of spray gone to ice in the air melt on my raw cheeks. Gavin buttons me up in his coat. Holds me close. The pill bottle like a rock between us.

"Come down to the shore with me," I say. "We'll spread the ashes there, at the rock."

Mist swirls around the contour of the eroded cliffs, driven over the rock by the waves and sent back by the wind. No idea of which way to go. The mist hangs there, like the spying gulls. Like Gavin.

"You can't do it," I say. "Even now."

His hand go to stuff his pockets. I'm wearing his coat. "And then what, Mairead? I go home. What will you do? You going to come back at here? You going to hurt yourself?"

"You think you're to save me?"

"I just want to be good for someone."

"What do you think is going to happen? We're going to get married? We're going to live happily ever after?"

"We can just live, Mairead."

"There isn't any living."

"We can try."

"You want to stay here? You want to be with me?"

"Yes."

"Come with me to the shore. We'll scatter the ashes."

"The tide's out," he says, like any one of his excuses and then he sees I'm not making one. "Mairead..."

"This is what you came here for."

"I came here to live. I want to live."

I pat the pocket thick with the ashes of his father. "This isn't living."

His face sinks. Bags under his eyes. So tired. I haven't seen it before. This bleeding pill bottle. So heavy. The jacket, soaked from the grief of the sea. I can barely move.

I hold out my hand. "Walk with me for this bit."

He starts to say something, but he keeps his words. Maybe he's tired of repeating himself. Lord God, let it be he's tired of me. His hands close around mine. His father's ashes.

"I can't do this," he says, and takes the pill bottle.

He goes back into the grass. I expect him to come back. I go down to the shore. Wet rock dazzles with sunshine. Slick. Treacherous. The storm left the coast less than it was. The metal of one of your boats tinks against the stone before me.

Mo leanbh. Mo stór.

I expect Gavin to come back, but he doesn't even into the night. I fall to the ground. This brutal earth all I have left.

○

Constant spray rains on the tarmac, eroded deep along its northern edge into the choppy waters of the bay. He'll be ginger on his landing, that pilot, or he'll be making a boat out of his plane. Gavin stands in the car park with his bag, waiting. The air buzzes.

Soon now.

Colm pulls in through the mangled gate. Colm pats Gavin on the back and his hand keeps there as the buzz builds again and this time it's the plane. A minute away. Maybe two.

The plane bounces off the runway. The wings jitter as he brakes hard over the ruts in the tarmac. Gavin looks back at the road. East toward the shore. Up here at the monastery. Does he see me. Will he wonder of me for the rest of his short days, far inland as the seas claim their first. He stares into the tower.

Get on the plane, Gavin. Live. One of us has to live.

Colm says something to him. Gavin's head drops and he starts toward the plane. The pilot clapping his hands. *Hurry up now it's time.* Dozens of stranded tourists flood the car park. Bags on their shoulders. Mad hope in their eyes. Gavin says something.

Of course he does.

The pilot contorts in objection, but Gavin badgers him into taking as many as the plane can hold. The older folks excuse themselves. And like that, the Italian family is delivered. Gavin almost gives someone else a seat, but there's no staying.

Not now.

Gavin leaves his bag on the tarmac to make as much room as he can, and then gets in. The buzzing builds again and the last plane to ever leave Inishèan climbs past the tower out to sea.

No rush in going back to the home.

No sense. There is nothing I can better there, or anywhere, but the shore. Yours is the only loneliness I can cure now. It's like a cut. A wound. It hurts and it frightens you, but you feel this energy. This adrenaline. This life. Part of you doesn't want it to end. Another wants it over. I'm bleeding. I'm dying, but I feel desire to feel this living and I'm lost. I'm so lost.

The dog scratches at the stone.

"Away with you," I say.

He trots into the beach grass. After a few feet, the dog looks back. Expectant, like. He wants me to follow. To where. For what. Go on. Go on and leave. He whines in protest as I keep my place. The dog waits at the edge of matted beach grass, his eyes cast downwards, as if in some way, he's disappointed.

CHAPTER TWELVE

Puckered lips of pink clouds kiss the back of a gentle, taupe sea. The sun summits the eastern shoulder of the island, and the moment is gone. The beauty of the world is that it will not last. The wolf's eye in Cassiopeia is brighter. Another star flares within it. The diamond of a ring. Saturn, the news says. Some probe the States sent years back captures the whole thing and we watch, Ma and I, unable to look away until Ma looks over at me on the sofa and grabs her chest.

"I thought you'd left, girl."

"I've been back, Ma. Since Da."

"She'll never come home, he said. Mairead. But I told him. She's too much of a home bird."

"I've been back."

She winces. "You're not here."

"I'm home," I say.

Ma goes back to watching the telly. Her confusion. Do you see this, girl? A wandering black hole? Do you know what it is?

Do you know.

○

Rounds. Pills. Vitals.

No pills. Only empty paper cups their dementia allows me to make full. There's nothing I can do for anyone but wait. Without anti-hypertensive medication, nearly all the residents suffer rebound high blood pressure. Without calcium channel blockers like the vera-pamil, or beta-adrenergic blockers like propranolol, angina runs rampant. Without aspirin, I have no defense against a heart attack. And yet they endure. This anger sustains us all. This injustice.

Getting pure thick, we are.

Saidbh calls me to the nurses' station. If ever she does, it's to inform me of some other disaster. She holds the receiver of the land-line up, this mortified look on her face.

"It's for your man," she says.

I take the phone. "Hello?"

Heavy static makes the woman hard to understand. "He said there was a nurse. I called the nursing home."

"You're calling for Gavin?"

"I'm his mother," she says.

I shoo Saidbh away from the station, and sit down in her chair. "Is he not home?"

She sighs. "No. He's not there?"

The receiver is heavy in my hand. Fat with a battery to keep its charge. I rest it on my shoulder. "He... he left."

"Last time I talked to him, he said he might never leave."

"We both thought... I thought it was best for him to be back home with his family."

"You must be her," she says. "When was this?"

"A few days ago. You've not talked to him at all?"

"He's not answering his cell phone. I don't know if there's any service. I barely get any here. He said there was a meteor."

"That was weeks ago. Loads of broken windows, mostly. There was just enough wood to board them up. Gavin helped," I say, not sure what I'm saying. "I'm sorry you can't get hold of him. I'm sure he's fine. He could be stuck at the airport in Dublin or New York, trying to get a flight. I'm sure."

"He helped at the nursing home?"

"He did."

He'd wake in morning, loose. Easy. Never tired. I was a nervous coil in his arms. Heavy against him. Heavier with every moment, the weight of the universe in a body barely scratching a hundred pounds. My ribs like the wrinkled, eroded beach rock but he didn't mind. He didn't want the heat, the press, the distortion of himself. He didn't want to be himself anymore. Adrift. He became part of the island, helping to board up the windows and fix the doors jammed in their frames. He became part of the island with me. He said so. I'd drawn him there. Captured him. And then I released him, ejected out of my orbit like the lucky planets and moons.

Newspaper crinkles on her end as much as the static. "Did you see this? Russia invaded Iran. Took the oil fields."

"I haven't seen the news."

"There might have been a bomb."

"A bomb?"

"Nuclear. Someone set off a nuclear bomb."

Residents shuffle past the station, slow and weak with pain. Hunger. A need for some resolution. "I'm sure he's fine."

"Maybe there aren't any more flights."

"He's rented a car. Something."

"Gas is seventeen dollars a gallon here. If they have it."

"He'll get there," I say. "He's persistent, like."

She sniffs. "You sound young."

"I'm in my old age, as it happens."

"Yeah, I can see the interest," she says. Dogs bark somewhere behind her. "When he was a kid, he loved space. All those movies. He wanted to be an astronaut. When the space shuttle blew up, he became obsessed with finding out why. He read everything. Cut out articles. Made photocopies at the library. Kept them in this shoebox. I couldn't understand it. It happened. What could he do about it?

When they first found this black hole thing, he was so calm. He told me all of this, all of this happening now in the sky, down to the letter. He knew what would happen."

I picture him, a boy, sitting at the library reading a congressional report on the destruction of this flying thing that to him had been a cathedral of wonder, but in an instant was reduced to dust. There is no worse betrayal than realizing the world is not designed for you.

The only design is failure.

There is no understanding the black hole. And yet the end of the world has been plotted to the precise second, confirmed with quiet assuredness as the black hole first started to tug on the earth, creating tidal waves and earthquakes to the ballistic shredding induced from the comets, asteroids, moons and planetary debris. There is something reassuring in the autopsy of disaster. Reverse engineering tragedies gives some kind of power over them, as if they can be undone, by just pulling on this or that string. If I had just done that. If I had just done this. Simple.

Easy.

"I've been going through all my old photo albums," she says. "Things you keep. You know. The shoes. The stuffed little things. I kept the napkins from the baby shower. I don't know why. Pink. Faded now. Like a wine stain. I've been making my peace with him being there and now I don't know where he is."

I grip the phone cord. "He's fine."

"I lost a baby," his mother says. "Miscarriage."

"Oh."

Her voice becomes more distant. "It was after him. Yeah. If you had time, you'd probably learn how to make it work. You read about these things. After 9/11. People meet, and share in their grief. They fall in love. It happens. It's happening to you. You just don't have any time. And I'm sorry for you. I'm sorry for you both."

I set the receiver down on the desk. Her phone whispers out of it. *You probably just want to disappear. We don't have the luxury, do we? Men can just disappear. And they won't let us.*

Are you there?

I pick up the phone. "I'm here."

"Don't be too hard on yourself," she says. "You've got to look at the big picture. That's what I always tell him. Maybe he was supposed to be there. And maybe he's done his bit."

The receiver is slick in my hand. "He's fine."

"We all think we're the symphony, but really, we're just the instruments. Some of us get a solo. Some of us never get used."

I choke back my tears. "I'm sure he's fine."

"I'm sure," she said turning the page. "What's your name?"

"Mairead."

"Mairead. I'm glad I got to talk to you."

"And you..."

Static breaks up the line. Voices ghost over each other. The line drops. I set the phone heavy back on its base. My fingers brush the plastic, like they might a cup holding a beer. A cocktail. Your hand, warm in mine. Day comes. Aoife to replace me. Mist hangs over the bay. The island scratching with sleet.

Fear.

○

A blinding flash goes off over the sea.

So bright I think the sun has come up early. Or another meteor. Much, much higher this one. I think about Gavin flying over the ocean home through the flak of asteroids and meteors. Best not to think of him. What is there to think about now.

The tide is fierce. The cold worse still. I trudge back home through the rabbit field. None of the lights are on across the harbor in Kilbanna. Who would be down there now he's gone, anyways. The street lamps are out. Normally the bowl of the island is constellated in stars. There's no glitter across the bay. No lights at the house.

Ma sits in front of the telly in the dark, murmuring to herself. She doesn't even know. I click on the remote. Nothing. There's nothing in the house working at all. The storm is passed; I don't understand.

Aoife bursts in through the front door, out of breath and drenched in sweat. "The backup is shite!"

○

Alarms ring inside the home as life-support monitors and ventilators burn off their battery reserves. Moira Kavanaugh lies on the floor of the lobby, cold and still.

Aoife shakes her head. "She just dropped over. Right when the lights out... she must have had a heart attack."

"She has a pacemaker," I say, as more screams erupt in the home. I grab a flashlight from the nurses' station. I take over bagging Roisin Ni Shealbhaigh from Saidbh. She clutches her sore arm and goes to the corner, crying. The fuck was I doing at sixteen. Saidbh has been pumping oxygen for half an hour. The fuel filters on the generator clogged. There are no spares. The bag crumples, Roisin's chest swells and unless we get power back she's got as long as our arms hold out.

I hear the jangle of all Colm's tools coming down the hall. That box he carries them around in old as he is.

"I thought you'd seen to the generator," I say.

"I'll look again," he says.

He goes off down the way and ten minutes later he's back saying maybe there might be some spare fuel lines around. He doesn't look at me as he says this, so I put no stock in it.

○

My arm throbs. My hand shriveled in righteous pain. Hours we've been at this. I wish Colm would just say there's no fixing the generator instead of shuffling the same parts around.

"I don't understand," Saidbh says. "The storm's over."

121

"It's something to do with that meteor," I say. "Nothing landed, though. I don't think. They'll fix it. No worries."

Saidbh strains her hand back to its original shape. "I can take over now." I hand the bag back to her. "Will it be soon?"

Colm shows up in the door, head down, wiping the grease off his hands with a dirty rag. Lord God.

"Have you any juice left in your mobile?" I say.

He hands it to me. 72% battery. I tap in the number for the office of the county manager in Galway. I go through the count in the medicine cabinet as the phone rings and rings. We're down to bones here. Cobwebs. I try again. The island darkens outside.

I punch in Gavin's number. Starts to ring. There's this click on the other end, like he's picking up. Please pick up.

"Gavin?"

The line goes dead. No bars now. Lord God.

I hand the mobile back to Colm. He puts his hand on my shoulder. "We've got to find a land line that works."

"There's no power anywhere on the island," he says, pocketing the mobile. "None of the phones work."

"They'll get power back on."

"The last time the islands lost power was years ago, and it was days before they got it back on. That was some trawler hitting the cable by accident. This is something else."

"It was a meteor, like."

He scratches his chin. "There was no explosion."

"It was high."

"Meteors don't generate any kind of electrical interference, so far as I know. I don't know. You see this light, and the power goes out right after. It's like an EMP."

"What you mean, EMP?"

"Electromagnetic pulse," he says. "Off a nuke, like."

"Nuke?"

The batteries die on the monitor. The alarm fails. The only

sound now the soft crunch of the bag as Saidbh squeezes it, the soft whine wheezing in and out of Roisin.

"Can we get the plane over?" Saidbh says.

"There's no calling him."

Even if there was, what would be the point? Roisin likely wouldn't survive the trip and if she did, then what? She rots on a gurney in the overcrowded corridor of a powerless hospital in Galway? The car park? And then what of the lucky one of us nurses who gets drafted to squeeze that bag on her across the bay for the next few days or weeks until we get power back?

I call out to Aoife. She comes in, red nosed and bleary eyed. "She's no other relations here?"

Aoife shakes her head. "They've all left or passed."

"You've got to get the generator back," I say to Colm.

"Mairead... I'm telling you, even if I replaced the fuel lines, the circuits will all be fried from the blast."

"What are you talking about a blast for?"

"I don't think this is a meteor."

"You'll be figuring out the generator, Colm. You'll be coming back in here in an hour telling me so."

○

Aoife massages my sore hand. My fingers. I look off at nothing as she does. Saidbh gets this hangdog look in her eyes. We switch off again. How many times now. Saidbh's eyes deadlock on Aoife's thumbs as they spread across her palm.

"They keep getting younger on you," I say.

Aoife's hands glide up Saidbh's arm. "It's my burden. What was he saying? About nukes?"

"He's daft," I say.

Saidbh nods, comforted. "Why would you set off a nuke in the air, anyways?"

"A test, like," Aoife says. "A warning."

"It was a meteor," I say.

"The news said there was a bomb in Iran, though."

"Aren't you finished?"

She releases her grip on Saidbh. "Finished, yeah."

Aoife leaves the room. The door to the loo slams shut. I keep pumping the bag, trying to become the repetition of it. The mindlessness. Forget everything else. Nukes. Generators. The failure of power on the island. In my own heart.

"I wish I could do for her," Saidbh says.

"Give it another hour."

"Sorry?"

"Nothing," I say.

I close my eyes. I forget everything but the crunch of the bag and sigh of Roisin's breath, the world collapsing and expanding in the darkness again and again and again.

He works all through the night, Colm. By torchlight. By candle. After dawn, he comes into the room and I know. He leaves without saying a word. Aoife's awake, still.

"She's been months on the machine," she says.

Saidbh sits up in her chair. "The lights will come back."

"I don't think they will," I say.

Saidbh stands up, in tears already. "And if they do, they'll charge the lot of us with murder."

"As if there'll ever be any inquiry," Aoife says.

Saidbh flees the room, sobbing.

"Go after her, will you? And close the door behind you."

"I'll stay with you," Aoife says.

"I'll be doing this on my own."

The door whimpers shut. I brush Roisin's hair. 84 years, this woman. Three boys and a girl. The boys all lost to the sea. The girl lost to a boy in Limerick. A grandchild. A boy, I think. Your age. A bit older, could be. Months on the machine. I take the bag from her mouth. She sighs, Roisin. Long, and full.

○

A disciplined set of men with the only dependable work on the island shoulders the casket through the cemetery. A boat, adrift in fog. All the islanders follow, tethered in black back down the road. Ma weaves in and out of the headstones. She pulls at the ends of the fluttering beach grass. Her hands fill. Ma looks hard at Da's stone. The memory of him, that he's gone, crosses her face like the shadow of a cloud. Her hair comes away in her hands, as if her memory lies in the white strands, in the grooves of her sunken cheeks, the blood that wells beneath the raked dry skin on the back of her hand.

"You should plant me," she says. "Before it gets too cold. Bury me, while there's still men."

"I should have them dig us both a spot while they're here."

"Not you," she says. "This isn't your place."

"What?"

"I heard this scratching. Do you know? I thought that bloody dog was at the door again."

"Ma... what?"

"He always comes round. The dog. Do you know, he's been in the house. I've seen him, I know I have."

Ma looks at me with a hapless smile. The woman never smiles. She pats my raw cheeks, like she did when I was a girl, and then on her tippy-toes slobbers a kiss on me.

"I want you to go," she says.

She trundles down the road home. My eyes follow the rim of the island enclosing Kilbanna, the cemetery and everything I have ever known. A crater the island is, flooding with the sea. Mounds of dried seaweed cake the inside of the stile. The cemetery unrecognizable, paved in fallen stones. Ancient graves turned sinkholes near the dunes. The sea is hungry. Impatient.

Where will my grave be?

○

Some on the island shrug at the absence of electricity, their memory elastic enough to remember a time without it. At the home, memory is as scarce as power. Drugs. Comfort. We cluster the residents between the sitting room and the dining room, and the only fire-places. Coal burns fast. We're poor in wood on the island. Trees go from rare to extinct. Down in Kilbanna the men form teams that break down the damaged homes and buildings. In a couple weeks, the harbor is as sparse as it was a century ago. It's a bit communist how they dole out everyone's share, but for the most part everyone is peaceable about it. There's no money for anyone to buy or barter with, anyhow. If we had money, we'd burn it. Aoife surveys the home, determining which sections we can cbreak down for kindle and in what order so at the end we're left in the dining room, whoever's left. We'll burn through our morphine before we burn down this building.

○

My only duty now is managing suffering.

Everyone on the island comes to the home for their ills. Malnutrition. Anxiety. Alcohol poisoning. How is it there's still drink left. My stomach growls. I excuse myself but the girls act like it's no bother. Hunger is just another sound here like the sigh of forced breath. Unforced moans. Dying alarms.

I'm starving.

○

The door handle of the staff loo strains against the lock.

I'm not asleep, but not awake. The handle is furious. Aoife calls for me from the other side and I know it's bad. She's hyperventilating.

126

Eoin Mac Cába got in a fit over not having his arthritis pills. His hands curled up into nautilus shells. She could do nothing but warm them, try and massage them. He cried about the pain until his heart gave out. This look in his old eyes like it was a surprise. The son comes for the body. The next morning, smoke falls across the hills like fog. Men form a line down to the shore and pass old kegs filled with seawater up the high road. I expect to see Gavin among them.

I am reliably disappointed.

○

Michael Burke gurgles loud in the dining room. I turn his head every fifteen minutes to drain the saliva building in his throat, but there's nothing else for him. His body shuts down now without the dialysis machine. This frost collects on his skin from the uremia. I dab his skin and hold his hand and turn his head and that's all I can do. I wait. Days this goes on. I expect him to pass quiet and easy but nothing goes easy now.

"Are we just going to wait?" Aoife says, voice a hush though no one can hear. "Until they're half in the box?"

"It'd be murder besides."

"It's murder listening to them. I don't know what's worse, listening to their bellies rumbling, or mine."

On a calm day a hooker can get into Galway Bay. Sometimes it comes back with fish. Sometimes it doesn't come back. Women stand on the rising shore waiting for their men to come back in body or evidence of death. The sea gives only anger. The promise that in time, the water will claim you as it did your love. All this time I've been waiting for you. *Mo leanbh. Mo stór.*

You're waiting for me.

"I'll do it," I say. "I'll write something, explaining."

"Explaining? They abandoned us, Mairead."

"All the same, I want it clear how and why we got here. I'll do it. It's my responsibility. It's my decision."

"It's been the two of us this far."

"You and Saidbh... I'll dismiss you, before."

"I won't let you live with the burden of it on your own, Mairead."

"I won't be living with anything," I say.

Aoife sinks into the chair beside the bed. Sometimes at night I hear this clenched sobbing of hers down the corridors of the home, from within some dark, cold and forgotten room.

"You were doing so much better..."

I sit down with her. She curls up in my arms, sobbing into my shoulder like she did after every shipwreck of a boy back in school. Most dangerous approach in all Ireland, Aoife.

"It's over," I say. "It's over now."

"There's got to be some other way..."

There's no other way. Three years. Three years this cancer has been growing in the sky and it's terminal. That's it. Nothing more to be said. Nothing to be decided but choosing the casket. No. I'm going to choose how my story ends. Not God. Not chance.

Me.

CHAPTER THIRTEEN

On my way to the home, I go up to Colm's.

The high road slick with momentary ice. Snow falls light, streaked with ash. This has gone on a week or more now. The sky dark with it. Colm sorts through boxes and bins inside the garage and he looks the same as he always looks, mad and dirty.

He wipes his hands on his coveralls. "How's herself?"

"You know. The same. How are you getting on?"

He limps out of the garage into the drive. "Damn arthritis has locked up my knees."

"The starvation will take some of the weight off you."

"This is your father's bedside manner I'm hearing."

"Has its uses." His pockets are full of loose wires. "What are you working on?"

"I have an old HAMM radio I'm trying to get working. No luck so far. Though it may be static I hear, anyways."

Clouds race against the shale sky, soundless of planes.

"Do you even want to know, Colm?"

He shrugs, a little. "Passes the time."

"Keeps you busy," I say, "tinkering as you do."

"It does." He shakes his head. "Sometimes, though. Sometimes I think I ought to leave well enough alone."

"How do you know when to?"

"It's me you're asking?"

"Who else can I ask?"

He scratches his chin. "Seemed you two were sorted."

I don't have to ask who he refers to. I know. We all know. "We were ahead of ourselves is what we were."

"Two lonely people. Tends to happen." His hand glances my shoulder. "Your Da used to come up here and we'd work on cars all day, and drink. Or we'd go fishing, and drink. Or we'd go to the pub, and drink. To dull our pain. This ache, in our souls."

I understand perfectly. I was Da's understudy, after all. While he was sick and dying, Colm and I both needed someone to fill that space at the bar, or here at the house.

"But you," Colm says. "You haven't had a drink since the day you found out you were pregnant. You're the strongest woman – you're the strongest person – I've ever known. It's me who should be asking you how to get through my day."

"How do you?"

"By imagining you coming up that walk," he says. "And me saying I'm sorry."

My cheeks burn with tears. "I need to be getting back to the home. I thought I'd come by, and..."

"You're strong, Mairead. You'll be the last of us."

This confusion dawns on his face. What does he see in mine. He always knew me. The birds circle the feeder, looking for a place to land. I look east, toward the mainland. Lidded in gray.

"Gavin made it back," Colm says. "I'm sure of it."

"Yeah."

"Whatever I can do for you, Mairead. Just ask. I know I can't... I'm happy to help. Whatever I can do."

"I know you'll have to break the house down," I say. "Could you leave the cot? I know it's wood, but could you?"

He ages years right in front of my eyes. I think he might crumble to dust right there in the drive, but he manages, Colm. He stands his pain, like he's always done.

He nods. What else can he do.

I go down the drive. I look back at the feeder. The cluttered yard and garage. Colm. *Seanfhear*. I wave goodbye. He blows me a kiss. The softy. There are good men in the world. Failures, all of them.

They are good because they endure.

О

The school is perched halfway up the bowl of the island on the high road. This is the new school, built in the aughts like the nursing home when the country was flush with money.

Why should you leave, Ma said. *There are jobs now.*

Never on the island, though we were always sore for something. Another doctor. Nurses. Teachers. I gave Dublin a go after I turned eighteen. Dublin was new. Dublin was the business. The indifference of Dublin made me sore. It was all so pinched together, the people, the streets, the row houses, snug up against each other like twins in the womb. It was too much city for me. So I did what I always do. I went looking for more.

Eithne continues in the school, even without power. She's nothing at home for her, I suppose. That's cruel. Ian left her after eight years and moved to Galway for some girl with tits like deployed airbags and they had a baby the spring after you. A girl. She won't see her next birthday. None of these children sitting at their desks in a cold and damp and dark school will see another birthday, or fulfill the promise of their youth. There is no more vile crime than the squander of a future.

The class has been eroding since the discovery of the black hole. Those parents who could leave, left. Those who thought an education was pointless pulled their children out. Others had the foresight and the resolve to pile the kids in the car, close the garage door and turn the motor on.

Now there are five.

I check their noses. Throats. Ears. Lord God. Have they ever put cotton to them. I make them stick their arms up in the air and when they do, I tickle their ribs. The ones that laugh, I pinch their noses. The ones too old and too cool to react, I make faces until they do.

The boy I thought was you on the road that day is too shy to do anything. He's too bashful. Beautiful boy. Eoin. I play keep away with my stethoscope. Cat and mouse with my light pen. He's terrified of me. He must sense it in me. The loss. The absence of you. The wanting to fill it. I tried making Gavin fit into this depression inside me. The boy knows it's still there. The boy knows I'm still wanting, even now. I'm still looking.

Do you know.

When I'm done examining him, I hug him. My arms just spring. His go flat down his sides like boards and he doesn't breathe a breath the time I hold him. His heart doesn't want to beat and I let him go and he runs back to his desk.

Eithne smiles her paralytic smile. I should be embarrassed. I should be ashamed. I am only sorry I didn't scoop him up in my arms that day by the seal colony, and give some of this love I will die with. A person should not die with love to give.

"Kind of you," Eithne says, walking me out.

"It's no bother."

"You're basically the doctor now."

"Only took the end of the world."

Her laugh, like everything about her, is exaggerated, as if she's on stage and I'm in the back of the house.

"Your father would be proud," she says.

"He'd be out of a job."

The hall moans with the breeze creeping in through the plywood Gavin covered the windows with. Drawings in what must be water-colors flap on the wall, taped up alongside banners celebrating Easter they never took down. The ceiling painted in finches. Butterflies trailing dot, dot, dot from one room to the other, one year to the next, one level after the other.

"How long will you go on?" I say.

She takes in this breath, like she hasn't thought about it. "Until they stop coming, I imagine. It's just a few hours a day now. A walkabout. Collect some wood. Pick up some trash."

"How are you, Eithne? Your health?"

She waves her hand. "Oh, I'm grand."

"You sound as if you've a bit of a cold."

The boards breathe in. The boards breathe out. "I think we're all a bit under the weather these days."

"Aye, yeah."

"I thought he'd stay. The American."

"Oh."

"I'd see him on the road and I'd say, 'I'll bet. I'll bet you'll be here this time next week,' and he'd smile. I'll bet. I thought I'd ask that man for his time one night. Why not. And then I found out about you."

"I should get on."

"Do you know what I thought? Good. Good for you. Good you're having some joy. Not joy. Not happiness, I know it wasn't that. Not even peace. But good. I was glad for you."

I try to smile. I am numb.

"I should let you go. Thanking you, Mairead."

"*Slan.*"

"A bit of sun today," she says, holding the door open as I step out of the school. "I'll take them for a walk."

"Where will you go?"

"You know, they've never been to the monastery. Not a one. Today is as good a day as any, I suppose."

"I could take them."

Now she doesn't even try to smile. "Oh, I don't know."

"I know the way."

"Thank you, no. I'm sure you're busy."

"I've got time."

"Thanking you again, Mairead. Thanking you very much."

The door pumps like a brake. She's gone back to the classroom. I'm just standing there, feeling sick. Feeling slighted some way and I don't know what that was just now.

I don't want to know.

○

Domnhall's cart idles in the intersection of the harbor and low roads. Three bodies wrapped in blue tarps rest in the back of the buggy. Their names scribed across each of their chests in black marker: LURGAN. JACKSON. BOGLE. I don't know them. Domnhall comes out the little gift shop tourist flytrap kitty corner the pub, with a bundle of rope. He sets it in the back of the cart. Rocks piled between the bodies.

He doffs his cap to me. "Fine day for it."

"What happened?"

He shakes his head. No. We won't speak of it.

I don't see a shovel. "Going to the cemetery?"

"Garda says: to be no more burials at the cemetery. The ground is not secure. I'm taking them to the pier."

"I see."

He climbs into the cart. "*Slan,* Mairead."

"Are we not to burn them, either?"

"We're to conserve all wood and consumables for the living. There was a meeting. You must have been up the home."

"I must have."

The horse ambles around the curve of the sea wall the short distance to the pier. Domnhall ties the bodies together with the rope. The end around a rock. The rock he tosses over the side and as the first body is pulled out, Domnhall snaps the reins. One, two, three the dead fall out into the water as the horse trots away. Domnhall tips his cap to me as he goes past, back up the road, looking for fares.

○

I wake up early.

Fill up bottles down at the shore. The quiet unnerving. I assign my anxiety to this being the last morning and that despite my resolve I billow with excuses, the same as someone does anytime they're hammered with some aspect of the fine print of a contract they signed without reading. Life gives you everything. In the fine print it says it will take it all back but you'll never know when, how or why. That's the deal. Everyone chooses the deal. Everyone cries foul.

I sing you your lullaby

Seoithín, seo hó, mo stór é, mo leanbh
Mo sheoid gan cealg, mo chuid gan tsaoil mhór

I imagine coming back out here tonight once I'm done at the home. I walk out on a scab of limestone crusting the sea. Seaweed mushes under my bare feet. The sharp edges of broken shells stab at me. My hands lift with the tide and I'm nearly there, Declan. Tonight.

Here I am.

○

Edna Malloy wanders out of the dining room. I let her go. She's the only one of the residents still mobile. Why cheat her or her good genes. Aoife speeds around me all day like one of those moons of Jupiter, tangled in my static, stretched and torn from *Are you doing it? You're not, are you?* and hours pass in the dining room with me in the medicine depot, counting out the vials of morphine. Ten for the residents. One for Ma. One for me. My skin feels taut, like I still have the sweat of my enthusiasm on me. It's right here. The shape of my life. The form. The symmetry. All this pain and suffering comes into focus and it becomes this defined thing, separate from me I can gauge and measure. I have found the limit of my grief.

○

Aoife plops down on the cot with me in the sitting room. Smirk on her face. A plastic zip bag unfurls out of her hand.

"Get yourself up, woman. Enough of this sulking."

"What's that you've got?" I say.

"It's the disco biscuits, like."

I sit up. "Where did you get ecstasy?"

"I've been holding on to it," she says, leaning into me. "It's my use only in case of emergency type stash. I'd say this here situation calls for breaking the glass."

"I'm an addict, Aoife."

"Not after we empty this bag, you're not."

I take the bag from her. "What about Saidbh?"

"We make her *earn* it."

○

The walls are pillows, like.

I am sinking into the walls. Pillow fort. We need to make a pillow fort, Aoife. YES. We'll turn the dining room into a pillow fort. We'll have rooms for the residents and an A.V. room and a dungeon, like.

A sex dungeon, she says.

Right now I'm more focused on the building it than I am what's going in it, so one thing at a time. We must be proper with this to ensure architectural stability. There will be no weak foundations in this fort. No building it from the inside out and destroying it trying to get out. This isn't going to be fucking Dublin, Aoife. This is going to be Paris, like. Loot the home of pillows and cushions. Position the furniture just so. No blankets. Too heavy. Sheets. Use sheets. They use blankets over on the mainland. The idiots. We'll show them. We'll show them all. Knock down this fort. Send your wind and your waves and your comets and your asteroids and knock down this fort.

I dare you.

I draw up the plans. I'm brilliant at drawing. Do you see this, Aoife? I've missed my calling, I have. Think of it all. Tortilla hammock brasseries. Origami strip malls. This love. A city of this love in me, deep and dense and strong from all the pressure pushing down on it. We have to be smart. Saidbh is our primary construction liaison/engineer/gateswide when it comes to organizing and such and you want it, Saidbh? Work for it.

She drags beds and couches together and arranges them all just so and sometimes she makes a mistake but seeing how she's our only manual labor I can't dispose of her like some nameless Egyptian slave despite Aoife's insisting I do, so I publicly shame her and occasionally her ancestors since this seems like a thing I should be escalating towards and then I send her back to work. She's young and fit and very fit now she's out of her clothes. Mostly. Aoife removes a piece for every infraction and pulls on the scrubs over her own.

I've never been in a sixteen year-old, Aoife says.

This is going well for us, I'd say.

The fort is fucking deadly. Saidbh suggests we vote on a name. Pillowtown is her contribution. We flirt with democracy but resources being what they are, it's best this remains a dictatorship. That way I can preserve the illusion of a stable, functioning government until the eventual collapse crushes all my critics and opponents with me. I do like Pillowtown, though. I consecrate the fort as Pillowtown and to commemorate the foundation of our downy empire that will last at least until the E wears off, we hold a parade crawl down the main boulevard. Then I force Saidbh to recreate scenes from the *Amsterdam Nights.* The fort consumes us.

I have all these plans.

What planning is there in Ireland? We can't even plan for the end of the world. There aren't stories as such of the apocalypse in the

Celtic legends. So much of our identity was in the church, but before that, we were pagans and people of a deep connection to the earth and sky. In our soul, the Irish believe life and eternity are knotted together and cannot be separated. No lines. No Armageddon, no Ragnarok, no kingdom come.

No life. No death.

I suppose that's why we are who we are. We've picked up our guns and set off our bombs but we've never had the apocalyptic drive of say the States. We are gentle. An eternal creature is gentle. You might say weak. Weakness is often confused for grace. We endure. So Da said. Listen to me. Here I am trying to convince myself. Our conviction found at the bottom of a bottle of the drink. Pills. This is the fucking business, the ecstasy. 'Tis, Aoife says. She licks my hand.

Tizzzzzzzzz.

Water. I need water. I've planned poorly. There's no water. I deserve to be punished. Punish me, Aoife. Take my clothes. Wait. Let me check your nails, first. Ah, you're grand. You're grand, Aoife. This will all be yours when I'm gone. My kingdom, for you. I'm sinking. We're sinking into the wet, into the slick, the melting in our mouths. Slow. Slow, now. Aoife. A-O-I-F-E.

Eeeeee-fahhhhh.

Your name is so strange. I love your name. I love you. Your round-ness. Softness. Your salt fluff. I melt into this wetness with you this smell, this taste, this being of the sea the sky the rock.

Saidbh pools between us. *I want some,* she says.

Aoife suits herself in Saidbh. Water. I need water. How do I get out. I need to consult my original plans. Where are my plans. I had all these plans. A way out. It all made sense.

I'm lost.

Edna Malloy crawls through a tunnel. I follow her to the armory, the library and the planetarium which being honest is just an open window but I believe in making use of found things. I found all these stars. Stars like old Irish families with too many children. Barren stars. Bereaved stars. Stars living on top of each other with all the weight of the universe on them and so they cave in on themselves, and take down everything with them.

This is a takedown.

A coup. They're trying to kill us. Aoife. Saidbh. They're trying to kill us, they're trying to take our fort, they're trying to take what's ours but they won't. There's no taking this from me.

Do you know?

There's no taking this from me. No breaching these walls. Everything I have is within these walls. I don't have you. Ma. Gavin. Lord God. Aoife. Had she given all the love she spread around to just one person, they would have built castles for her. We need to extend the walls. Fortify our position. This will all be yours. I'm giving you the world, Aoife. I'm trusting you with the world. You've never let me down. You've never quit on me. Ever since we were girls you've been right there and I left you for the States and I rubbed your nose in my 'success' and it was all shite, Aoife. I was a fucking blubbering mess sore for home and I should have come home sooner. I should have had more time with Da and Ma and you and it would have been different. It all would have been different, had I come home even though she nags at me, New York does, like the lover who could have been the one, should have been the one.

I find Gavin in the catacombs. "You've come back?"

"Is this a pillow fort?"

"It's class, yeah."

He shrugs. "Is there a password or something?"

"Password... what's the password?"

"How many guesses do I get?"

"I'm asking you, like."

"Um... 'Don't start?'"

Fuck's sake. "This is all too analog."

He takes my hand. He's strange. A gelatin skeleton. That rhymes. "I heard you screaming."

"You did not."

"I heard you all the way in America."

139

"I don't do that. The neighbors."

"This seems like a pretty heavy trip."

"Tizzzzzzzzz."

"Let's get you some water."

"We have to be quick, like. We've a planning session in a few minutes. We're going to extend the walls out around the world. I have concerns about the long term viability of the project, but so long as the girls don't union up we'll be tits."

"We can make this work," he says.

"You're just like Colm. You think you can fix anything."

"I'm not very handy."

"You sell yourself short," I say.

"You kind of have to pick a lane."

I kiss him. "You left your bag."

"My bag?"

"On the tarmac. I brought it home."

"I'll have to come back for it, then."

"That would be something now, considering."

"If something is easy, I won't do it."

This is very true. "If only I lived down the street, like. You'd have nothing to do with me at all."

"My actions are often disproportionate to their aims."

"I wouldn't mind," I say. "If you came back."

"You don't want to kill yourself?"

"I want..."

He takes my hand. I'm so tiny in his hands. Small enough to be inside everything. I feel everything. The satin burn of the sheets. The folding tongue of the outstretched floor. The pull of the waves. The waves lick at me, tongue their want against the frozen stone of my body and I'm stuck. I feel so young. I feel alive.

A-L-I-V-E.

Sounds so strange. I feel everything. His kiss. His hands. His fingers. He traces the curve of me down inside my knickers. I fall against him, helpless. He fingers the elastic, round and round, teasing and his hand dives and finds me and God, Lord God his hands are quick with me, slick with me and I feel him, I feel us, I feel so young I feel so alive I'm alive alive ALIVE.

"I want to live..."

The fort shudders from my screams. I thrash and pull and I feel him on the other side of the sheet and don't let go, please come back and the sheet comes off him and it's Aoife trying to lift me as she always does but I keep screaming. I want to live. Lord God, I want to live. The curtains fall on Aoife.

I need water.

The surf rushes in over my ankles. Low tide leaves the beach naked. The salt coarse on my tongue. An ocean of undrinkable water. All we're left with. Nothing to drink and nowhere to stand. Blood scars the eastern horizon. Stars scattered like buckshot. The cold of the water settles in me. The sober clarity of the air. The dog lingers beside the rumpled rock, his eyes heavy on the shadowed mainland.

"Let's go home," I say.

○

Ma sits in front of the telly. Dark as the sky. She pounds her fist against the arm of her chair. She throws the remote.

It lands at my feet. "You're making a mess, Iris."

She forgot I wasn't there. "Is that you, Ma?"

She falls at me in this exhausted embrace. Her clothes need changing. She smells like a car that's never been cleaned out. How long has she been sitting there, clicking through channels we no longer get. How long has it been since I cared.

○

As the water cools in the tub, I peel off her heavy, stained clothes. She giggles like a girl. Her nudity embarrassing. Have I ever seen her naked? A glimpse here. There. For the first time in my life I truly see my mother. Pale. Veined with blue. This tiny, fragile, shivering thing. I get out my clothes and guide her into the tub with me. She squeals at every trickle of water down the back of her neck. She shakes the soap out of her hair like a dog and if I could wish her in the sink. Hold her in my arms and make it all go away with a kiss.

"Caoimhe," she says. "Caoimhe, Caoimhe, Caoimhe."

"Ma... who was Caoimhe?"

She goes on repeating her name. A song now. She never mentioned her in the past, so far as I can remember. We've no relations by that name. A friend, like. A schoolmate. Maybe Da knew her. I wish Da was here. I wish I could have done this for him. I wish I could have done so much more for you. I wish I could have done so much better. I failed you. I failed all of us and I'm failing us all now wanting to live when there's no hope. When you're waiting for me.

Aren't you waiting.

"Stop your crying, girl," Ma says, and kisses me.

I kiss her back. This beautiful stranger.

I wash the grime from her face. Her hands. I pour water over her head and her face rises, like a flower to the sun. For a long time I just hold her. We prune, Iris and I, and I hold her still.

CHAPTER FOURTEEN

His bag sits at the end of the bed, where it has since the day he left.

I keep thinking he'll come through the door and I'll hand it to him. *A yo-yo, you are.* Very organized, Gavin. Everything rolled and tucked in place. Economical. I pull on one of his shirts. His sweaters. This smell to them from not being washed in ages now. Sawdust. The sea. Sweat. In the inside pocket, I find a journal. I shouldn't. Flowers tucked in the pages. Strands of my hair. His passport.

Lord God.

He left it. There was no getting on any plane without it. There was no getting home. Gavin. What did you do.

Do you know.

○

"Do you think he could be still on the mainland?"

This shit eating grin peels off Aoife's lips. The tension in her releases and she unspools across me in the cot we share in the sitting room at the home. I don't know why we bother sleeping. We have all of eternity to rest and yet here we are, in our last days, exhausted and spent, trying to get a few minutes of kip. Some warmth. Some distance from the dark.

"He must be," she says.

"What do you think he's doing?"

She shrugs. "He's money."

"He's alone."

What did he do when he realized he didn't have his passport? Try and get back here? Did they lose power in Dublin? What did I do to him. Everyone who touches me. What did I do.

"Do you think he left it on purpose?"

She rests her head on my shoulder. "He'll come back."

"Would the plane still work? With the EMP?"

"You think that's what it was?"

There haven't been planes. There hasn't been anything since that night. The only business in the sky this demolition.

"You don't think Dublin, though?" I say.

"Why would they nuke Dublin? It's no place to be on a Saturday night, but a bomb is a bit excessive."

Why would they do any of it. Who would. The *eejits*. All of them. They couldn't fucking wait. The tides have gone mad. The earth is opening up. The sky is falling. And we're not to be left out. Never to be out done, us. Off go our missiles, as if to say: Show me your best apocalypse. We'll do you one better.

"You don't think New York?"

She kisses my cheek. "He'll come back.You'll hear that plane coming over and you'll run down the road to him and it will be just like a fucking movie, it will. And then it will be just the three of us."

I pinch her tit. "And Saidbh?"

Aoife shrugs.

"You may have unlocked a secret level with her."

"She's sixteen."

"Hardly matters now."

"I don't think it will be a viable defense, like."

"I see her looking at you."

Aoife squirms, uncomfortable. "She's only beautiful."

"Give it a go."

She snorts. "You're telling me, give it a go?"

"The circumstances aren't the same."

"Aren't they? Aren't I wanting for someone else?"

I pinch her again. "It doesn't have to be love. It doesn't have to be anything. But it can be good."

"Her parents may object."

"I don't see why. You're only twice her age. You only gave her ecstasy. And then molested her. Repeatedly."

Aoife crosses her arms. "Like you remember."

If drinking helped me forget, I'd never have stopped. I remember everything. My mind this clutter I keep turning over searching for what I really want and can never find.

"It's been weeks, Aoife."

"He'll come back, Gavin."

Do I want him to come back. Didn't I want him home. Isn't this why; this speeding downhill now toward our end. A year, they say. We don't have a year. I don't think we have months.

What did I do.

○

Apocalypses pile on themselves, all waiting their turn. Unnatural clouds, heavy with the ash of volcanoes or nuclear blasts or both lid what daylight there is. The days endless despite their brevity; day in name only, the day a long plow through darkness to an oasis of a lesser dark only to trudge, helplessly, into a more bountiful one. It's as if the black hole has already swallowed the sun, and now the earth circles the event horizon, time stretched out thin and far as we spiral around and around into the passionate darkness below.

○

I become the stink and the squalor of the house. Ma runs amok through the upstairs and downstairs, the garden out back, the road out front. My energy and will to deal with her gone, along with any sense of time. She is a child. I am old and tired.

We are all dead, fit for graves yet to be dug.

○

Spray rains down in ice pellets on the low road. Birds flit inside a house near the pier, exposed to the elements from a boulder the waves must have spit ashore. The boulder doesn't seem limestone or shale, or any part of The Burren. Was it some chunk the ocean bit off from Greenland? Iceland? America? Or was it something the sea had swallowed once long, long ago and now finally spit out in its death rattle? I reach for my mobile. Life real only in pictures. Bloody thing doesn't work anymore.

I wonder if he's called me.

○

Snow buries the island as never before. You never saw snow. Drifts make the roads and boreens treacherous back and forth between the house and the nursing home. Wind licked curls hide depressions in the ground. Lagoons form from the ocean spray showering on the cliffs. I melt the snow to drink at the home, knowing it could be contaminated with radiation, but if so then we're all soaking it in every bleeding day. No obvious signs of radiation sickness manifest on the island, but cutoff from the mainland, there is no way of knowing the extent of the war or even its veracity, though no one doubts the sky.

○

I burn the remaining coal. Then the old, dirtied newspapers papering the floors of the house. Then books. All my books. Clothes. Whatever will give us warmth in the home. Ma sits in her recliner, curling her hair with her finger and watching the dead telly. No idea where she is. Days without pills now. All her words like gibberish.

It's just waiting, now.

○

I press towels against the cracks of the doors, and against the porous edges of the windows to try and keep the cold out. My breath clouds the air. Ma goes behind me and puts them all in the hamper. Her arthritis flares unabated in the cold, until finally I find her rickety and crumpled in the yard out back. Aoife helps me get her inside, into her bed. I try to get some water down her. I dab the sides of her mouth with a cold washcloth. She smacks her lips. Blubbers nonsense at me.

"*Baaaa daaaa soooooo.*"

All night long. I sit by the bed, listening to it unfold.

"*Ahhhhh emmmmm ohhhhh.*"

There's no medicine. No food, really. I know this is happening and I don't want it to. I should be thankful she will not suffer through the worst ahead of us but I don't want to lose my ma. I hold her hand. Wipe away drool. Pretend I'm not bleeding terrified. I sit there, staring into the white space of her hand. My mother a blank page to me even now. The words don't come. Hours. Days. Her story is her story. Most of it will die with her. How she ever allowed Da to share any of it with her, I'll never know. All I have are questions now. Things I never thought to ask before. Now it's too late.

○

The last sheep go to the knives. The last cows. Some of the farmers have moved on to their horses. Very little of their butcher makes it beyond their own plates. No one has money or anything of value to trade for food, except more and more, room and board. Those in the low-lying houses abandon them, going to family or neighbors higher

147

up the steps of the island. Water creeps up the road. Splashes against the style at high tide. The cemetery is said to be under, most of the day now. I will not be able to bury Ma there, like she asked me to.

Like I promised.

O

The island shrinks but in the space left, island gossip seems thicker. Juicier. Gossip keeps us full, hours each day. Aoife knows all the business. I imagine her going door to door before she comes here, collecting news like honey and then rubbing her legs together, distracting both our fears with the sound of her own voice, her own inexplicable relish.

"You awake?" she says, sipping on fish soup.

I open my eyes. "Hmm?"

"You're nodding off on me."

"I'm listening."

"I'm boring you."

Every morning she comes to check on Ma. Every day she has some new dirt. We never did this before. Always it was down the pub at night. I enjoy our mornings. The sunshine of her voice. It delays the pain waiting, lurking, ticking away at the clock until I bed down, strip down, and the pain goes to work on me again, all through the night into the morning until she comes.

"I'm not bored," I say.

She smiles with relief. "I'll just go home and sit there in the dark with them, anyways."

"How is she, then? Saidbh?"

"Getting on, I suppose. We're... sorting it out." She winces. "I may have woken a beast, Mairead. I'm not proud."

I smile. "Let it be her kills you, then."

Her lip curls. "It's not safe out here, for either of you. You should be up at the home."

"This is home," I say.

Aoife looks down into her soup. "Saidbh asks me. If we're going to pass out the morphine at the home. If we're going to be there. She asks me about people dying. All the time."

"She's just... thinking ahead. I'm sure."

"Do you? Think ahead?"

There isn't that far to think ahead. I can see all that is left in our lives out the window, in the closing distance between the house and the sea, creeping up the island.

○

Colm casts out his line from a cliff that had been the ledge of a dale, brooking an old grazing field near the rim of the island. I don't know how the man managed such a feat, climbing down karst steps calved from the face of the cliffs hundreds of feet over the mad sea, or what possessed him to even try. Hunger, I suppose. Or sheer boredom.

"Have you got a death wish?" I say.

He bobbles his rod. "I could ask you the same."

I ease down the steps, slick with spray and all of them so big you have to go flat on your belly to get down to the next. Colm reaches up to catch me, his hands on my legs and I come down in his arms. Twenty years go between us.

"If I had any wishes," I say. "I wouldn't spend them on myself."

"If you've got three, the first two should suffice to account for the good of everyone else. No black hole, peace on earth and a personalized check for one billion Euro hand delivered to me by Helen Mirren in a black lace teddy."

"You've thought of this before," I say.

"I've plenty of time to think out here."

I follow the arc of his lure across the shale horizon. It's been weeks, maybe longer, since I've seen the azure blue of day or the royal blue of night. Since I've seen the stars or the trouble the black hole had made of them.

"How's Iris, then?"

DARBY HARN

I sit on a shelf of rock. "She's close now."

He nods. "I'm sorry."

"I was ready, you know. To do it. For both of us."

"Aye. And now?"

"All I want is to be there in the cemetery with Ma and Da and... I can get out there, at low tide. If I stay, the water will sweep me away and I think that's what I should do. I should bring Ma down there and we can both..."

I stifle my cry in my hand.

Colm reels the line back in. He bends over to his tackle box – knees not bending at all – and switches out lures. The old man is always tinkering, adjusting, trying to make things work. He keeps going over the same thing again and again, certain he'll figure it out. He'll find life in the line again.

"I've told you about Katmandu," he says.

"You have."

"The Hindus, burning the dead on the river." He scratches his chin. "In Hindu thinking all the universe is divine, and everything in it is a manifestation of divinity itself. A manifestation of God. You can predict a Catholic man's response to this. The question becomes, is death divine? Brutality? Indifference? Cruelty? All of the suffering in the world. And the answer is, in the end..."

"You have to say yes to it?"

Colm reels in his line, slack, and then slings it back to the water. "You have to accept it."

"How can you accept any of this, Colm?"

"Because it is."

This flash of heat goes through me. The cold gone, in a snap. All the soreness in my body. It is what it is. Easy for him to say. He's lived his life.

"People were starving before all this," I say. "People were dying, every day for some war or some disaster somewhere else in the world. Was that just the way it was?"

"It doesn't mean do nothing, Mairead."

"What does it mean then?"

"It means live. Participate. This is. You are. This is who we are. This is what's happening to us. We have to say yes to our story, our failures and our regrets, or else we don't have a story."

"Is that what you think about Declan?"

Colm reels in his fishing line, and rests the rod against the stone as he sits beside me. The wind blisters us with spray. I shield my face but he doesn't. His cheeks are raw. Red. His hands white. Calluses across his palms. He's as naked as the rock out here, and as battered. As persistent.

"I have to accept what happened," he says. "I can't change it. If I could go back in time and make it so it never happened... would I go back and make it so he was never born? Your father never died, and the two of us were never drunk and lonely? Would I change it you were never born? I wouldn't. I can't. I can't untangle our joy from our misery, Mairead. No one can. I have to accept it."

I shake my head. "I can't..."

"And once I had... once I embraced the pain... I could see beyond it. I could see the good memories again. The joy. All the good he brought in my life and he was there again."

I look behind me, toward the shore. "He's waiting..."

"This is all there is, Mairead. You already know that. You've always known it. That's what spurred you to New York, and what drove you through the doubt of raising that boy. This is life. This is living. Our joy and our eternity is here, now."

"He's waiting for me..."

"He's here," Colm says, his voice breaking. "He's with you, wherever you go. Just like your father. Iris. Gavin."

A cloud of birds morph through a series of increasingly frantic shapes over the manic sea. Something is dead down there, beached on rocks swamped in foam and seaweed and tide. The ocean swells beyond Inishèan. Waves build and crest toward clouds, distorting the horizon and shrinking it seems the distance between the island and an America I imagine quiet. At peace.

I take Colm's hand. "Aren't you afraid?"

"Terrified."

"But you accept this?"

"I have to," he says. "Doesn't mean I like it. Doesn't mean I won't come out here to get as much fish as I can for as many people as I can. Doesn't mean I won't imagine slipping and falling and being relieved of my worries. But I get up in the morning, because the morning is there. Just like you do. Just like you will, so long as you're able."

"Colm..."

He squeezes my hand, and lets go. Colm throws his line out again, as he has done since he was a boy. Hours we're there on the ledge. These fish, they've caught on.

Every day the same: breakfast with Aoife, sit with Ma, walk down the road as far as the tide allows. Some days I sit at the crest of the hill going down into the cemetery. Some days I fall into long trenches of remembering you, deeper and darker the further I go, your voice echoing back and forth between the narrowing walls of my hope and my fear. Some days I find myself knee deep in water without remembering how I got there. Some days the sound of my own voice jars me out of my fugue, and I look at Ma, stranded in her bed somewhere between life and death. Consciousness and dreams. We're stranded. The sky never loses its red. The sea its anger. The island its secrets.

Ma calls out to the dark. "*Weialala leia...*"

She doesn't eat. I keep a bedpan nearby for her, but Ma passes nothing but nonsense. Her hands shrivel to knots of bone. Her cheeks sink and her face becomes riven with the lines of her age, the stress and endurance of her life, the surface of her tortured and stretched, pulled and pried apart from the collapse of human will within.

"*Wallala leialala...*"

"Ma..." I brush her thin hair. "Ma, do you hear me?"

"*Weialala...*"

"Do you remember?" I say. "The day he was born? Only time I ever saw you cry. I had to fight you for him."

Drool courses the channels in the corners of her mouth to pool in her chin. I wipe it away. I caress the hair out of her eyes, clenched shut, and put my hands to her cheeks, constantly inflating and deflating with random noises and sounds.

"Maybe I put too much on you, asking you to look after him. I should have had you all at the home, like. I don't know."

"Maaaaaa..."

"I don't know anything anymore."

"Raiiiiii..."

"Colm talks about saying yes to this, but... I just want us to be together. I close my eyes and I see Declan. The sun in his hair. He's reaching out to me. I don't know. What if there's nothing else? What if this is it? We should act like it. I should have acted like it. We could have all been together. I think I'm going to be the last person here. I'm going end up like one of these shells out on the beach. Just pieces. Picked up and left here from God knows where. Powder."

Ma gulps. I squeeze her hand. The engine keeps on chugging.

"You're so strong," I say. "Whatever strength I had was your strength. I need your help, Ma. I need you to look after him again. Would you look after him for me? For now?"

Her breathing slows. The fierce pumping of her cheeks and the mashing of her gums. This sound sighs out of her. I wait for her breath to pick up, but it never does. What peace there is in our house breaks with my sobs. This scratching at the door.

○

Fire eats the roof of the house.

In minutes it's gone. The home I grew up in caves in on itself. I stand on the road with the dog in quiet observance. Neighbors come with pails. I wave them off. The trickle of people up the high road becomes a funeral procession. Iris was well known on the island for her cantankerousness; if anyone would make it to the end, she would. Even in her sickness, people saw the island in her. Strong, battered, defiant against the tides. The old rock of Inishèan.

Is folamh fuar e teach gan bean.

All who can stand on the low road in the snow and wind and rising tide and hold hats and hands to their slowing hearts for what has passed and will never come again. Their voices rise like glasses in toast, tired, ragged, one at a time and then all at once.

Fainne oir ort! Slan, Iris.

Inishèan has lost its strength. The end comes quick now, like death on a body void of will.

CHAPTER FIFTEEN

At low tide, I go down to the harbor to fill bottles.

The air rank with the rotten egg stench of seaweed the tides left behind last night. The sky the gauzy brown on marshmallows before they catch fire. I never understood marshmallows. Such a strange taste to them. Of course I want one now. I want just about anything. I reach in my jacket. It's a shit picture of Gavin on the passport. The flash brings out all the red in his skin. His eyes. Still and all. He smiles. He's excited. He's hopeful, Gavin. Is it involuntary, this hope. Could we deny it, if we wanted to. We must not be able to. People can survive fucking cancer. They can survive losing limbs. Being lost at sea. Going without food for weeks.

People can't survive losing hope.

I hear this scratching. The dog, I figure, but when I look across the water, it's not the Collie. A raft bobs against the swamped pier. Inflatable. I get this start in me.

Gavin.

I go down the pier as far as I can. The raft is big enough for five or six people. An outboard motor on the back. Serial numbers along the sides, along with strange backwards letters. Angry waves roil in

Galway Bay. The mainland a blur beyond. No one came across, not in that thing. A rope tethers it to a stake in the concrete. A tripod-like thing. Machined. More serial numbers. More strange letters.

Russian. I think it's Russian.

Colm slouches on the stool next to the car in his garage, staring off into space. Bottom lip droopy as that pot belly of his. Nothing left to tinker with. He sees me coming up the drive and he near hits his head on the open hood of the car.

"I found a boat," I say. "Down at the pier."

"What kind of boat?"

"Military. I think. A raft, like."

"Not Irish, I take it."

"Russian. I don't know."

"The tides washed it ashore."

"Absolutely not."

He scratches his chin. Whatever spirit he got from seeing me alive and well drains out of his face.

Colm goes into the back of the garage. "Ever fired a gun?"

"No..."

He lifts the tray out of an old toolbox. A revolver and a semi-automatic pistol underneath.

"Where did you get guns, Colm?"

He checks the chamber on the revolver, and then he hands it to me. "You understand the safety?"

The gun weighs in my hand. "I do."

"Blind man's guess, it's supplies they're after. Food. Medicine. They're on foot. They'll be going house to house."

I grab his arm. "We have to get back to the home."

There's gas enough left in the car to get us down the high road to Kilbanna. We creep along, looking down the hills at the houses below, looking for Russians. What would they look like, anyways? What would we do? Colm's riding down the road with the gun in his lap like he's John fucking Wayne, and any Russians we find are sure to blast us to smithereens the second they see us. The fuck am I supposed to do with this thing? What's happening. Why is any of this happening. Lord God. What did they do.

○

A man stands outside the entrance to the nursing home, layered in black and slung with a machine gun. The instant he sees us pull in the car park, the soldier grabs at the walkie-talkie hooked to the belt crossing his shoulder.

"Colm," I say. "Jesus."

"Stay calm," he says, and parks the car like he does any day he comes up here. The soldier stands at the door, watching. Waiting. All I can see of his face are his eyes, blood red and frayed. Another two soldiers come out the home. Christ.

Colm gets out the car. "How can we help you lads?"

Blood Eyes says something in Russian.

"I spent a week in Moscow once," Colm says. "I took the train, all the way from Paris. Didn't pick up any Russian, unfortunately. Well. I might have picked up a girl or two."

"Yeda?"

"Any of youse speak English? English?"

"Yeda," Blood Eyes says.

"We don't understand," Colm says. "I'd invite you all in for a big sit down but you've already helped yourself, I see. I trust disciplined men like yourselves have been good guests."

Enough of this bollocks. I get out the car. "What are you doing in there? The fuck are youse doing? Aoife? Aoife!"

The soldiers all grip their guns. Colm reaches for his and Lord

157

God we're all going to get fucking shot in a car park and at the last second Colm thinks better. He puts his hands in the air as the Russians shout at us both. I've no clue what they're saying. Blood Eyes points at the ground.

I'm on my knees. I'm going to die on my knees.

Colm goes to his, gingerly. "Just go along."

Blood Eyes drives his knee in Colm's stomach. He folds over and the soldier shoves him to the asphalt. He takes the gun tucked behind Colm's back in his belt and searches him.

He comes to me. "It's in my pocket," I say.

Blood Eyes fishes the revolver out of my jacket. He hands it off to one of the others and then starts patting me down. His hands not as quick as they were with Colm. Tosser. He searches through every pocket in the jacket inside and out.

Blood Eyes stabs a finger at me. "*Ty amerikanets?*"

"What?"

He shoves the passport at me. "*Amerikanskiy?*"

The passport confuses Blood Eyes. Colm. Blood Eyes gets on his radio again. We sit there waiting on our knees on the pavement with guns in our faces and I could have done it. I could have walked out to the sea and taken control and now I don't have any control. He has such anger in him, Blood Eyes. The passport bends and wrinkles in his closing fist. His breath clouds the air between us. His breath frosts to my skin.

Another soldier comes out the home. The leader, I take it. He rubs away the soreness from his grayed temples, forcing out a long, angry sigh. Blood Eyes says something in Russian and they go back and forth, the leader acting like *What are you bothering me with this for?* and Blood Eyes hands him the passport.

Now's he interested. The leader kneels before me, flipping casual through the pages of the passport.

"Husband?"

"He's gone," I say. "He left."

He smiles. "Without passport?"

Colm spits out blood onto the pavement. "Fuck off back to Russia and leave us be, Boris."

Blood Eyes drives the butt of his rifle into Colm's back. Inside I hear screaming. Aoife. Saidbh. They're at the windows. More soldiers inside. Two or three of them.

"Are you trying to start a war?" I say.

The color drains out of the leader's face. He stares at me, his eyes small in his head, like the rims of bullets. "You not know?"

"Know what?"

He rubs his chin with his thumb. "Where is he?"

"He's gone," I say. "Just take whatever you want and go. We don't have anything, but take what there is. Leave us alone."

"You Mairead?"

"What?"

"You head nurse?"

I look at the windows. Aoife quaking with sobs. "I am."

He smiles, like it's all just a big misunderstanding. He takes my hand, and helps me to my feet.

"Yelchin," he says. "Captain Yelchin."

"*Céad míle fáilte.*"

"*Preevyet.* We need nurse. You help us."

"Fine. Fine. And then you go."

He wraps his arm around my shoulders and guides me to the door. "Inside, yes? We go inside."

Aoife's every movement in the mirror casts a shadow on the door of the staff loo. The dog rests on the end of the cot with me, head crooking with each interruption of candlelight.

I scratch behind his ears. "Do you believe him?"

Her voice is still hoarse from crying so. "Those men are starved... grieving. They've nowhere to go."

"He didn't know how it started, though. Why."

"Would he?"

"You don't think New York, though. You don't think Dublin."

Aoife comes out of the bathroom. "Christ."

"Maybe it was just a few. They stopped it, before..."

She sits on the end of the cot with me. "You should have told Gavin you were pregnant."

"For fuck's sake, Aoife."

"What did you let him go for?"

"What did I let him go for? Are you high again? Gavin needed to be home with his Ma."

"This was his home. He told you."

"It's my fault they've done it, is it?"

"You knew it was all going to shit – "

"It had all gone to shit, Aoife!"

" – and now they're going to rape us and kill us – "

We fall into the cot together, exhausted from our grief. I cradle her close. Brush the hair out of her eyes, wet with all her tears and snot and always a mess, Aoife. I should be a mess. I should be running around like a chicken without its head. It's over. They've done it. Everyone out there in the world is dead.

Aoife holds me close. "You're not going out there, are you?"

Better I go with them back to their submarine than have over a hundred Russian sailors come to shore. I don't know what they think I can do for them. We've nothing left in medicine or supplies for their injured. I don't know what choice I have.

"I'll be fine," I say.

"I'll go with you."

I see how the Russians look at her. Saidbh. They're staying. "How many Americans are there up at the B&B?"

"A dozen, like. I don't know."

"I want you to go up there, Aoife. I want you to take all the Americans up the old way to the monastery."

She goes tense. "Mairead..."

"You stay there until I come back to get you."

"Send Saidbh. I'll go with you."

"I'm trusting you to do this."

"I'm afraid."

"I know. I know."

"The Russian thinks youse were married."

"Gavin isn't here," I say. "He can't hurt him."

Her arms coil around me. Her fingers clutch the dry paper of my scrubs. Her nails sink into my skin.

"I'll stitch them up," I say. "They'll be on their way."

"I can't believe it..."

I kiss her cheek. "They'll be gone tomorrow."

She rolls on top of me. Her weight, her heat pressing into me and if she could, she'd never let me go.

"I love you," she says.

I kiss her. "Don't start."

○

The sky in the west takes on the hue of raw meat. Aoife is slow up the high road to the B&B. I stand with the dog outside the home as she vanishes to a silhouette against the evening.

○

I can't swim.

All my life on an island and I'm no better than a cat. This raft goes over on a wave and I'll be with you. I should want this. I should be glad I've no choice but to go out to what has to be certain death, but I don't want to. I don't want to leave. I want to stay, and keep to the death I had planned.

Somewhere, God is laughing.

Yelchin sloshes back to me. "In."

The raft scrapes against the vanishing pier. The Russians no weight in it. Their submarine is a few miles out in Galway Bay.

There and back, he says. And then they go.

I toss the bag holding what's left of the home's supplies into the raft. "I'm not kissing anything to make it better."

He makes this frown, Yelchin. His whole face wrinkles. "You – *dusha*. Spirit. Make good sailor."

"I don't suppose you have women sailors anyways."

"Not on submarine."

He's just going to let me go. They're just going to leave.

The motor of Colm's car echoes off the emptied buildings of Kilbanna. He pulls up right at the end of the pier. He gets out with his took kit and a bottle of whiskey.

"Good," he says. "You're still here."

"We leave now," Yelchin says.

"I know you lads probably have a taste for vodka, but let me tell you, you've not had a drink in your life 'til you've had Irish whiskey. Keeps your warm. Keeps you moving."

Yelchin reaches for the bottle. "*Spasibo.*"

Colm tucks the bottle in his tool kit. "I figure you boys can use a hand. I'll take a look around. See what I can do."

What are you doing, Colm.

Yelchin laughs. "You? Fix sub?"

Colm shrugs. "Wires are wires."

"We have engineer. We have electrician."

"That's as maybe. I'm coming."

The smile drains off Yelchin's face. "No room."

"I'll take a look." Colm slaps his hand on Yelchin's back and moves him back to the raft. "We'll have a nice, stiff drink. It's the least I can do for such fine guests as yourselves."

Yelchin's in the raft. Colm's in the raft. Like that, I am and we're drifting away from the pier. The island. That dog. He runs down the pier, chasing us like he'll leap into the water after us but he stops. He sits there, head crooked in confusion. This whine coming out of him. The island recedes, a tide I expect to come crashing back in but it never does. The light of distant fires twinkle from the shrouded peak of Inishmore. They shrink, and vanish in fog. I'm going the wrong way. The raft lifts under a swell and I come crashing down inside it hard. Water soaks me head to toe. Colm grips my hand.

He smiles, but it's no ballast.

○

All of the Russians have some type injury.

Cuts and bruises, mostly. A few broken arms. Legs. Collarbones. I set what I can and make do with a folding split meant for an arm. Yelchin doesn't say how they came by their injuries. I don't ask. There isn't room for questions. The sub like the hollow of a bone. A mute, fluorescent green tint to everything, even the metal, like we're inside some morgue you see on the telly. Valves barnacle the bulkhead. All these boxy gauges, piled on top of other. The interior reefed in kit. Switches. Knobs. Caged light bulbs. The whole thing dripping with condensation.

○

I skin some fish they've caught. Soaked with radiation, I'm sure. Everything we've been eating and drinking since the lights went out probably. So it is. After, I scrub the paring knife in the mess. I think about tucking it up the sleeve of my sweater. What would I do with it. Who do I think I am. Crewmen watch me. They stare. Some of them, it's easy to know what they're thinking. That stiffness in their face. Others are just sore for home, I think. Girls like me dead now. Wives. Sisters. Mothers. I am all of these girls to them and they want to fuck me. They want to hug me, save me, bury me for later. They want to be boys again, but they've done their boying and all that's left is for me to clean up after them.

Yelchin comes in the mess. "Ah. *Ryba*. Stay. For dinner."

"We'll be getting back," I say. "It'll be dark soon."

He pats the seat next to him. "Stay."

163

○

After dinner, the Russians pile up in the mess. One of them has a guitar. He plays some Russian songs that are sad, if loud. Blood Eyes glares at me. The smell of burnt fish in the air.

Colm covers his mouth as he whispers to me. "It was a Brit sub. The Russians took a torpedo. There's no leaving for them."

Yelchin claps with the music, leaned back in his chair, foot up on the table. He passes a cigarette around with the others. A couple of them nod off to needful sleep.

I lean forward, my head down. "Did they get the Brits?"

"They did not."

The Brits are still out there. They could be hunting for this Russian sub right now. They won't give a toss who's on it.

"We have to get out of here," I say.

The boy with the guitar comes over to me. He presses the thing into my hands. "You," he says. "You."

"Thank you, no."

Yelchin's eyes light up. "You sing?"

"Not really. Not anymore. We should be going."

"Sing. Sing for me."

He's not exactly asking. Christ. I take the guitar. I sing *I'll Tell Me Ma*. I've not sung for anyone besides you in ages. As kind as the guitar is to my fingers, I can't go on.

"We should call it a night, I think."

Yelchin offers me a cigarette. I can't stand the things, but I take it. "You good singer. I like."

"Thank you."

"You singer? Make record?"

Records, he says. "I never did."

Smoke funnels out his mouth. "My mother was nurse."

"Was she?"

"How you say... pediatric?"

"What's your mother like?"

164

He laughs. "Not good fit for babies."

"Oh. Well. It takes a certain nature."

"You have mother's nature."

"Kind of you to say."

"You – children?" I just shake my head. "My boys. Eleven and twelve. Strong boys. Fun – funny? Funny boys."

"I'm sure."

"You no children? With American?"

"He's left, I've told you."

Yelchin nods. "He leave you? Your husband?"

"He's not my husband. It's none of your business."

"He run," Yelchin says. "Like coward. Americans – cowards."

"He was going home to his family. To the States."

"The States..." Yelchin lights another cigarette. He roasts the end over the flame slow like. Lord God. He's gone. They're all gone. "Island your home?"

"I want to go now."

He puts his hand to his heart. "Odessa." Tears flood his eyes. He flicks away the ash. "Very much we want to go back. We no go back now. No one go home."

This chill that's been hanging around finally sinks in.

Colm stands. Stretches. "Been a lovely evening. We'll be off now. You lads help yourselves to the rest of that whiskey."

Yelchin just goes on. "We not start this. We defend ourselves. *Da?* What happens now – not personal. My obligation to my men. My family."

"But we didn't..." What did I do with the knife. Why didn't I bring the knife with me. "I don't know about any of this, we didn't know any of this had happened. He's not here."

Yelchin nods, like he understands. "He run, your American. He hide. *Da?* But he suffer as I suffer. He lose as I lose. I take his family, as he take mine."

It's so calm, the way he says it. So matter of fact, like. Unfortunately at this time you do not meet the minimum criteria in order to live. Our apologies. Have a nice day.

I shake my head. "The residents need my help."

"You help my family."

The sound is so loud I'm inside the gun barrel, like. I didn't see Yelchin draw his gun. Colm plops back down to his chair. This look on his face, like someone's just told him his son has died. His shirt goes red. The white in his beard.

"Colm..."

Yelchin points the gun at me.

Mo leanbh. Mo stór.

CHAPTER SIXTEEN

The sea explodes inside the mess.

Yelchin vanishes in the flood. The sub feels like it's coming apart. Lord God. I grab Colm. Choking blood. I drag him behind me into the press of men through the portal out the mess. The light gone from green to red. Water up to my waist. Dead cold. My elbows bruise against the wall. We're listing.

We're sinking.

The fuck is going on. I'm under water. I lose Colm. Every dive below a dive into sharp glass. A tangle of arms and legs and belts and slings. I scratch. I kick. I claw. My hand gets around the hilt of a knife in someone's boot. The water goes dark. I surface. Just enough room for me to breathe. I'm freezing. I'm drowning.

I can't swim.

Get out. You have to get out. I pull myself along all the greebles on the bulkhead back to where I think the bridge or whatever the fuck it is was. However I got in here. How did I get in here. Colm. Where are you. Thunder in the water. Muffled screams. The thrash of drowning men. I keep following the sailors in front of me, bobbing up every minute or so for air and the sailors in front of me disappear.

The sub disappears.

Water burns in my lungs. My feet touch something. The sub. Oil clouds the water. The ink of my own blood. All this way. All those starts to never finish. There is no letting go. There is only the loosening of your dead fingers as the current rips you away from the thing you've held most dear.

Mo leanbh. Mo stór.

I am caught. This force pulls me like a lure upwards and the steel rung of a ladder descending down through the parapet of the sub jabs me in the ribs. I recoil into the water. The tide sweeps me back in and I grab hold of the rung and hold on with everything I have left. Every muscle in my body is frozen and yet I shake from the cold so much I can barely climb the rest of the way. Waves crash against the sinking submarine, blasting whatever strength I've got left right out of me.

I keep moving.

This muscular, determined force seizes me and I move, rung to rung. Minutes and waves between each one. I surface. I shout. I scream. The most honest sound I ever make. Colm is on the ladder above me, white as a cloud. One hand on a rung, one hand with a death grip on my jacket.

"Colm..."

"Go," he says.

The raft floats on the water close, tethered still to the outside of the parapet. I pull myself along the cable connecting them in and I climb in. I reach back for him.

He's gone.

Colm. The parapet sinks. The raft going with it. Lord God. This bleeding cable. I can't undo it. I hack at it with the knife. I hack and hack and hack until the cable breaks. The cord lashes me across the cheek and I fall back in the raft, alone.

I crawl back to the motor. I yank hard on the pull cord. The engine sputters. There's no fuel left. Water and steam geyser into the air. The submarine a whale, surfacing but she sinks. The sea gurgles. Men scream. Torpedoes streak under the raft like sharks. The sea heaves and I fold in with the curve of the raft. The darkened island expands out along my view. The tide takes me out into the bay.

Declan.

I scream for you. Let my voice be the fuel to get back to you. I'm going out. I'm too far now. The arms of the island open to the emptiness of the sea. There's no way I'll last out here. Maybe the tide will sweep me back. I try to use my arms to paddle. The cold shrinks me back into the raft. There's nothing else for it. I try again. Come on. You can do this. You've got to do this. The raft lifts under a swell and I come crashing down inside it hard. I'm soaked. Head to toe.

The island reduces in the distance. So does my hope.

○

This deep cold sinks into my bones.

The way it did the house when I was a girl and the heating would go out. If you didn't get in the anti-freeze before the first frost, the heating would go and there'd be one part, this little blower kind of thing you'd have to go to Galway to replace. An entire day gone to it. Up at seven Da would be to catch the ferry and then all day to wait to come back in the afternoon and it would be seven at night when he'd come in the front door. I always wanted to go with him to the mainland. *Take me, Da.* Ma never let me. Such a fearful woman. Her fear strong as karst stone.

Mo leanbh. Mo stór.

○

A rainstorm wakes me. The morning shy. The world only the sea. The tides heave in anger. I am thrown. Where am I. Gavin. I'm in his shirt but it's so heavy with wet and I can't get warm. I curl up in my own arms. Gavin. You're holding me. Running your hands through my hair. I'm in your lap, in front of the fire.

Keep me warm, Gavin. Keep me close.

○

The day dies in red haze. Night falls on me and I'm lost again in darkness. A day. A day off the island now. They must think me dead. Hold on. I'm coming back to you. eclan. I'm coming home, I swear to God. I wish I had one of your little boats with me now. A way back to you. I try to paddle again, but I've no sense of where I am or where the island is and I've no energy in any case. I'm a lump of ice in a freezer. My arms like weights tied to my body and I sink into the raft, in and out of consciousness. My mind goes to better places. Sitting in the chair with you singing you to your sleep.

Seoithín, seo hó, mo stór é, mo leanbh
Mo sheoid gan cealg, mo chuid gan tsaoil mhór

I wake in an inch of water. Sleep a distant country. I am lost between worlds. Stiff with cold. My body aches. I struggle to lift my head above the edge of the raft. Nothing but water. Endless water. I think I've gone out to the ocean. The raft will drift all the way to Norway, if it stops at all. The Arctic, like.

I'm finished.

Maybe I'll go around the south of Ireland, to Dublin. I'll find Gavin there, at the airport. We'll steal a plane, and he'll fly it back to the island and they'll all be waiting for us on the tarmac. Aoife. Ma. Colm. Saidbh. Eithne. Loads of people. Just like a movie. Roll credits. Take me back to Dublin. I'm never long in Dublin.

I'm in Dublin.

I'm walking the couple miles from Heuston Station down the quays to the boat. I need the air and the life back in my legs after the train from Galway. I'll make the walk faster than the buses, besides. The ghosts of truant buses, all No. 13, flicker in windows of the empty storefronts on Dame St. Grocery bags and crisp wrappers everywhere. What does it matter collecting trash now? Paying taxes? We've just learned our doom and straight off we're done with the maintenance of life. The veneer of civilization. The stillness of the island grates at me most days, but the closer I get to the city center, the queues waiting for me I know at Connolly, the train waiting for me and this pain waiting for me, I miss it. I miss the quiet. The expectation of the expected. The vastness of our isolation.

Trinity springs up out of the knotted streets at the pitted core of Dublin. The age of the place compels. The seeming permanence. Everything old fascinates me now. I ask the skinny bloke with his Morrissey coif at the ticket desk for the library if he'll just let me in for a minute, to see if the smell still lingers. That ancient musk of the old books going to dust on the shelves. Something is comforting in that: even as what was precious decayed, it did so naturally. With purpose.

"They emptied her out three weeks back," Morrissey says, leading me through the barren gift shop up the stairs into the Long Room. The creak of the floor under my feet echoes through the hollowed chamber. "It's been loads of vandals ever since the news. They moved all the books somewhere safe."

"Safe? Where's safe?"

People brush past me in the piss of a July rainstorm out front of the library. Students. Tourists. Going on about their business like nothing's happened. What's happened. A few months ago some scientist sent a tweet. *Rogue black hole in solar system. Pluto already gone. #thetruth.* Then the next thing you know the President of the United States is sweating through her top in front of some green screen running the same computer animation of the black hole chomping through the solar system like the fucking Pac-Man.

Three years, she said. *We have at best three years.*

I wind down toward O'Connell, determined to make the boat for Liverpool. A half day at sea, and then. A woman comes at me on Westmoreland, holding a half-eaten chocolate bar. A baby wrapped up in a pillow sheet slung over her shoulder, the same fabric as the scarf around her head. I can't make out her accent. Latvia. Estonia. Ukraine. One of those places.

All I have, she says. *All I have.*

"I can't help you," I say.

She reaches into the sling, and starts to take the baby out. She's shoving the baby at me. Into my arms.

All I have.

I push on through the crowd. The woman melts into all the others. I come to the bridge. Under a calved lamppost, a man stands beside a fold out chair with these obvious self-made books laid out on the seat. He holds one flat against his chest and shouts on repeat about the great conspiracy behind the black hole. How it is all a lie.

Can you even see it, he says. *This so called doom.*

"The sky, like," I say, pointing to the comet of the day as I inch my way through the crowd. "Or can you not see that?"

"They've got their probes, don't they? To visit comets and aster-oids. The world can't sustain 8 billion people. There's not food, there's not water, there's not oil enough. They got to thin the herd and best we kill ourselves as they walk in behind, collecting all the tokens. The fuckers."

"As theories go, it's decent."

"You'll buy me book, then?"

"I'm poor as Jesus."

He looks at me. "You up the pole?"

I pull my sweater down over the curve of my belly and I keep on. The crowd delivers me to the north side of the river. An angel looks down on me. Hand on her heart. Resigned. Restrained. That dog at her feet, like all us Irish dogs. Begging. Looking for something more than we will ever find.

I keep on.

I try cutting across the median. The woman from before, *All I have,* coalesces out of the crowd. That sling of hers empty. She's confused, like. Stupefied. She opens my hands, and places the sticky, melted bit of chocolate bar in my palm.

"Where's your baby?"

"All I have..."

"Lord God, woman. What did you do with him?"

I run around the terraced base of the monument, thinking she had set him down. No one knows what I'm talking about. I drag her back with me back to the bridge, searching the crowd, anyone with a bag or a stroller or who's stopped in confusion. I scour every inch of the bridge up and down both sides and the Bachelor's Walk down to the Ha'Penny Bridge and back again and I look over the edge, down into the Liffey, the pale blue color of frosted glass. Brown paper bags floating past. Protest signs. The body of a dead dog.

"What have you done?"

The woman lists against me. "All I have..."

"Why did you come here..."

Her head shakes. "All I have."

The WALK signal goes off like the timer to some homemade bomb. Traffic flows as it always does on O'Connell. The crowd propels me off the median, away from her numb confusion and I stumble on the 90. I fall into a seat. Usher's Quay is next.

An old woman says, "Why all the blood?"

"What?"

She nods, precisely, downwards and for the first time I feel the tautness of the dried chocolate on my hands.

Lord God. I'm covered. "I tried..."

She sighs. "There's no sense killing yourself."

"I didn't – "

"We all have the same pain. We all have jobs. If you don't, find a job and keep yourself busy. Always keep moving."

My mobile trembles in my hand. Ma picks up, bothered by the ringing as always. "Ma... I've changed my mind." Her voice scratches at me. "I know, Ma. I didn't want to do this. I want him to live. I want us to live. Please, Ma. I'm just for the train. And then home. I'll be coming home."

I close my eyes. I imagine myself in the bath back home, warm and floating in stillness and peace, you afloat within me. This life and purpose I never had. You're all I have. I imagine giving birth to you. Your first days and nights and your first walk and your first word and you're coming into your life like the flowers on the island in May, straining through the grikes to the sun for the little living they'd get before the rains of the summer drowned them. I imagine you so beautiful. So perfect. So flush with life and energy and joy you will not be denied, not by fear or circumstance or the jealous sky.

I imagine all these meteors and comets missing us. The black hole. The tides lose their fever. The sky. I imagine you leaving the island a man for your life in the world, spared, and I imagine I am not sad or sore but proud and vindicated in my living. I imagine all my mistakes and missteps and false starts justified. I never finished anything so I could start with you. Declan.

Mo leanbh. Mo stór.

I imagine scrubbing away all this mess and dirt and fear. The water red with it. The water is red. Like the ocean has gone to rust. The water sloshes in on me with every movement.

The water is getting in on me.

Salt crusts my lips. I must have fallen asleep. Still dark. I don't know if it's been hours or minutes. The raft a little paper tray for chips, floating down the Liffey toward the sea.

The rhythm of the waves quickens.

One comes fast after the other. I go up and then down and I know I'm going over. Any second now. I hold on the grip hard as I can. I'm weak. So weak. Days now without food. Water. The monster in me starved. All this ocean and still I can't drown this thirst. I can barely close my fingers around the handle. It's slick. A wave comes.

Lord God.

I'm not going to last in the water. This is it. The ocean swells beneath me. The raft teeters. I vault right out of it, over the side, face first into a bed of fierce rocks.

My lips bleed into the water pooled in the bored rock beneath me. I hear the punch of water colliding with rock. The call of seagulls. I push up on my arms. Land. I'm on land.

Lord God. Thank you God.

I crawl up the shore, propelled by the frustrated waves chasing after me. Somehow I find the strength to make it off the rocks up some scalloped earth to soft, flat land. I lie there and quake with guilt.

Where am I?

I try and sit up, but I can't. All my strength gone. The ground is so soft. Warm, even. I close my eyes. Don't close your eyes.

O

Spray flicks me out of my sleep.

It's near dark. I crawl away from the beach. High tide rolls in fierce. The raft long gone. Shells litter the ground all around me. I crawl on all fours along the ground and then I am crawling through a yard. I'm in somebody's yard. That's not the beach out front; it wasn't before at least. I stagger up to my feet, using the wall of a gutted house to prop me up. I get out of the yard, into the street and the broken hull of a yacht juts out of a two story. A couple barefoot kids excavate watches, rings and coins, any shiny thing, from out the heavy silt caking the street.

"Help," I say. Do I even make a sound.

A boy, five years old at best, salvages a laptop from the muck. The other kids howl in jealousy. The boy runs away from them, clutching the mud-caked thing against his chest and runs right into me. Dirt smears his chubby face. His entire body, like he came out of the ground. He smiles toothless at me. Such a beautiful boy. Undimmed even in all this ash and dark.

"Help me..."

A stringy girl, a bit older than the boys, fishes through my pockets. "She's no money."

"Help... I need help..."

"She's gone sick," another boy says.

"Don't touch her, then."

"Please... I need to get back to the island..."

The girl looks out at the vicious coast. "What island?"

"Inishèan." Their mouths drop. "Where am I?"

As soon as I ask, I know it's not one of the Arans. The ground is too soft. The air is different; less warm without the Gulf Stream. Less clean. I'm on the mainland, somewhere.

"Westport," she says. "This was Westport."

A frothing hell swallows the housing development behind. Westport, she says. Westport is miles inland of the coast. In fucking Mayo. I'm fifty miles north or more. If this is Westport, then all the lowland areas, Barna, Inverin with its airstrip, Rossaveal with its harbor, they're all gone.

There's no getting home.

CHAPTER SEVENTEEN

Eleven miles and three days later I make it to Castlebar.

Soaked through. I just kept moving, driven to get back as fast as I can and Lord God. I'll be in Galway the next day. I'll find the pilot and I'll be back to the island the day after.

Three days. Three days to home.

My legs throb and my hands are numb but I could keep on going, all the way through. Nothing will stop me. As I cross the bridge over the lough, my confidence dies. Hundreds of people line the high street, all of them carrying pillowcases and grocery bags stuffed with clothes and food. More pool in the interchange beyond. Some on bikes. A few horses and carts. Oases sprout in alleys and car parks, under canopies made of those large umbrellas you'd find just inside the door at Marks and Sparks for five euros. No one says hello. No one asks after me. We all look the same. Frozen. Haunted.

I bunch up against the clot of people in the interchange. No one is moving. I don't know why. I'm too short to see over everyone. A skinny teenage boy in a Dublin mandated tracksuit perches on the pedestal of a street lamp.

I go over to him. "What is it? What do you see?"

"Police," he says, shrugging. "Soldiers."

"Russians?"

"What you mean, Russians?"

"Ours, then?"

He comes down off the lamp. "Where you headed?"

"Galway," I say.

"You're going the wrong way."

"The coast roads are gone."

"How'd you get through the checkpoint?"

"Checkpoint?"

His face screws up in confusion. He drifts off into the crowd, looking back now and then. Unsure. I chat up some others. Most are headed to Connemara and the mountains. Many are headed to relatives or friends. Some have no idea where to go. Anxiety sticks to all of us. Rumors move faster than the refugees. The loss of power and the strange red haze in the sky produces endless theories. For the folks here from Dublin – they've walked across Ireland – the most common is a solar flare had struck the earth. The sun rent in spasms from the black hole. The more people I meet come from the border counties, the idea there had been a nuclear war becomes more prevalent. Flashes in the north. Across the Irish Sea, in Scotland. I say nothing of what I know. What do I know. I don't know anything other than I am getting home. I am getting home to you.

I'm coming home.

○

Dozens of soldiers armed with assault rifles man a roadblock in the interchange between the high road and the N5, going east. An older tractor from the 50s or 60s sits in the roundabout behind them. Bullet holes riddle the rusted chassis. Blood stains the seat of the open cab. The concrete below. On the far side of the roundabout, coming from the west, there's another river of people trying to get through. Lord God. The state of them. Old, rusty bandages. Their clothes like they've been sleeping in ashtrays. Soldiers escort them off the road down another.

I don't know where.

I come to the head of the queue. A soldier points his rifle at me. My hands go in the air. I've had enough of this for one lifetime. Another soldier pats me down.

The soldier lowers his rifle. He's twenty, if that. He looks as much a mess as the rest of us. "Destination."

"I'm trying to get to Inishèan."

He sniffs. "You hit your head, mate?"

"I'm not any trouble. I just need to get back home."

"Back?"

"It's a long story," I say.

"Identification."

"I don't have any."

"Gimmie your license, c'mon."

"I don't... I don't drive."

Snot flies out with his sigh. "Where you from?"

"Inishèan, I said."

"You sound a bit North."

"I don't."

"Yeah," he says, wiping at his nose. Stepping toward me. "You do. I can hear it. How'd you get through?"

"I don't know what you mean."

He calls over another soldier. What is this. What the fuck is going on. The other one is even more scraped than the boy, down to the raw red skin around his eyes.

"Identification," he says.

"I told you, I don't have it."

"That's a problem. Where are you going?"

"You know what's going on."

"What's going on?" He says it with a straight face. He has no idea. None of them have any idea.

"Why are you blocking the road?"

"Martial law has been declared. Haven't you heard?"

"I'm trying to get home."

"Belfast?"

"Are you not hearing me? Inishèan. I need to get to bleeding Inishèan and you lot need to come with me. There's Russians. They've taken over the island."

They both snort.

"Put her with the illegals," the other says.

"The fuck you mean illegals? I'm not going anywhere with you. I need to get home. They need me. You have to help me."

"We'll get you looked at, alright? We'll get you a nurse, yeah? You'll get a lie down and some protein in you and some of this will click back into place for you. On you go."

The one with the rifle puts his hands on me. I shrug him off. "You put your hand on me again and you lose it. I'm a citizen of this country. I have rights."

He grabs his gun. The other one puts his hand out.

"I don't know how you got through the checkpoint, or why you are trying to go back and I don't care. You're not a citizen of this country. You are here illegally and we are at war."

"I'm not from Belfast."

"You're giving your vowels a stretch, just because."

"It was my Da."

"Take her away."

"Please... just let me pass. I have to get back."

He sniffs, the boy. "You're better off here."

"Please," I say, but there's no arguing. He grabs me by the arm and pulls me through the checkpoint down a side road where all the people bandaged and bloody coming from the north and east are stuffed behind a fence in a car park. I try to run away. He chases me down. He pushes me down and then he's dragging me across the pavement, my nails shredding and my knees scabbing and I'm coming home, Declan. I swear to you.

I'm coming home.

The Defence Forces reclaimed an old barracks building in Castlebar. A hundred soldiers or so guard the barracks, turned into a detention center – or as they say it, a 'hospitality zone' – for refugees from the North. They man the checkpoint and patrol the streets, sometimes on horse. Mostly they seem to be waiting. For orders, I suppose. They put me in a room with a handful of others in the basement of the barracks. Most of the people here are from the suburbs around Belfast. Bangor. Holywood, Carrickfergus and Whitehead. Belfast is gone to a bomb. There may have been others as well.

Lord God.

Panic lurks in the room. Fear. There are some foreigners as well. Germany. France. America. I half expect to see Gavin in here. He was on his way back, and got swept up with the rest of the illegals. No passport. It makes so much sense it has to be. Give me this. Give me something.

He's not here.

I ask around. Have you seen this bloke from the States? Gavin? Bald? Every time you turn around, there he is. No one has seen him. A few of the Americans came from Dublin. Dublin did not see a bomb so far as they know, but expecting one, they left. There were thousands of people on the N4 out of the city after the attack. Hundreds of thousands. People scattered across the countryside, fleeing the failure of civilization only to catch in its web.

The Brits sit together. Five men, all Gavin's age or older. Typical pub guys. Cannons of beer bellies poke out from under their T-shirts. They keep up a verbal assault on the guards outside through the night, expanding my vocabulary of British slang and keeping anybody from sleep. Not that I could sleep, anyways. The Brits try recruiting me into bum rushing the guards the next time the guards come in with food. I decline.

The hothead Brit walks toward me, armored in body odor. "I thought we was supposed to be friends."

I ignore them. The guards ignore them. The prisoners ignore them. The Brits needle this woman. Australian. A long, thin curl of string of a girl, always bent at her hip, leaning a bit to the side as if to disguise how tall she actually is. The Brits call her the Leaning Tower of Pisa. *You tip over make sure you do it over here. You're as long as any of us.* She keeps looking over at me through hours of their bullshit as I slowly become part of my folding chair. To rescue her, maybe.

There is no rescue.

○

They let us out in the morning for some air. Soldiers watch us as we mill around the boxed in courtyard, the frustration of just standing out there no less than sitting in the room. I'll be coming home. I'll be right out of this prison and these soldiers will be escorting me back to the island big style. Do you hear me. I'm talking helicopters now. Paratroopers. The bleeding Seal Team Six, like. You'll be defending your country. You'll be trading me in for a Russian.

You'll be trading me in.

Tempers flare. The Brits engage in a passive aggressive hour of insults with the guards before the hothead escalates from screaming in the face of a soldier to giving her a shove. The other guards fire into the air, and the shouting is over. They beat the man savagely with Billy clubs. We all get marched back to the basement and as soon as the door slams shut the Brits try and coax the rest of us into a mutiny.

No one takes the bait.

○

Every day, more refugees flood into Castlebar. There aren't soldiers or space enough for them all to be prisoners. Just my luck, I guess. Thousands settle into migrant camps. Hundreds shelter in train cars. Buses. Schools. The soldiers attempt to filter out the non-nationals, which by turns is both easy and impossible. They get wise I'm a nurse. Everyone needs a nurse.

"Only if you let me go home," I say, as if I've a choice.

I spend more and more time in the tent they put up outside that passes for a triage. I have only the loot of the local pharmacies and I ration it for those I know can be put to work in the kitchen or the fields or the breaking down of the abandoned houses for their wood. The only thing I accomplish is seeing what the soldiers do outside. Anyone obviously foreign feeds the hungry bureaucratic machine the soldiers maintain to avoid their own boredom. Less obvious people go undiscovered in the tent cities, either by oversight or design.

Stories pass between the soldiers about Irish hiding British, French, Americans. Presumably people they've some personal connection with. Rumors there are refugees protesting for the soldiers to release us spread among the prisoners. The tension among the Brits screws tighter into the barracks with every passing day. No one can ignore the strain they put on everyone with their bitching and whispering and plotting to get the lot of us killed.

I curse the speed with which I got to the city.

If I had run into trouble along the way. If I hadn't sent Gavin home. If I had just done what I meant to do and I was with you now. I dream of it. Every night. The water grows heavy on me. I feel myself sinking. The current snakes between my legs. Pulls me further from the shore. I don't know where the shore is. I don't know where I am. Where I'm going. I'm afraid. I'm so afraid. But I hear this sound. This ripple in the water, like scratching against stone.

Here I am.

You come into my arms at last warm and alive and smiling. Declan. *Mo leanbh. Mo stór.* The weight of you carries us down. The water so soupy with weed it feels like suckers on my legs. I sink beneath the surface. The sun a distant, distorted hope. Willowy flowers flutter on the sea bottom like curtains in a gentle breeze. We descend, into the bed of our country. We fall and I hold you in my arms the way a mother does, the way Mary holds her son in the Pieta.

Almost.

My entire life. Too early. Too late. Never at all. I become as bitter as the cold setting on the country.

I become as indifferent.

○

The next morning in the courtyard, the Brits get into a shoving match with themselves. Hothead blows his top about some remark one of the others made, which turns into a rant about our confinement and he starts in on the female soldier again.

This is it. I know.

Part of me wants to disrupt their coup. Part of me wants them to succeed. Part of me wants to get killed. I'm half way into the court-yard when the female soldier's rifle comes right out of her hands. Shots. Screams. Blood channels the stone.

I spend the rest of the day picking bullets out of the wounded. Two of the Germans. The Australian girl. Tilly. She's disappointed she wasn't killed.

I have nothing for that.

The female soldier I can do nothing for, but spend a vial of morphine. She breathes, the routine drilled into her. Another soldier, a boy I think she was soft on, holds her hand. He tells her it's ok. She can go, and she does.

He says her name was Moira.

The gang of Brits do not get treated. They are taken out of the barracks into the fields. Birds scatter on the gunshots. The soldiers come back, their faces pale and drawn.

Are there any injuries, I say.

○

The soldiers march us out to a farm down the road near dark. A horse and cart ahead of us carrying the rigored knot of the dead Brits. They put shovels in our hands and we dig a long, shallow trench in hard, brittle earth. I expect to top off the mound of bloody, dirty bodies we pile into it, but we live. Somehow we live.

I don't think I'm coming home.

○

"You know, this is the perfect setting for a sitcom."

We're down to the last of the cigarettes. Tilly and I pass the final stub back and forth, taking empty drags off the filter. Her hands calloused and blistered. I cough with hollow lungs. Snow trickles down on the courtyard. No doubt hot with radioactivity. Indifference turns within me. A key testing a lock. I hold the handle of the door hard.

"Six young stranded tourists," she says, "And we're constantly trying to get out of this prison. It's sort of *Hogan's Heroes*, but it's the end of the world."

"Except I'm not a tourist," I say.

"Neither am I. Exactly. I suppose I'm nothing."

"How long had you been sleeping in the rough?"

"A couple years," she says.

"Lord God. What brought you to Dublin?"

"Seemed really far away from Sydney. I had a job. I had a place, for a while. And then, I don't know. It just went away."

"Do you miss home?"

She puffs off the cigarette. "Who's Gavin?"

"Sorry?"

"You say his name, in your sleep."

"I do not."

She smiles. "You have to talk to them somehow."

I sigh. "He's an American. A writer."

"Was he stuck on your island?"

"More or less. What do I say?"

"I think you're telling him you're here. 'Here I am.'"

I take the cigarette from her. My hand shakes. From the cold. When I pass it back, her hand steadies mine.

"Don't tell me he was writing a book," she says.

"If he was, he didn't say."

"Wouldn't be any point."

"If it's what you do, I suppose that's all the point there is," I say. "He was desperate. To write. To finish something."

She nudges my shoulder. "You were a distraction?"

"I was, indeed."

"Sex was good?"

"The sex was fairly spectacular. I don't mind saying so."

"Well. Live your truth."

"He was good to me... he was a little much, sometimes. A lot of the time. Clumsy. But honest about it. Do you know what I mean? He was honest. And I punished him for it. I punished him."

The cigarette shrivels between her fingers. "We want to be punished," Tilly says. "Don't we?"

"For what?"

"This guilt... over living. Existing. This conscience we're cursed with. Knowing. We know we're alive. We're dying. We fix on this fear of the end of the world, but we want it. All these films... these books... since Revelation."

"I don't know," I say.

"The longer we go on, the more we want to be let off the hook. We want to be rescued. Don't you think? That must be it. We're prisoners, Mairead. This is our prison."

"We're getting out of here."

"We're afraid of being homeless but... sleeping rough or sleeping in some five star hotel, it's all the same. It's all here on Earth, isn't it? Same prison. Just different cells. We die and we're truly refugees. We're homeless. We're free."

Lord God. "I don't know, Tilly."

"That's why it's a black hole. Nothing will survive. Nothing will be left. Not even guilt. Not even bad dreams."

Our lives have always been buttressed by knowing something of us lives on in blood and memory. Life goes on. The black hole drains all of our life. All of our time. The dinosaurs got an asteroid. The world survived. Life continued. Humanity got an interstellar Shop-Vac. Gone. Down to the last atom. The black hole made it as if we never were. Not Shakespeare, Harriet Wheeler, a baby boy from Inishèan. There is a cruelty in it, beyond the act itself. A meanness to it that felt personal.

"What else do I go on about?" I say. "In my sleep?"

"I don't mean to pry," she says.

"Apparently, I've left the door open."

She offers me the last puff. "Your son, I think."

"Anyone else?"

"I don't think so."

"Not my Ma?"

"I don't hear everything, Mairead."

I finish the fag off and flick it into the snow. My cheeks burn. The list Tilly always seems to be in carries her into me. She rests her head against my shoulder, her hands shaking. Her entire body. I put my arm around her. She's cold to the touch.

"What's the worst thing you've ever done?" she says.

"Time to confess?"

"'Maintain always a blameless conscience both before God and before men.' Or words to that effect."

"I ignored people when I shouldn't have," I say. "And I wouldn't leave them alone when I should."

She coughs through a laugh. "Off with her head."

"What about you?"

"Same here. I wouldn't leave well enough alone."

"Why did you leave Sydney?"

Snow falls like ash in the courtyard. The moon somewhere behind a blanket of gray that never lifts.

Her breath rattles. "Do you think we're forgiven?"

"We're going to get out of here, Tilly."

"We're all dead here. This is the world of the dead now."

○

We go through town to find things to burn.

Magazines. Mail. Furniture. Doesn't matter. If it burns, we take it. We strip Castlebar clean and what we don't burn we leave in the streets, on the floors, the city a landfill behind us. Weeks of this. The soldiers loot the tent city as well. I treat cuts and bruises the soldiers dole out as they take whatever will burn.

One ash morning, my throat becomes sore. My neck. I start to cough. Sweat. Shake. I'm shit for collecting any thing more, so the soldiers throw me in the back of the cart with the rest of the kindle. The refugees brought everything they could carry with them to Castlebar. Books. Photo albums.

Pneumonia.

CHAPTER EIGHTEEN

The damp and cold of the barracks settles in my clothes. My chest. An endless, restless cough rattles through me. I lose days in fever. I don't know. I never leave my cot but I walk the eastern shore of the island, through the beach grass out to the rock. The mainland stretches out before me like the painted backdrop of a school play and I look out from backstage, Aoife in the wings, always in the wings and I make my entrance. The gelled sun glints off foam rocks. Cardboard waves bob at the edge of the stage. Faces I can't see in the crowd. Everyone waiting for me. You're all waiting for me to come out.

Here I am.

I hear this scratching. Something's at the door. Do you hear that. Hello. Is anyone there. Declan. Are you come for me. Am I to go now. I meant to be home. I meant to be so much more.

Gavin comes up through the floor of the stage. "Hi."

"Like a yo-yo, you are."

"Will you help me?"

He uncaps the pill bottle. We kneel at the edge of the stage and the ashes make a mushroom cloud in the air above the band pit.

There is no release in him. Just an emptiness. A void, empty as the pill bottle and he lets that go, too.

"I wish I could help you," he says.

"I wish I could help you, Gavin."

He takes my hand. Don't let go. The scene behind us winds to another and the mainland materializes across the bay, a stranger country than it had ever been before. Ireland disappears with my fever. The dog sleeps on the end of my cot.

He does not leave me.

○

I wake up in a different room in the barracks. Swimming in my clothes. Mouth the inside of empty, dried out can of paint. The dog gone. Gavin gone. Half the prisoners gone.

"Where's Tilly?" I say.

○

I make a marker for her from a round, heavy rock I find down at the river. *Tilly, Forgiven.*

○

As soon as I have enough strength, they put me back on grave detail. Why go through the effort. There won't be enough of us left to dig soon. Pneumonia cut through the refugees and soldiers alike. Castlebar stinks with death. The odor of the dead and dying has this mass. Texture. I think about the maps weathermen stood in front of. They'd point to a big H or L. Pressure systems. That's what the smell is. A municipal decay. I should be lucky I can lift a shovel at all. Hundreds fall over into their graves and I am unfelled. I inspire as much fear as hope among the dying. How. How do you do it.

How do you go on.

I'll be going on, I say. *I'll be going on home.*

No effort is put into any more markers. I remember the names of every person whose grave I dig. Holness. Lowe. Barry. Ayoade. Some illegals make a run for it. Distant gunshots find their way back to the barracks. The runners never do. Bodies pile like the debris of stripped houses. Trash everywhere.

○

The days lose their rhythm. The sun its track in the sky. It might be December. I don't know.

○

There aren't enough soldiers left to keep any kind of cap on Castlebar, let alone their makeshift prison. Reinforcements never come. Orders never come. Some desert.

I could run.

I could just keep walking on one of my searches through the town for food and medicine. There'd be no one to stop me. How far would I get. My cough sends tremors through me still. The pallor of my skin like a zombie from one of those interminable movies. I could leave, sure enough and I could drop dead not a mile down the road.

I make the shape of laughter, but not the sound.

The want to die sweeps like an unseen current through the city. I don't know how many suicides I bury. The further we go into Maybe December, the stronger the current becomes, sweeping along the weakest to quick deaths. Those who resist are brutalized, day in and day out, both by being a piece of debris speeding along the surface of a torrent barreling toward a cliff and by our own confusion for life.

I run into this strangeness every day, in people who have found an understanding not just in their own private grief but the collective grief over the fate of humanity. An acceptance. An alien peace, like. They seem alien to me. Replaced. I want to be replaced. I want to be

put back, without this pain. This suffering. I want to scream. To run
through the empty streets of emptying Ireland, screaming the truth.

I want to give in to giving in.

○

Down a quiet lane of small cottages across the river, I find a walnut
tree growing in someone's backyard. The ground littered with rotted
and pilfered husks. I stuff my pockets with what's left. Gray squirrels
flick their tails in the branches above. The squirrels go off like a car
alarm and come out of the tree at me. I'm running. From squirrels.
Nutshells fall from my pockets and roll across the pavement as they
chase me out of their kingdom, down the lane back to the road.

○

Thunder wakes me in the night.

Lord God. More bombs. Gavin talked about Iowa thunderstorms.
I'd never seen a proper one. Thunder in New York always seemed to
be confused with other sounds. I crawl out of my cot to see meteors
shred the sky. Thousands, like. A dozen or more go off like the one
over Tralee and whatever windows were left in Ireland go to these
terrorist rocks. I scramble under the cot and I pray for dawn.

○

The bombardment leaves the dawn nickel. The sun a bloody smudge.
I go down to the courtyard. No one. I go to the triage. No one. I can't
find the soldiers. The barracks are deserted.

○

Northern lights try to catch the meteors in a gossamer jade web as I
scavenge for food. I've never seen aurora in broad daylight. The sky

feels strange. Off balance. The moon unrecognizable after the meteor storm. Even the sunlight seems skewed, but there's so much dust and haze in the air the days have become diffuse. I cross the bridge back to the east side of the river, having pillaged the west. The high street long since looted. I might be the last person left in Castlebar. Even the squirrels have abdicated their kingdom. Lord God.

I'm alone.

○

I know from previous searches the hospital yields nothing in medicine or supplies, but I decide to scout it again on the off chance some refugees took up there. Maybe somebody is here yet. Maybe they have food. I need food if I'm going to walk out of here back home. It's miles to Galway. Days on foot. I can barely stand as it is.

○

An oxygen fire erupted in the aftermath of the loss of power, destroying much of the emergency room. I find nothing but charred twists of patients in beds burned down to their frames. Flowers left on some of the bodies. Over a month of rain and snow and wind had left the first floor mildewed and rank. The upper floors I'd been through before; there's only below.

The basement drips like the inside of a dark, wet cave. Pipes vein the walls of a long, concrete corridor running under the hospital. The smell of death thick. I cover my mouth as I inch toward a door at the end of the corridor. The handle turns, but the door is jammed.

I put all my vanishing weight into pushing it open. The body of a nurse blocks the door. Her skin hard and brown like some dog chew. Five others slump over a conference table set up in front of a blackboard at the back of the room. Carbon dioxide. Had to have been. A small generator rests behind a blackboard.

They probably thought they were safe.

I break out the few windows in the basement to let the air clear. I think it had been a supply room. They turned it into some kind of command post, I suppose, to manage the disaster that unfolded in the wake of the EMP. There's papers and dossiers and charts and graphs. One of the dossiers is labeled DISASTER PLAN.

Some nice theories about an orderly evacuation. The rationing of food and conservation of water. A brief bit about the state commandeering of salvageable farms for the greater good. Reference to a NATO command post to be set up at Shannon Airport, assuming it's not destroyed. At the end, there's a dangling bit about marshaling able-bodied men for an army that 'given the necessary conditions' would be under the command of NATO, most likely direct command of Britain. Must not have gotten the memo here.

Long, hard hours go in dragging the generator out of the basement. The generator ran on petrol. Fuel had been scarce for months before the war, but after the bombs dropped what gas there was became useless in Castlebar. I know the soldiers had some reserves at the barracks they intended to use once power had been restored. The petrol reserves amount to a piss jar but I enjoy the hum of the motor. The soft rumble of the generator, inducing a tremor through the floor like a dryer did as it reached the end of the spin cycle. Light bulbs had burnt out in the EMP. The TV shows nothing but snow. The generator gives little more than heat, but I am grateful for it. The absurdity of finding it now, when it can't benefit anyone but myself, undoes me. The generator powers little in Castlebar beyond my screams.

Air service to the island had been run out of Inverin for ages, until the airline started to gouge on the contract and suspended the charter. Private planes gave it a go the last few years before the black hole. The pilot flew out of the airport in Galway, on the Carnmore Road a few miles outside the city centre. He can get me home. If the bloody plane even still works. It has to. I've no money. I've nothing.

I've got to try.

○

Bicycles litter the city.

I blow the tires up on my own air. This takes an hour out of me. I fill up the rest of the gas in jugs I strap to a rack I rig over the back wheel. Among the mounds of bikes in the tent city I find dozens of improvised hitches and wagons. One of them just the right size for the generator. This will do us well at the home. This will do us brilliant. I set out on the N84 south, the last person to leave Castlebar. I'm coming back to the island.

I'm coming home.

○

Seaweed litters the road.

Electrical wires dangle in the wind like broken clotheslines. Cars float in ditches turned moats. The same for miles. For hours now. If I were a nurse – ha – I'd give myself days of bed rest and lots of liquids before even skirting the idea of minimal physical activity. I don't have the luxury of time. I have all the strength I need.

You are my strength.

The tidal damage here is less than it was even just a few miles north, as I'd hoped. The Aran Islands provide a natural breakwater against the Atlantic for Galway Bay, so if I'm blessed the city has been spared the bulk of the havoc visited on the lower lying areas up the coast. Lord God, let it be true. Give me something for once. Get down to the harbor and find a boat. Find something. There'll be something. I'll wait for low tide and get back. I survived the crossing.

I'll do so again.

○

The city is a city only at low tide. A city of wet dunes. The smoke of long smoldering fires in Salthill curls into a kind of barbed wire over the wall of rain clouds fencing me off from any perspective on home. Any escape. I know the island is just on the other side. Aoife and the residents and Colm are still there, waiting for me. You're waiting for me. Our peace.

○

Along the canal, the river is rusty with leaves.

A lone duck paddles along through the amber weed, his wake rippling gentle like far behind. A pair of swans idles at a lock just short of O'Brien's bridge over to Nun's Island. Immaculate. The beauty and grace of the world unspoiled. A little pedestal rises on the span above the lock, engraved with a poem.

And the flowing

of waters below

too many years.

Nine hundred years the Children of Lir kept their form as swans. Time meaningless to them. Take another shape and time loses its grip on you. I always loved that story, and more after I sobered up. The bell of the new God tolled and the curse finally wore off. Time found them again. Death found them quicker. The children aged rapidly, as if they had been preserved deep beneath the sea all that time and when at last they made contact with the air again, they turned to rust. It had to be so; their world had gone. Everyone they knew and loved. A kind monk buried the children together, in a single grave.

I always wondered: did any of the Children of Lir want to live?

The old stories always giftwrap you the ending. Untie the ribbons of fear and suffering, and inside your box, new and shiny success. Vindication. None of that used, hand me down human doubt. Were the children true, at least one of them would have gone kicking and screaming to their death.

Ah, you know it.

It seems like I've been here forever, though I know it's only been a few hours. The stillness draws out time. The absence of others. Of life. Without life, there is no time. No ticking clock. If I stayed here, alone in the lost city, would I age? Would I become Pan?

Only girls play Peter Pan.

I wander back into the streets in a daze. Night coming on. High tide. Where do I go? The human delta of Galway has evaporated. Left behind are the empty channels of High St., Manguard and Market. I expect the shadow of a person along the wall. A shout in the street. The bright reds and blues seem dull now without the light of life. Sandbags pile in the doors of shuttered shops, topped with shattered glass. Some attempted to board up their storefronts with plywood, but left it undone. Trash lines the roads, studding the silt accumulating against dozens of abandoned taxis along the rank opposite Eyre Square. A few have boots on them, as if the authorities tried maintaining some order before saying to fuck all with it.

There is no one.

All this could be yours someday, Da said, in one of those vapory conversations about my future.

We'd come over for a new television. The one in the sitting room at the home now, running only Ma's reflection. She wouldn't come. She'd never come. I loved to go across with Da, and he wanted me to leave. All that possibility. The forked paths life could have taken, all draining toward the same dark sea. The stream of youth and ideas from the university joined up with this river of tourists from all over the world in a delta of streets branching through inner Galway to the bay. In the summer came the flood. There in the clogged streets between Eyre Square and the Spanish Arch you'd find packs of American girls checking off their Irish Bourbon St.; buskers vying for location; Italian girls over for the weekend with their effeminate boyfriends or companions or whatever is they do in Italy, sipping on espressos out front of the coffee shops too cool to be swept up in the mayhem passing by.

The tide creeps up both sides of Eyre Square. Pinching me in. Lord God. I won't be making it to the airport tonight. I have to find shelter. I'll go in the morning.

I've got to try.

○

The verdigris capped dome of Galway Cathedral glints within the envelope of winter fog surrounding it. Deserted cars ring the cathedral, along with rows and rows of tents all left without thought. The cathedral looks a bit like a prison up close, with sheer stone walls and turrets like guard towers.

The door opens with a bit of a shove. I half expect someone to be behind it. Failing daylight illuminates enough of the cathedral interior through the stained rose windows to show my solitude. Sleeping bags patchwork the marble. Yoga mats, like. No one would leave the church like this. The women of town polish the gold altar and communion railing after each and every service. At least they did. The cathedral echoes with my every nervous breath. I look around every pillar, down every row of pews, expecting someone to be lurking in here with me.

Mine is the only sound.

My first trip here, Da and I came during Sunday Mass. I was five, like. Six. We didn't plan on going into the church. I don't remember now why we did. Was it the time we got the telly? Must have been I wanted to see it. Whatever I wanted, he gave me. Da held my hand and we stood with three or four men at the back of the pews near the south entrance, though there was ample room to sit. This one man in runners and sweats fidgeted back and forth, as if he didn't know to sit or stand. I asked Da why we were all standing and he hushed me. I murmured along with the prayers, but like him, I did not close my hands, did not kneel, and did not tithe as the basket came around.

Churches no longer move me, even one as grand as this. See enough people off in church and you understand what this place is. A harbor. A port. An airport waiting room. A transitional place where no one stays and everyone passes through. I imagine God must be on the other side; the ultimate vacation. Rest and relax. Unplug.

It's only the waiting that chips away at us, erodes our defenses against the consideration of what this all truly is. In churches we try and give shape and form to what we can't understand. A blind person's image of the world. Then you know: all that matters is how we see existence. Our lives. The future is already within us; we spend our lives trying to focus on what is distant and we are resolved only to bring clarity to our moment.

This distant rumble snaps me out of my fugue. I go to the doors. High tide rolls up the city like an old carpet. I run up the stairs into the organ room. The pews tumble through the well of the church like ice in a glass. I'm so thirsty. Hungry. Please, God. What did I do? What did I do to make you punish me so? I am what you made me. A gluttonous craving for life wrapped up in a tiny little bit of flesh and bone. A fishing boat drifts through the church. Even now I want.

Even now I hope.

Painted angels support the dome above on their outstretched wings. The sky heavy on their backs. My chest thunders with all my dread. I'm never getting home. I'm going to die cold and starving in a ditch somewhere and I didn't want this. I wanted my peace. I had my peace. I had you and Da and Ma and I had it all there, waiting for me and he started with me and I let him. I should never have let him.

Why. I wanted more. God forgive me. I wanted more. Here it all is. The world. Empty and mine.

Moonlight flares through the painted windows off the tiled mosaic of Christ on the wall on the far end of the church. Christ stretches out to the thin lines of his crucifix, head folding into the spaghetti string of his arms. Angels float above, waiting; a skull rests beneath the cross, its foundation. Beside her son, Mary holds vigil with her head lowered toward her meek left hand. Always Mary has her hand out to the faithful. Here I think it's to shield her view.

I slump to the floor. The strain of stone and steel against the water, the pressure building up within the city, twists up all the tension within me. I don't sleep.

There is no rest.

○

Morning comes. Low tide leaves the city a little less than it was. I bike out to the airport, which takes hours thanks to all the debris the water left in the roads. Several of the cars in the park burned. Some down to their charred frames. The glass doors into the air terminal splintered from bullet holes. A rental bike rests against the wall, the type you'd see here, or in Dublin. The taste of wet smoke curdles in my mouth like vomit, just barely choking the reflex to gag over the smell of burnt flesh. Torch marks scar the walls, stabbing out from this deep black scab on the floor just inside the door. Melted glass curled within it.

Molotov cocktail. Must have been.

The remains of a body shriveled outside the public toilets. On the wrists I see a pair of cufflinks still pinned to a sleeve once white but now stained, like a smoker's teeth.

Lord God.

This sound builds in the distance. Like a smoker having a coughing fit and then it evens into this labored buzz. Fuck. I run through the terminal out through the gate to the tarmac just as this old turboprop races down the runway. Wait.

"Wait!"

The plane takes all the runway to get off the ground and even then, it doesn't seem she will. She labors into the sky, turning west slow and deliberate out toward the sea.

"Wait..."

The buzzing dies. A terrible quiet in Galway. I sit on the tarmac and I wait for the pilot to come back. He won't be gone long. He's delivering someone home, or supplies to someone in need. There and back. I'll beg him. I'll promise him whatever he wants. He'll get me home. I'll be home tonight.

I'll be home.

Morning comes without the plane. Hours I wait in the terminal. Days. The plane never comes back. One last, cruel rubbing of my nose in it. Almost. My life in a word.

Lord God.

There's nothing. There's no way home. Seven miles. Seven miles and it may as well be the other side of the world. The sound I make. The force of it leaves my lips bloody. I don't think there could be another, but it pries itself out of me from down deep and leaves me gutted inside. My grief echoes through the night. Galway. Ireland.

Mine is the only sound.

CHAPTER NINETEEN

A battery of vacant shops and stores piles on my mood.

I trudge through silt-laden streets, past burned out cars and the rotting masses of dead fish back to the docks. I come to the boat slip at last. I hurry up along the wall, toward the masts. All of them jutting out of the water. Every last one of them, dashed. Scuttled. I stretch out to the park shadowing the bay. There's nothing else. Nothing at the old, battered docks. A cruise ship lies on its side across the mouth of the bay, the white of its hull charred and streaked from fire.

At low tide I make down to the seaweed draped causeway to Mutton Island, lancing out in the bay from the city like one of those booms a plane connects to refuel in-flight. I stand on the edge of Ireland, facing home. Home a shard of darkness across the horizon. I cry for you. I scream for you. Hear me.

I'm coming home.

I'm going the wrong way but I'm going home. The documents in the dossier I found at the hospital in Castlebar seem official enough.

Shannon, then. This command post. They'll have helicopters there. Planes. They have to. There's nothing else.

They have to.

I'm coming back to you. I'm frightened and alone and weak but you are my strength. You are my hope. You will see me home.

You will see me.

I love you. *Mo stór*. I blow my kisses to you and I wrench myself off the shore somehow, and Lord God, I make my way.

○

I go up the Hedford Road to the shopping mall. In the mess of the men's department I find a backpack and water bottle. There's nothing for food but I toss some random batteries in the backpack. Either I can trade these or use them to power something or other on my way. I'll find food on my way. I'll need something to protect myself, like. There's no Swiss Army offerings, naturally, so I'm back to the kitchen knives in the housewares department. I break open a set and take the big ones. I find a road map and I plot my way south to Shannon.

The coastal roads are gone, I know. How far inland has the sea come. There's only one way of knowing. I get all up in my kit. I button up the coat tight. I can do this. You can do this.

You're going to do this.

○

There's no way through Oranmore.

The N18 swamped. I double back to the M6 though it takes me east. I'll cut south near Athenry. Down to Craughwell. A lightning bolt of roads all the way to Shannon. Abandoned cars and trucks make the M6 a gauntlet. Loads of vehicles left everywhere. I make great time. At Athenry, I turn south down the R347. Less cars. Empty houses. Fields of nothing for miles and miles. The road like a bunched line of string until it disappears under the surface of a flash flood. The signs and markers lost to water too far and too deep to cross. I'll have to go back. Keep on the M6 and try the R349 I suppose. Miles. My legs are concrete. I'm so tired. I'm so hungry.

Get on.

You've got to get on. You're not dying here. You're getting home. You're getting back to the island.

Sheep graze on the shores of impromptu lakes. Baby hills become candy coated bolts of popcorn. The hinds of the sheep painted green and red to mark their owner. I miss popcorn. The dagger of hard kernels in my gums. The pain of eating too much too fast. I'm days without proper food.

I need food.

One of those sheep, like. If I can get close enough. I've got the knife. I can build a fire from the thrushes of pine trees fencing off any friendly way across these fields. I can make camp. Roast some lamb. Sing some ancient songs from the radio. It will be some good old *craic*. I can do this.

I bike until I find a stretch of the ditch beside the road that's not a lagoon. I climb the fence and slowly make my way back a quarter of a mile across the marshy shoals of the field. There's no telling how deep that water is. I'm no swimmer.

You're not dying here.

I cleat a clump of earth out the ground with the knife and toss it in the water. There's a sinking, heavy sort of plop as it goes in. The noise startles the sheep. It's a merry-go-round, the sheep island. They rearrange themselves on the hillock, circulating down to the water's edge and then back. Sheep in general will not cross water if it's too deep, or if there's nothing of value for them on the other side. By the looks of them they're a wool breed, like we have on the island. This lot is long without seeing any sheers. Full fleeced.

Fine then, lads. Drowning it is.

I stab out more clumps and throw mud grenades into the huddled herd. This dance begins within them, where the ones at the top abandon their perch and circle down to the rim of sheep along the shore. The ones running from the earth bombs twist back up to the top where I plop them again and on it goes until they get so agitated they barrel through the fence of the ones that can't be bothered along the shore, right into the water.

The sheep thrash and try to get back to their island but I keep raining agitation down on the ones bringing up the rear. There's no getting back for the early outs. They paddle furious. They bob and sink and surface and then unable to find their balance or the bottom they drown. They float like popcorn in beer. The dead sheep disperse and my luck does not extend to the water delivering one of them to where I stand. Fuck it. I'm wet already.

I get out of my coat and wade in a bit. Lord God. The cold. I'll never shake this cold. The water rises to my waist. I'm too small to go any further. Come on. Come closer. A little one floats near. I reach out. His wool brushing my fingers. I get my fingers in some strands and my feet flutter. I go weightless.

Lord God.

I'm drowning. I'm drowning I can't swim I can't swim I can't breathe the water is dark and cold like sucking on me like mud dead sheep down here carcasses like cobwebs hung on trees caught with mud and shit and death I'm drowning get back get back get back GET BACK the ground I feel the ground that's the ground up up UP God damn you GET UP you crossed Galway Bay in a tray for fucking chips you're not dying in five feet of water in a fucking field God knows where you're not dying here.

You're not dying.

The air stabs a thousand daggers in my lungs. A good, clean pain. I claw my way back to the grass. Stupid. What were you thinking. The dead sheep floats away on my wake.

There's no getting him now.

○

I cut some branches from pine trees and build a little fire under their thrush, off the road far enough hopefully someone won't see. The fire is nice and my pride in making it warms but I can't get this cold out of me. I wrap up tight in his shirt. The smell of him still in its fiber.

Where are you, Gavin. Are you home. Be home. Be safe.

I won't get as far tomorrow. I'll be lucky to get back to Athenry. I'll put up there. Find some food. There has to be some food somewhere. Don't go out in the country again without any plan or energy. Two days. Two days I will have been at this and all the farther I will have gotten is fucking Athenry.

I have to get on.

I have to get to Shannon fast as I can and get a helicopter or plane to get me back to the island. I'll tell them about the Russians. Go and defend your country. Charge of the light brigade and so. So hungry. I'll be home. I'll be home for Christmas, I know. It's not Christmas yet. Is it? I've no idea.

We'll be together for Christmas.

Night drowns with its muddy dark. I'm so tired. This is no country of rest. So much restlessness. So much yearning to leave and spread wings we haven't got feathers for. And then this pull. This tide sweeping us back home. All that leaves returns. *An tús.* I'm so scared. This fear. This cold. What is there beyond numbness? Nothing. I can't feel my fingers and toes. I can't feel anything but the cold.

○

I wake up covered in snow.

Lord God. An inch of it at least. Get up. This pain. It hurts so much. Get up. I can't even see the road. Where's the road. I follow the line of the pine trees heavy with snow and shrugging off their burden but I can't see the way to the road. I don't know the way to the road. I walked up here a good ways from where I left the bike. Where did I leave the bike? That dog of his drove me mad, but if he was here. He'd see me out. I'm so alone. I want to go home. I want to go home. What am I doing? What the fuck am I doing out here in the snow in a fucking field I'm going the wrong way. God.

I want to go home.

The snow slushes. I dip into a puddle. Christ. Water again. I back up so fast I fall down. The cold of the snow so deep it burns. I can't see the water. The sheep complain somewhere close but I can't see them. The world a white out. I walk from the sound of the sheep. Back toward the trees. I find the trees. I follow them to their end, and the fence along the side of the road. A foot of snow in the ditch. Ice cubes in my shoes. The snow slithers around my socks and mashes to cubes and melts slow against my coldness and I'm walking barefoot in an icebox down the road, an inch at a time looking for my bike along the fence, hand over my face in a blizzard.

I can't find the bike.

This feels too far. I've walked too far. Where is it? Where the fuck is it? Did someone take it? Why didn't I take it over the fence with me? Lord God. Calm down.

Breathe.

The snow drifts. The accumulation breaks like ice around my ankles. Up and down the road I go, in and out of ditches keeping water like a secret. Every few minutes I think I see the outline of the bike under some snow and I scratch off a fence post. Up and down I go. The same stretch a hundred times. The snow never quits. The wind screams at me, walking back and forth in the shite like a fucking chicken. Up and down I go and finally I keep on down, back up the road toward Athenry.

I have to get on.

O

The feeling in my feet gone.

The snow impassable. Somewhere I come on a roundabout. A few cars and trucks left there as if to block the ways on and through. All the doors on automatic locks. I break a window out of a coach van with my elbow and climb in the back. I've no blanket or any way to warm myself so I just huddle up in the aisle between the seats in my coldness and I think of myself walking out on the tarmac at the airport in Galway. The plane taxiing out.

Wait.

I chase after it and this time, I'm quick. I open the door and it's Gavin at the controls. He flies us back to the island and I'm in front of the coal fire back home, sitting in his lap. Happy and sweet in his arms. He loves me and he warms me and I'm warm and he never left. I never lost my place. I stayed home safe and warm.

I can't get warm.

Dull light illuminates the coach. My breath frosts to my lips. A morgue van, like. My bones crack like ice as I crawl to the window. Lord God. Drifts over the hoods. Three feet of it or more. There's no biking in this. I lost the bike. There's no walking. I can't walk. I'm so cold. Sleet scratches against the glass. I'm so hungry. I'm so lost.

Mo leanbh. Mo stór.

You have to forgive Ma. She tried. She tried so hard. I'll find you. No matter what I'll find you. Stay safe with Da and don't worry about me. Don't worry. It's not where you die. Not how. This is just a body. I am just a body. I will find you in spirit. Nothing can destroy the spirit. Not the black hole. Our spirit is beyond gravity and consciousness and the limits of the world. It can't get us. It can't get us where we're going. The wheel broken. We're going to live forever and ever together you and me and Da and Ma and Gavin and the bleeding dog we're going to be a family I promise. I promise.

Declan.

I'm with you. I'm with you now. I'm in the cold and the dark and I won't leave this time. This time I'm staying. Here I am. This is the same cold. The same dark as yours. Snow buries the windshield.

Scratching against the glass. The coach. This is my burial. The whole earth the same grave. The world is a grave.

All this way.

All this way to die in a coach in a roundabout in the country in the snow, in the cold so cold in the dark I'm in the dark the cold the sound of the world breaking I am the sound I am inside the breaking this is the breaking now baby I

am

the

light

within the coach the snow glinting diamonds swirling inside the door is open someone opens the door someone is inside the coach. A cut of dark. Not this. Go away. Please. Dark. They climb in the back with me. A Russian doll of coats and scarves. No face. Dusted in snow. I try to speak. I don't have anything. Go away. Don't hurt me. They start to unbutton my coat.

Don't.

They're opening the coat on me. My shirt. It's all I have of him left don't take it and they unzip their coat as well and the one underneath and the fleece underneath that all the way down to the shock of dark hair within a baby sling.

Lord God. It's a baby. She has a baby.

Her scarf unravels a little as she hovers over me. Asian, like. Beautiful dark eyes. She lies down next to me on the floor with her back to me like we're spooning. Doesn't say a word. She peels the gloves off my fingers. My fingers are purple. Almost black at their tips. She puts them in her mouth and she bites a little and Jesus it hurts but there's blood. She massages them in hers for a little bit and then she slides my hand down her belly past the stretched elastic of her knickers.

She's warm.

She pulls a blanket out of her backpack and unfolds it over us. This warmth grows between us and slowly it flints to my chest my arms my thighs my legs and I burn with pain but she's warm and I'm warm and I hold her close. I hold her very close.

I can't make out the words. My lips glued shut. Thank you. Thank you. Thank you thank you thank you thank you

thank

you

O

Wind shakes the coach. She's facing me. She cradles my head in her hands and puts my lips to her naked breast. *Drink,* she says, her accent very heavy. *You must drink.* She's swollen with milk. Blue with veins. Instinct strips me of all pretense. I wet my lips and put them soft to her. Milk dribbles out. I lick it away from her skin. So hungry. A little sweet. This soft cinnamon aftertaste. I tasted my own milk when I was nursing you. You get curious. I don't know. Mine was a bit nutty. I take her full in my mouth and settle in under her arm. The pressure in her breast eases. The pressure in her. I float on her warmness. Her sweetness. The baby thrashes inside her sling. Jealous, like. I touch the baby's cheek. The color back in my hands now. The baby grips my finger so hard it hurts but I don't mind. Such a tiny pink wonder. All gummy grimaces and drool. I brush her cheek and she sucks on my finger.

Lord God.

I fall asleep to her taste in my mouth. To a dream of a milk bubble I float in with you, laughing, kissing, being children both of us like we're in some chamber of Willy Wonka's Chocolate Factory, if he had built it inside a womb.

O

"We cannot stay here," Sumi says, her every word measured, as if she poured them out in cups. Such calm. Poise. If I had you out here in the snow and the shit I'd be right out my fucking mind. She seems catatonic. Medicated, like.

A line of houses marks out another road off the roundabout going north. "We can wait for the snow to melt in one of those," I say, hoping the people inside are as hospitable as Sumi. Somehow I think I've exhausted my luck in this world. "With the weather here, it won't be long before it does."

"There will be more water after."

"I think water is all we can look forward to."

Sumi situates the baby inside her sling, and then begins the process of pulling on all her layers of coats.

"She's beautiful," I say. "What's her name?"

"I have not given her a name."

She can't be more than a few weeks old. "Still debating?"

"I will not name her."

"Why?"

"I do not want to get attached."

"I'd say you're attached."

"I could not leave her. I tried."

"What you mean, you tried?"

She stares off into nothing. "I was confused. I was in an alley. A kind of door, between doors. I was screaming."

Her eyes glaze over with memory. I'm looking at myself, in the worst of it after you died. She says her husband was a doctor at St. James in Dublin. He studied abroad a year in Osaka and after he came home they kept up on email. Finally he wore her down – a shock, this – and she packed her entire life into a suitcase and moved to Dublin. The day it all went to pieces he put her in a car with some clothes and money and told her to go to where they holidayed near

Salthill, in Galway. He needed to oversee the cardiac ward got to its safety point and then he was going to meet up with her.

I'll be right behind you, he told her.

The car died with every other on the N4 at the exact same moment. There was a flash in the sky, she said, out over the Irish Sea. She followed people back into the city but by the time she got to Maynooth, smoke shrouded Dublin and she thought the city might have been bombed as well. The roads became veins surging with panic and fear. Not knowing what else to do she went back to the car. She got her things and eight months pregnant Sumi started walking west, toward Galway, toward where he would meet her.

A couple weeks back, in a town somewhere on the M6, she delivered the baby in that alley. Alone.

"The alley was like an echo chamber," she says. "I heard myself screaming, and I could not tell if it was from the moment before or the moment to come. And then my screams became her screams and I knew I was in the future. But the future was the same as the past. Time has become confused. We live in fear of comets and waves but these are minor compared to the ruination of time. A dog came along. It ate the afterbirth. I watched. I felt like he was eating me and but I was not eaten. I was dead but not dead. I had become someone else and I was a baby again."

What do you say. I take her hand. "It will be ok."

She looks at me, her eyes wide in surprise, as if to say: you stupid, stupid girl. Nothing will ever be ok again. It must have been the same look I gave Gavin when he told me the same.

"Soldiers came. A man helped me. I left."

Poor woman. She was alone here except for her husband. She's been through hell. "I'm sorry."

"I think this must be what eternity is like," she says. "Where time does not exist, because it exists in every state. I think we are dead."

"We're alive," I say.

"There is no one here. Everyone has left."

"There were loads in Castlebar."

"Where are they now?"

I sigh. "We're alive, Sumi. We're going to live."

"We are not meant for eternity. We cannot stay here."

"I'm going to Shannon. You're coming with me. You and the baby. I'm going to get us home. All of us."

Her face is infinitely stoic, but something changes in her eyes as I tell her my plan. This distance grows behind them. I thought the prospect of a safe, warm place out of the cold would lift her spirit, but she sinks into this sallow.

"It is not realistic they would do this for you."

"They'll be defending their country."

"The country is lost. Everything is lost."

"Nothing's lost. We can make it together. You and me and the baby. They'll help us. They will."

She nods as I go through the plan again, making it real in words, her eyes settling out the window at the falling snow.

CHAPTER TWENTY

The snow is light today but there's so much.

A field of feathers up to your knees. You could lie down and go to sleep in it but don't you dare. Don't you dare. Don't die here. After ten minutes I'm wiped. A trail of sick dotting back to the coach. The houses are farther away than I thought. Miles. So quiet. Not a sound except for the wind speeding against the countryside. Black birds perch on dead electrical lines toggling above and watch as we trudge through the snow. Waiting. I hold their gaze as we pass, as the birds tick to the sides to keep us in view.

Waiting.

○

The first house we come to, an older man meets us at the gate with a pair of cutting shears, like.

"Move on," he says.

"We're freezing," I say. "We're starving."

"So is everyone else."

"She's got a baby."

"I don't care what she's got. We wouldn't be in this mess if not for these Chinese people. Get out of here. Don't try any of the houses here. I see you stop I'll come running."

We go on. I don't know how far. Until I can no longer see the smoke from that man's chimney. We are deep in the country. The sun shy behind clouds that move and curl swift as cigarette smoke. We are headed north this road. I think it's north. Aren't we going back to the M6? To Athenry? I don't know. We come along to another cluster of farms, across a rail line. Smoke puffs out the chimneys of some houses. Out in the fields I see the blurry silhouettes of men shoveling and dredging the ground for peat. We keep walking. Night comes. We sleep in a car off the side of the road, our warmth all that sustains us.

"I am not Chinese," she says.

"Never mind that old git."

"He thinks China is responsible for the war."

"It doesn't matter."

The baby cries. Sumi seems not to hear.

"In China they used to set baby girls out in the cold to die. Perhaps they still do. Girls were unwanted. I used to think this horrific, but now I see the practicality in it."

Lord God. She's cracked, like. "How?"

"We talk of life as if it is something singular and precious, but it is not. Life is like grass. It grows everywhere and sometimes you must trim it, or it will overrun you."

"Sumi..."

"Perhaps this is why the black hole has come."

"What are you..."

"There is too much life here. I read once it is possible the universe formed from a black hole. The death of a star, in another universe. It is possible there are many universes, infinite universes, created from the plunge of gravity through space and time. The process repeats itself, endlessly, light and darkness never able to defeat the other because darkness begets light and light darkness.

There are hundreds of billions of stars in our galaxy alone. Hundreds of billions of black holes, potentially. Hundreds of billions of universes. Death begets life. Life begets death. There must be balance. Weight."

"There's this theory," I say. "Information can't be destroyed, like. Anything that goes in, it has to come out."

"We reach for theory as we once reached for God."

"This Hawking bloke. He said this thing... Gavin told me this thing Hawking said, about if you end up in a black hole, don't give up. You can get out. We can get out of this, Sumi."

"You have a great yearning in you. I hear it in your voice. I felt it on your lips. You are still hungry for life."

"I just want to get home to my family."

We're going to find a place out of the cold. The snow will melt. I'll get to Shannon and get back home.

"There is too much life here," she says, as the baby cries.

○

Around midday we come to a house with no smoke. I knock on the doors. The windows. I wait for an answer and then sure no one's home, I bust out the glass of the back door.

"Hello? We need help."

The house is empty. A family lived here, by the pictures. A pretty young couple and their baby. A boy. On the mantelpiece a wooden block engraved with the word GAGHERTY. I tear up some magazines and books and toss them into the fireplace. We sit in front of the fire a long time in blissful warmth.

Sumi stares into the fire. "Mairead? Are we dead or alive?"

"Try and rest. We've walked a marathon."

"How would we know?"

"I'm going to see if there's any food."

Rotten, withered fruit and veg frost over in fungus on a platter on the kitchen counter. Nothing to salvage. Shriveled bags of sugar and

216

flour guard some traces. A box of stale cereal. A packet of tea in an old Barry's box. I fill a teapot with some snow and hang it over the fire. We drink some shite tea and munch on cardboard corn flakes. She nurses the baby.

"Thank you," I say. "I just wanted to say thank you again. For helping me. I don't know if I did before."

"I was alone and afraid."

And there's no Santy Claus. "Thank you all the same."

"If I had not been, I might have been that man we saw with the scissors. I might have left you to die."

"You didn't. You're strong. You hear me now? You're going to make it. We're going to make it, the three of us."

She blinks. Tears skip down her cheeks.

"It does not matter if we live or die. We are the dust of a dead star drifting across the empty field of the universe."

She was so kind to me. So caring. And she's disintegrating. She must have been before. What caused her to stop at the coach? She was afraid, I suppose. It's no deep mystery. Fear motivates everything. I don't know what to do. I don't know how to help her. I put my arms around her. I kiss her wet cheek. Such a pathetic gesture compared to what she did for me back on the road.

"Get some sleep. Do you want me to hold the baby? Why don't you let me hold the baby, and you get some sleep?"

"It is all the same," she says, and passes the baby to me.

Sumi stretches out in front of the fire. I pull the blanket over her. Later I'll go up and bring a mattress down. I'll try and seal up some of these doors and windows and insulate the room as much as I can. All that can wait. Right now I've got all I need. Right now I'm holding you. Ma's holding you.

Mo leanbh. Mo stór.

○

In the fields behind the house I find a cow in the snow. Her ribs form a fence in her hide but I get her back to the stables. Milk comes hard and thin and but there's enough for me to boil and then churn for butter. Back in the corner of the stables I find a dog. A Labrador, like. She reminds me a bit of the dog back on the island. Border Collie. I miss him. Strange. It's been weeks now since I left. Months. It's near Christmas. I'm sure of it. The dog is very pregnant. Barely able to move. I give her some of the milk.

"I'll be milking you next," I tell her.

○

I pick a day I think is Christmas and we celebrate with some bread and butter. Christmas without you. I never thought I would make it this far. I give Sumi my thanks. I have only my gratitude. Sumi gives me the baby and stares into the fire.

○

We have been in the house for over a week.

The sky falls in snow. The towels and blankets I line the windows with grow hard with cold. Our dishes and trash pile round the mattress. The toilet crusted with our waste and my sick and Lord God the smell. I wake up sick every day. I wallow in fear. Sumi disappears into this haze in front of the fire. Our entire world reduced to this room, this clutch at the hearth, staring into the light but it's not light she sees but the darkness it begets.

It's not hard for me to imagine her headspace. Still I can't know it. There is no measure in grief. Every person's grief is its own world. It's own universe. She's trapped, in one of her universes, living and dead at the same time. All I know is she's lost. We're both lost. The longer we stay here the darker your mind gets. Your soul. The house groans with complaints we can't voice. This is the worst winter I've ever seen in Ireland. Snow to make New York blush. We have to get on. I can't make it with all this snow. The snow hangs around like a bad lover. The days slip through my fingers.

The weeks.

O

The dog gives birth to seven puppies. She struggles and I help her along, pressing them down out of her, pulling them into the chill of the world. I name them after Snow White's dwarves. Such tiny things. A pinch of life. They moan for a tit and she lies there in the straw, arm curled in the air, letting them find their own way.

I rub her head. "Ah, they're class. They're class."

O

All the books are gone.

Newspapers and magazines and inn tables and chairs we don't use. Most of the hay in the barn. I leave some for the cow and the dog and the puppies. The runt died. I couldn't help it. I go out to the trees lining the field and hack off some limbs. We are destroying the house and the world around us to feed this room and this room is a stomach of fear. A cave of shadows. Sumi stares into the cold fireplace.

I can't take this anymore. "We can't wait for the snow."

She shakes her head. "It is all the same."

"Sumi. I think if we can get to proper help, for the baby and... I have people, back home, waiting on me. Depending on me. And I need to get back to them. I do."

"It makes no difference if we are here, or Shannon, or this island. The past or the future. Alive or dead."

"It makes a difference. We need to think about the future. For your baby. For mine. My future is waiting for me back home."

She blinks. "You have hope. Even now."

A dirty word, hope. I never let myself think it and yet what was I sitting there at the shore for, if not hope?

"We need to get on, Sumi."

"My mother once said hope is ignorance."

Sounds like her ma and mine would get on. "We need to go."

"There is no hope. I have seen cities burn. The sky burn. My country no longer exists. It is lost to volcanoes and tsunamis and now nuclear anger. Japan is a myth now. I regret I married him. Do you regret your husband?"

"I regret..."

I regret everything. All of it. But it happened. God help me, it happened. I can't change it or rewrite history. We're not living in the history branded on us, or the future still hot on the poker. We can still choose. We can make our lives. All I can do now is get home and make what I can of what's left. I wish you never died, I wish he never came but I want to go home. I want to be home with my family. Please God let me get home. Let me make peace of this.

I want peace.

"A couple months ago... I was where you are now," I say. "I was staring into the fire. And then... I didn't want anymore in my life but... I opened my heart for a moment and now here I am."

"Lost," she says.

"I don't know. Maybe I am. Maybe I should be angry. But I was going to die there. I had tried so many..."

"Then why go back?"

I don't know what to say. "It's my place."

"You are living to die," she says. "I am dying to live. I think about killing myself. I want to die, but I am dead."

"Then why bother feeding her?"

She winces her smile. "You are feeding her, Mairead. The same milk and butter you are feeding to the dog I smell on you. You are wrong to put a dog before yourself. Or a baby."

There's no telling her. She's lost. Part of me thinks I can talk her out of it the way Gavin did me, but she doesn't want out. I wanted out. God help me. I wanted out.

I stack the limbs in the fireplace. I rub our flinting sticks together and breathe fire into the wood. Nothing changes on her face or in her demeanor. There is no difference to her now, between warmth and cold. Light and dark. I scoop up the baby and I sit in the recliner and I rock her to sleep.

○

The next morning I go out to the barn to milk the cow. The puppies float in the pail. Bloated chunks of flesh like doughnuts left in coffee. I want to scream but I don't scream. I have only thanks to give Sumi.

She will get nothing more.

I go back to the corner. The dog rests on the hay. This shame on her face. The glue of tears in her eyes. I sit with her and I stroke her saggy belly. There's no way.

There is no fucking way.

○

Out at the tree line I hack up the wood for her fire of the universes. Nice, thick clubs of kindle. Full up I march back to the house and in the bunker we made of the Gagherty's living room I set down the bundle of sticks, less one. Sumi stares into the darkness of the fireplace. The stick trembles in my hand.

I drop it. "I'm taking the baby."

I grab up some butter and bread and everything I think I need and Lord God I'm leaving. I'm leaving with the baby. Someone else's baby. She never tries to stop me, Sumi. She never says a word. The snow hasn't melted. The cold hasn't lifted. If I go now, I go on foot in the frost of winter's last breath. My chances of getting far are slim.

I don't look back.

CHAPTER TWENTY-ONE

Hours I walk.

A lidded sun makes embers of clouds over the countryside. Forget going back to the M6. I can't go so far out of my way just to track back. We'll find a way south. I will get you to a better country, I swear to God. I cut through fields. Branches of developments. I go house to house searching for food. Sometimes there's a forgotten bag of crisps or bag of coffee grounds and I make due. I don't feel hunger as I should. Once a person reaches a certain stage in starvation, you stop feeling the need for it. Your body digests itself. I must be starved. You must be. I have to stay strong for you. I have to stay healthy. I think about going back and doing what I need to do with the cow. The dog, even. But that would mean dealing with Sumi and I'm hungry and I'm furious with her but I've no stomach for blood.

All the signs and markers have gone to snow and water. Branches scratch cracked windows. Downed power lines slither across pavement. The fields mud. Every step a battle. Every mile a war. I win, but what do I lose. Days. Hope. I limit our walking to only a few hours each day. The days grow longer but they aren't proper days, like. Gray hangs in the sky. Ash streaks the snow. I don't know if this is the ash of bombs or volcanoes. Radiation terrifies me and we lose full days inside one house or another but I can't risk us getting sick. There's no getting to Shannon if I get sick. There's no getting home.

I'm coming home.

○

You get used to your now.

The torture of not being home, of not seeing their faces every day gives to this acceptance. Your mind mimes the shape of your hell to protect you, to insulate you in another layer from the daily shock, the constant pin and prick of waking up hungry and cold and alone out of dreams where he's come to get you. I wake up in the dead night and he's there, Gavin, come from the island to find me here. *I found the pilot,* he says. *We've flown all over searching.* He lifts me up in his arms and carries me out of the country like he did the shore and he's carrying us, the both of us.

I have to get on.

○

The drip of melting snow plops from the roof down to the front stoop. Ireland shines in the crystal of shrinking snow. The road goes slush but we get good walking days. The air warm, and the breeze invigorating. Birds drop pins on where mice and other little bitty things come out their burrows and I become a bird in mushy fields, waiting, watching and diving. So long as there are birds there's no radiation.

Steady on now.

○

I roast rabbit and squirrel and mice and I'm good with a knife. Da taught me a thing or two, throwing lines off the shore. We will be good and full on the road tomorrow. We will be sturdy on our legs and we'll make up all this lost time. We'll get home. Hold on for me, baby. Buddy. But you're here.

You're here with me.

○

In the morning I see the first people since Sumi.

Limping ghosts under dirty blankets. A man and a woman, I think, walking north toward us on the road. Fear surges through me out from behind some door I didn't even know I had yet. I'm a woman and an infant trying to get home in a shambles of a country at the end of the world. I have everything to lose. I hide in the ditch with the knife in my hand and wait for them to pass.

Why are they going north?

○

From the road I see smoke.

A town. What town I don't know. I think I'm past Craughwell now. I'm reluctant to go into town, but we need supplies. Out in the country people keep to their houses and shelters but in a city, even one so small as this, I fear it's going to be Henry St. in Dublin the day before Christmas. Everyone will be pushing and shoving and grabbing and no one can move because there's nowhere to go. There's nothing else for it. We need food. I can find a bike. Something. I can keep us going. I don't know what day it is. It's been a week since we left Sumi. Since what I thought was Christmas. Is it the New Year?

Lord God. It's Gort. I'm in bleeding Sort.

I'm on the N18. I'm south, like. I let out this squeal. It's embarrassing. I've never been so glad to be so embarrassed. The river flooded over the banks. Security fences curl up in tatters over the busted doors and windows of all the shops in the town square. I don't bother going in. Mousetraps. I go through the refuse bins. I follow the dogs. I might have to do with one of these dogs.

People make lumpy figures out on the steps of the church. A man and a woman under ash stained blankets. I think it's the two I saw on the road the other day. But they were headed north. We all look the same now. They see me. No point in hiding. The woman waves at me, meek like. I wave back.

How easy you forget.

Lord God. The state of them. Someone bandaged their burns, or they bandaged themselves. Either way they did a shite job of it. Jealousy greens their eyes. I am long in need of a bath and a change of clothes but I have health. Strength. The frayed ends of posh clothes flare out from under the borders of their layered fleece. Once polished and manicured shoes flop like the mouths of dead fish off the edges of their soles. These are people who lived in condos and river view apartments and did not look at me on the train but down into their mobiles, listening to their sounds or updating their status.

The man coughs. Gavin's age. Under weeks or months maybe of dirt and scabs and sorrow he looks a much older man.

"Have a seat," he says.

I shake my head. "Thank you, no. I have to get on."

"Sit down. You've been walking a while."

"Just a Sunday stroll. And yourself?"

"Couple Sundays worth. Where you from, then?"

"I don't suppose you know where I can find any food?"

"You some kind of comedian?"

"Shall I tell you my life story?"

"Can I see your baby?" the woman says, and just invites herself to do so. She peeks under the blanket I've got over you and I take a step back. "Is that your baby?"

"I have to get on."

"Where did you get it?"

"A stork. Don't you know?"

"You've come out of the north," her man says.

There would be no telling my direction from their perch here. These are the same two. They've followed me. Why am I so afraid. The two of them are sacks of potatoes on the steps, like. Bags of air inflating and deflating with weak breaths.

I keep the knife tucked in my sleeve always. The blade against my arm. The grip in my hand.

"I'll be going," I say.

"Where?"

"All the best to you."

"You don't want to go south," he says, and coughs again. He spits scarlet on the walk in front of me. "Trust me."

I take a step back. "You've come from the south?"

He rubs his hands. "We seem to be talking past each other."

"Did youse come from Shannon?"

"Don't bother with Shannon."

"Why not?"

"There's nothing back the way we came."

"I heard there was a command post."

"There's nothing. No one."

I don't know if I believe him. "There has to be..."

"It's not safe, a woman being on her own as you are. You should come with us."

"Can't think of a single reason why I would."

"We can use a laugh." He says it like it's already decided. Like I'm going with them whether I like it or not.

"I'll be leaving you now. *Slan.*"

He sheds the blanket like it's a cocoon and passes it off to the woman. A sliver of a thing layered in three or four hoodies and still she shivers to her bones.

He has a gun in his hand.

"How about we do this," he says, cocking and uncocking the hammer. "I ask you a question, you answer. You ask a question, I answer. Seeing how that's all either of us have got right now."

I grip the knife in my sleeve. "If we had answers, we wouldn't be here on the steps of a church, now would we?"

"You are a comedian. Funny lady."

"I kill people dead."

The woman shifts under her blanket, a wary look in her eyes. The man dangles the gun nonchalantly.

"You're not seeing the big picture here. Maybe you're a little foggy in the head, yeah? All those days walking in the cold without food. Maybe you're spent. Tell you what. How about you give us the baby. We'll take care of it."

He's serious. "Now who's the comedian?"

"It's not your baby," the woman says. Angry, like.

"What do you want her for?"

The man points the gun at me. "If you would."

"Over my dead body are you taking this baby from me."

"No need for this to get violent," he says.

"I'll just tell you. I've had guns pointed at me. And I know a man's nerve. You've none. If you wanted me dead, you'd have done it instead of playing at whatever scene you saw in one of your disaster films. Are there even bullets in that gun?"

He snorts. "I don't want to have to hurt you."

I drop the knife. "We've an understanding, then."

This look of anxiety shimmers across his face. "What do you think you're going to do with that?"

"Hurt your woman's feelings."

"You think you're smart, don't you?"

"I know where your carotid artery is."

"Go," the woman says. "Just go."

A smile burns like an ember on his lips. "Yeah. Go."

"*Slán*," I say, and get moving.

"You should put that baby out," he says. Like she's a cigarette. "There's no place in this world for babies now."

I keep on. Always keep going. Every minute or so, I look back to see if any one follows. I walk into the night, nearly backwards. Hand on the grip. I don't make any camp I can't pick up in a hurry. I don't build a fire. I don't sleep. Don't worry. No one's taking you from me.

I'm never letting you go.

○

"Don't say it," Ma says.

I haven't slept. I haven't eaten. I'm hallucinating, I am. A fire sprouts virgin from the ground and she's right here with me in the trees off the road. The lines of her face washed away in the soft, lunic glow of the flames. She's so young. Look at her. She's a beautiful young woman, my mother. Strong.

"What's happening?" I say.

"Another baby? Oh, you don't listen. I may as well be talking to the rocks. So I told your father."

"They'll see," I say, and look toward the road.

"That woman he's with has some sense. Leave sense to the women, I say. A man can only be trusted to follow his blood. Though to be a man. Flush with blood. I would have liked to have been a man. Sex shouldn't be skin. It should be like clothes. Something you can take on and off. Don't you think?"

"Who are you?"

"That Japanese woman was lovely," Ma says. "Broken, but lovely. She took you in, by God. To your knuckles."

"Lord God."

"I've never seen you blush so."

"Please. She's not the first girl I've had a hand in."

"You were always quick. I suppose you had to be. You didn't get all the time your father and I did."

"I'm fucking mental, like..."

Ma sighs. "Where do you think you're going?"

"Shannon."

"For what?"

"To get home."

"I told you," she says. "I don't want you here."

"Why are you doing this to me?"

"Go where the road takes you. But let me go. Let us go."

"Ma..."

"We're all hung with the stones of the dead but we're not tombstones, girl. We're not epitaphs. We're that bit between the dates. Most of us forget that, but you're one of your birds, aren't you? Free. You're free, Mairead. Do you hear me? There's nothing or no one here needs looking after now."

"Don't..."

She touches my face. My mother. "You're free."

"Everything I'm doing is to come home..."

Ma peels back the layers of my coats a bit, so she can get a proper look at you. She smiles, the woman who couldn't be bothered with children. She smiles big and bright.

"Not everything," she says. "A girl. I knew you were a girl. It's not that I didn't want you. I didn't love you. I feared for you. Your joy. But you had such courage. You wouldn't be told... you found joy in your life. You found hope."

In the blink of an eye, she becomes the woman I left weeks ago. Old. Tired. Confused.

"I'll never forgive myself... sometimes I sat there and wondered did I envy your joy so much I... you showed him so much love. Where? Where did you find the courage to show..."

"Ma."

She kisses me. "Don't cry. Girls cry."

"It's ok to be a girl, Ma."

"You were my girl."

"Stay with me."

"Don't worry for us. And don't look back."

"I want to come home. Please."

The light of her goes out. We're alone again in the dark. No telling how long until morning. Until the day that isn't the day, and the dark that's only a lesser dark than this.

CHAPTER TWENTY-TWO

Here I am.

Alone at the end with a baby. As I was. I hold out my arms for you and my arms fill. All this love. All this life, again and again. It just won't end. There's no end to this drifting. Like the snow, I am. I dig at every strange mound. I throw back the lids of the trash bins uncollected since before the war. Dead cats cool in their morgues, trapped inside trying to get some food. Diamond flakes glint in the sunrise as I let them thaw. We've not had any more accumulation in days. I think the worst of the snow is over.

Let the worst be over.

○

Voices wake me.

A dozen or more people headed south on the M18. Men, women and children. They draw knives and clubs when I come out of the trees. I'm no trouble for them. They're headed to this same sliver of hope I am in Shannon. *You'll be safe with us.* At some point I ask the woman beside me if she's trying to get home. She laughs.

There's no home for us to get to, she says.

○

Growing up on an island, you know when the sea is close. Before we are properly in Shannon, I know she has gone to the tides. The airport. The city they built around it. There is no command post. No helicopters. No planes. No getting back. I don't know if I accept this, or like the sea, reality just imposes its will on me.

○

For some, this is as far as they go.

There is nowhere else and nothing left in them, besides. A man strips off his clothes and walks out to sea. The brutality of a wave denies him his grace. He is simply run over and dragged back to shore, unwanted. The sea will not take us on our terms.

Ireland erodes before me. So does my hope. I am a fool to come here. I am a fool to think I was ever getting home. Seven miles away, I was. I could see the island.

Almost.

What did I do so wrong to be punished like this. Who did I hurt. What crack did I step on and where to break all our backs like this so we are fucking moaning and paralyzed as the end washes over us. You are cursed to have found me, baby. You are quick now to your end.

We all are.

○

Some say there are people in Limerick. A relief mission or maybe the NATO has relocated there. I know this can't be. Shannon is the airport and if there's nowhere to land, then there's nowhere to land.

Where would anyone go now, anyways. What isn't drowning is burning. What isn't burning is freezing.

What else can I do.

I chase hope. On I go, following the river toward Limerick. The opposite direction. Lord God. If someone had told me before I'd die in Limerick, I would have thought I'd be nineteen and pissed so I choked on my own vomit. I should be so lucky now.

○

We reach Limerick with a glimmer of light left in the day.

The river laps against the gray stone walls of the castle on King's Island. Torch fires burn in the courtyard, illuminating the turrets as they must have done on medieval nights. Fires flicker behind buildings climbing the drumlin of the island. I turn off the bridge to the castle. All of Ireland pools in this one wounded place. Thousands of haggard faces line the street. Strangers huddle together under blankets, shelters made of shopping carts, each of them hung with an address or advertisement of who resided within.

EMMETT ROURKE, BANGOR. EVA and SIOBHAN MAGUIRE, ARMAGH. JAMES O'HAGAN, FATHER of MARY AND KATHLEEN, DROMORE, EVER HOPEFUL.

The smell of gangrene and infection curls my nose. Mounds of people torn and unspooled like overburdened trash bags set out for collection. Shops and storefronts have become murals depicting an apocalypse and exodus in blood and shit and anything that could be made paint. Mushroom clouds of orange and blue. Skeletons marching through the evaporated Falls Road. The living drifting across the horror of the north, breaking against a peace line rent as a wave curling over their heads right before it drowns them all.

THERE IS ONLY PEACE IN DEATH. PEACE IS COME.

Some gibberish. *Ónen i-estel amar, ú-chebin estel anim.* As many hold their hands out to me as offer me the petrified crust of bread, or a tiny mandarin orange from a tin, cupped in their hands like a little baby fish. Not for me.

For you.

You suckle on the orange piece and I gush in my thanks. I have nothing to give in return. Nothing but you. *Mo leanbh.*

All I have.

Headstones prickle the surging river. Light glows within the windows of a large church. This sound emanates from inside. A relentless, piercing hum. Numbing in its pulsation. Hundreds line the floors. No speck of marble visible. The majesty of the pipe organ swells within, filling the white walls, the wooden canopy stretching high and far above like a forested night, its cubbies of hushed prayer, its gathered suffering, its wafting and sickening despair.

"Is NATO here?" I say, deep in the bent grass of lost humanity. "Is there a relief mission?"

As I walk through the pews, stepping around and over the people laid out under cardboard signs naming them to lovers and family and friends or blind hope, I realize everyone has come here with the same question. Everyone has found the same answer.

I sink to an open spot on the floor. I sit there with you, with nowhere else to go. An old man holds a radio to his ear. He motions me closer. A voice crackles from the speaker. Hope flushes through me. Batteries. Voices. It's the government. NATO. They're still broadcasting, still communicating, still there. I put the radio to my ear, the voice low and difficult to hear with the organ. It's a woman. Irish. She sniffs, like she's crying. Paper ruffles in her hands. I think she has small hands.

"And now for today's death notices," she says, and my heart plummets. "Once again we will relay any notice reported from anywhere. To anyone within the sound of my voice, please report if you can. There are a great number of us on the road this new year, and we here at this location will make every effort to announce all Irish who have made their way home. Christopher, if you're listening... I hope you can hear me and I hope you can let me know. I hope you all can hear me, in Dublin, in Galway, in Cork and Limerick, in Belfast... wherever life lives still."

Lord God. I take the man's hand.

"This broadcast is transmitted on radio waves radiating into space. They will carry a long way, and a long time. Our voices will be heard, even after... I read now the known dead, as reported to this location. I pray this message either brings you hope or peace."

Sobs quake through me. I'm undone, the same as all the others here in the church, seeking salvation and hope and finding only the cliff's edge of reality. You find the curl of my finger. Squeeze with your little hand. So strong. So much heart. Such spirit. Such life. You had such life, Declan. I sat there at the shore, waiting. Searching. I couldn't feel you. You were just gone. I wanted to come home. I wanted us together. The same earth. The same cold. The same dark.

But you're not there.

You're not dust. You're the ache in my legs sore from walking to you. The blood on my dry lips. The scars you left on me. The milk that beads on my nipples, even now. My body flush yet with the kiss of your life. *Mo leanbh. Mo stór.* Declan. I feel you. You're here. You're with me.

Here I am.

○

I help the wounded as I can. There is little I can do but soothe fear and hold hands. The city the nursing home. This wounded country. Aoife. Are you there yet. Did you hold on, or did you do as I told you and empty the cupboards of the morphine we'd been holding on to.

I can't think of it.

I didn't think I could bear watching all my love die, but I can't bear this. I can't bear this not being there with them now at the end. This exile. This not knowing what becomes of them. This immunity to death. I cannot drown. I cannot be swept away down the river out to sea and back to home, not for all my tears.

Gavin.

The both of us wanting for a home. The both of us pulling each other out of our orbits. The heart has its own gravity. Weak or strong. Right or wrong. If I could have held it all. If I could have been strong enough for us all.

I wasn't.

That song. The Sundays. What did she say. I used to sing it in bars in the city as the people were talking on their cells. Drinking their drinks. Dreaming their dreams.

If he'd lived. If he'd lived, and Gavin had come to the island. But would we have met. We were never going to meet any other way. This was the only way for us.

At least we walked it together for a bit.

○

A girl blinded in the death of Belfast asks me where she is. Limerick, I tell her, but she doesn't know; she's English. Nottingham. I ask her about the forest and she laughs. There's no forest. I describe the town to her, the island, the river. *Sionann.* Granddaughter of Lir. A goddess. She came to Connla's Well for wisdom but life being what it is, the well burst and she drowned. The girl wrinkles her nose. Such are Irish stories. If you're a goddess, expect to drown.

○

Church bells wake me.

Everyone trickling outside. I gather you up and follow the crowd out on the street. This flutter in the air. The sound gets louder and louder. This drumming echoes off the buildings, off the street, off us and then a helicopter lowers out of the sky over the swelling banks of the Shannon, down into the courtyard of the castle.

Lord God.

A thousand people surge down the narrow street toward the

castle. An apocalyptic Pamplona. I fight just to get back in the church to avoid getting trampled. Some aren't so lucky. I hold you close as I rush through the emptied church out the side. Not as many people have come this way. The way open and clear for us. I dash through the car park for the castle. The helicopter blades like machine gun fire. I fight my way through the crowd to the castle gates, where a vicious bottleneck forms. The kindness and generosity that has marked my time here evaporates in seconds.

Through bars of people and iron, I see the helicopter. Huge, like. Two rotors, on either end. The back opens and lowers into this loading ramp. Men inside. They've come for us. Lord God. I'm here. Please. We're here. Don't go without us.

I'm pushing and people are pushing on me and the iron gives and we flood into the courtyard. Soldiers come down the ramp with machine guns. They fire into the air and most everybody drops to the ground. I keep running. Another soldier throws out boxes of food on the cement. Bundles of blankets. Litres of bottled water. The helicopter starts to lift off.

Please.

The soldiers signal for the pilot to get going.

Wait.

I fight my way through the crowd, on their feet again. Boxes of food shred in people's hands. Flaps of cardboard become weapons. They punch and kick and claw over bags of flour. Army issue rations. They won't let go. Some die for their hunger.

Wait.

People swamp the ramp. The soldiers fire more warning shots. Wait. The helicopter sags back to the ground. I push and claw and fight through and the soldiers fire right over our heads. The crowd parts. The helicopter rises. I take you from the sling. I don't know. A plea for mercy. The baby.

Don't leave the baby.

A crewman is on the edge of the ramp, his hands out, imploring the people rushing at him to stay back.

I lunge to the ramp. The edge hits me in the stomach and you pass from my hands to his. He cradles you in surprise as the helicopter climbs away. I stand there with my arms to the sky as you rise. You rise away. And then you're gone.

You're gone.

Mo leanbh. Mo stór. All I have. My arms go slack, strung out and thin from holding on so long.

CHAPTER TWENTY-THREE

Days pass without any telling.

The sky off kilter. Speckled with comets collided across the night. There are no more helicopters. No more food. No more possibilities of escape. The streets rivers of suffering and misery. Death hangs over the city like a pungent fog. My own stink. I don't dare go in the river to wash. Bodies float through it like driftwood. Dogs pick at the beached dead. People kill the dogs for food. All night this scratching and gnashing and I keep to the church.

I think I will die here.

○

Dogs sniff through the church. Struggle echoes off the marble. Desperation. I move up the altar, my back to the organ, where I can get a look at the church in front of me. My hand on the knife under my cuff. And then I see him.

The dog.

The Border Collie. Looks just like him, anyways. I stand up out of the sleeping and the dying massed in the church and I call for him. He scurries out the doors, spooked.

I run after him.

I don't know why. Can't be him. I left him on the island. I'm seeing things now. Days without food. Proper water. Rest. I have legs in me yet. The dog scampers into a thick, low fog masking the street. I haven't dared leave the grounds of the church since the food drop. What passes for civility ends at the walls of the old church, at least among people. The dogs and rats don't observe any rules there. Glass shatters in the distance. Screams shatter the stillness. This isn't the dog. I'm just acting the maggot.

I'm just so desperate I think it's him.

The dog lingers in the fog beyond. A shade of gray. Waiting. Wait. I drift after him. He scampers down the street. Always leading me on. People. Bodies, at least. I clutch the handle of my knife. They line sidewalks and stoops, under blankets and slats of cardboard. Voices. Whispers. Everything close and everything a million miles away. The island. Nine miles away. Another world. Another life. What if I got back? What would be left of me? What use would there be in digging a grave for so little a scrap of humanity?

Some people sit on the curbside. Lost, like me. Where do you go. What for. The dog sits in the road, right beside them, as if he belongs to them. I step back, ready to run and the dog takes off into the fog again. A few of the people on the curb go after him. One man stays behind. A lump on the pavement, like breached bags of trash pilfered all up and down the street. I dawdle there in the street, torn between following the dog and racing back to the church. The man pushes up off the curb. I back away. Fingers squeezing the knife.

He resolves out of the fog, half the man he was. "Mairead?"

His clothes hang off him. Torn and dirty with grease and blood. Hands black with grime. But that's Gavin, under all that hell. He stares at me, like I must do him, each of us convinced the other is a phantom. After a moment, he reaches out and touches my hand. I flinch and so does he.

He nods, like he's mulling something over. "Am I dead now?"

If I am. I'm dead. Delirious. "Is the dog with you?"

He shakes his head. "Dog?"

"Gavin... is it you?"

He reaches inside his coat pocket. The pill bottle comes out in his hand, still full of his father's ashes. It's him. He's here. Alive. He falls to his knees. Tears streak through the grime on his cheeks. His head droops and he sinks to the ground, sobbing, a mound of defeated humanity again. The knife falls out of my hand. I kneel beside him, my arms open and I don't believe it. I don't accept it until they close around him. Until his heart competes with mine. His breath.

His relief.

O

His story after Inishèan comes in dribs and drabs, like the sunlight peeking through the fog days. All his words are heavy. Always so much to say. He doesn't have to say. I don't want to break the spell or chase away his ghost. Days go in Limerick without a word between us. Sometimes he thrashes in his sleep and I know his journey back to the island was as terrible as mine.

His journey back to me.

Inishèan was home to him. I knew that, and that's half the reason I sent him away. He had this peace there. This comfort. This sense of place that had been ripped from me and I was angry. I was sore. I wanted him to live, but not in peace. Not if I didn't have it. Lord God. He could have died with his mother, under a rain of bombs in Iowa. Gavin could have had his peace, but he left the airport in Dublin without boarding the plane.

He speaks slow, his head shaking sometimes like he can't believe what he's saying. He got in a taxi. There was a flash over the sea, like Sumi had said. The taxi died on the road. I was pumping life into Rosin's lungs and Gavin was walking, into the city. Fires breaking out. People running like mad. Planes falling out of the sky.

I don't tell him about the Russians.

Electrical fires had broken out all over Dublin after the bomb shorted the grid. The whole city burning, he says. Roads jammed. The only way west was the route he'd taken before. Airport, Heuston Station, a train, if there was one. The 90 bus to Heuston Station had been abandoned at the north foot of the O'Connell Bridge. An inflatable dam lay across the Liffey like a spent condom. Miles of defeated sandbags top the quays all the way down to the harbor. Bodies of suicides. People jumped from the tops of construction cranes. From the bridges, into the river.

Until Dublin, his father had been the only person he'd seen die. He's more ready to talk about this. The paramedics got him back after the heart attack, but Gavin says he had been without oxygen for over fifteen minutes. There was no brain activity. A ventilator kept him alive another three days as family gathered. I've been through this at the home a few times. The tears. The hanging on to hope. The final relinquishment, sudden as a parachute deploying. His family decided the machine wasn't what his father wanted, even though none of them truly had any idea what he wanted.

A few minutes, the nurse said. *It should only take a few minutes.*

His father kept breathing for four hours. His children sat around his bed, waiting. Encouraging him. *You can let go now.* And he wouldn't. His dad quit on a lot of things, but those four hours in the hospital room, his last breaths bubbling out of his lips, he wouldn't. Gavin sat with him the entire time, desperate to talk to him, to unload everything he had carried his entire life unsaid. The weight and the volume of it prevented that. He had kept his silence, swaying in the chair with the tide of labored breaths, winding down and then finding energy again.

"You don't have to say, Gavin."

He takes a breath. "I just kept walking."

Along the Liffey, he came on across one of the stations for rented bikes. Some still in their docks. The station terminal was dead. No way of unlocking a bike. Gavin spent an hour trying to dislodge one without damaging it. He got on the bike and pedaled down the road to Heuston Station. Buses and cabs left empty out front. Shouts echoed out of the building. Gunfire.

He biked on.

He kept going, past the War Memorial Gardens, onto the N4 and out past the Liffey Valley Centre. Fires on the Wicklow Mountains in the south. He came on the interchange for the M4. *An lár.* City Centre. *An Tuaisceart.* The North. *An tIarthar.* The West. Miles and miles of abandoned cars stretched into Ireland quiet. His only way west the bike. A few days. A week, tops.

"And then what happened?" I say.

Gavin stares off into the shadows of the crowded church. Months of strife in his eyes. Of hell.

I kiss his dry, broken lips. "You don't have to say."

He touches my cheek, like he still can't believe it. "I take it you didn't come here looking for me."

The words are as heavy for me. My story as terrible. His fingers brush my lips. I don't have to say.

His hand hovers over his heart. His fingers claw at his soiled shirt. "Do you think we're dead? Maybe I am."

"Gavin..."

Gavin looks down at his hands, scarred and callused. "I came to the island to scatter his ashes... I went up to the cliffs. I was going to do it. Who would know?"

"About the ashes?"

"I thought I would come to Inishèan and... something would open in me. Something would lift off, but... nothing happened. There was nothing. I felt empty and void. Everything was void. I was just going to step off the edge, you know. "

What do you say.

"But I didn't do it. I went back down to the village, to the pub and drank alone. Ate alone. Watched TV alone. Got up the next day, like always, did it all over again... and then I saw you, out in the cemetery. I saw you everyday. This fixture. Everything was slipping away from me. Falling apart. But you... I was lost. I found someone who was lost and I thought... I don't know what I thought."

"You thought of me," I say.

"I was so selfish..."

I take his hand. "We're here now."

"I'm sorry."

"We're here."

He grips my hand. "We are."

We don't deserve our fortune right now, finding each other again. We don't deserve this hell we've been cast into. We don't deserve our good or bad, we just receive it and I don't know why. I don't know why any of this has happened. God help me.

God help me receive it.

I slump against him. I don't have the strength to cry anymore. To stop him from speaking his heart. He doesn't have to say. He needs to say, somehow, and in speaking free himself.

He holds me close. "We'll get home. We'll find a way."

I look west into the church, toward the island. I look into gray, impenetrable stone. "There is no way."

"We didn't walk all this way to stop now."

I shush him with my fingers. "Walk with me for this bit."

With him, I feel safer wandering beyond the church.

We leave King's Island into Lower Park, looking for food. Medicine. Water. All the houses picked over. A fair few of them torched. We go on, energized with each other to the Shannon Fields. No one here in the green marsh along the riverside. Exercise stations rusting along the bike path, overgrown with weeds. The water seems calm. Clean, as far as rivers go these days. We take our clothes off and wade out to our waists. It's bleeding freezing. I squeal and splash and he laughs. It's the first laughter I've heard in longer than I can remember. He pulls me close. Cups water in his hand. Pours it over my hair. I don't care if we're dead. I don't care if it's a hallucination.

I like hallucinating us.

○

"I talked to your Ma," I say.

He drapes his shirt over the bars of an exercise station to dry in what little sun there. "You what?"

"Right before," I say, and choke back this sob. Everything hangs on those words. His mother's voice. The ruffle of her newspaper on the other side of the world. Ma, sitting in front of the dark telly, not knowing I'm gone or not.

Gavin sinks to the bench. "I don't understand."

Fog clings to the riverbank, hiding us from others. My shame. "She called for you... she was thinking of you."

His head goes into his hands. All those thoughts trying to get out. If he'd been there, to talk to her one last time. If I hadn't sent him away. If none of this had ever happened.

"I'm sorry," I say.

"What did she say?"

I barely remember. I don't know why I brought this up. Better to have not said anything. He sits there, all the lightness we found this afternoon gone. All the joy.

"She said... we all think we're the symphony. But we're just the instruments. We have a part to play. That's all."

He smiles. "Sounds like her."

I kneel before him. I peel his hands away and rest his head on my shoulder. "She sounded like a strong woman."

"She is," he says.

Gavin lets go of me. He goes to the exercise station, and reaches inside his jacket. The label is near worn off the pill bottle. The white of the cap long faded. The ashes this dark mass inside, solid and heavy in his hand, even now.

He looks toward the river.

I feel it, too. The gravity pulling us all back to the earth.

I go with him, down the path, through the grass. Branches silhouettes against the fog. The haze clearing with the day. The sun glints off moss covered rocks. A skinny tree splits the path. A burm of island sprouts in the river beyond. Tall grass. Trees. Gavin stops. He drifts off the path to the shore, into the water. His hand slips from mine as he unscrews the lid from the bottle. There's no hesitation now. No indecision. The ashes become a cloud of mud in the water. A cloud of fog. His father sinks into the bed of our country, to his rest.

CHAPTER TWENTY-FOUR

The sky changes.

The sun no longer rises in the east, but to the north. Weeks pass without a moon. The clouds flicker with aurora borealis or the war in the sky. Ash falls with rain. Snow. The tides lose the plot completely. The rhythm of high and low tide disintegrates into a hyper-furious march of battering rams of waves which swell the river.

Earth breaks with every hour.

People push deeper into the mainland. Many stay. Where else is there to go. Gavin and I talk about leaving for Galway. The plane is gone from the airport. He might have come back, the pilot, but I know he didn't. There's no way over to the island.

I don't think we could make a walk back to Galway. We're shreds of who we were. Our clothes a tattered flag hung from a rickety old pole. If there's food out there on the road, it's in someone's belly or deep in their bunker. Any boat we'd try and use to cross those tides is expelled from its moors, pushed up with the rest of the coast inland and we're here.

We're here now.

I am no longer sure of the days.

The sky never clears. The sun a memory. Days like suggestions. Hunger becomes a daily pain, like the numbing cold. Dogs prowl the church, unimpeded. Gavin and I sit with our backs to the wall, his arm locked across my chest like those safety bars in amusement park rides. What do you call it? The Tilt-A-Whirl. Except we're not moving. Nothing moves here, but death. Fear. Hope, out of every person, swift ahead of the knowledge this is it. This is it now.

One by one the homes of Limerick became pyres. The city twinkling with the stars of ancient nights, when people first came. When the smoke clears, when the sky breathes for a moment, the stars are all confused. Brushed aside with comet tails broad and white as sails. *Mo leanbh. Mo stór.* I'm coming to you.

Ma is coming, soon.

A shudder goes through the earth.

I come out the church with Gavin. The sky in the east shimmers. The light builds into a long pearlescent sheen across the sky, expanding and rising, rising, my eyes drawn up and up until my neck hurts, until the crest of the wave eclipses the sun.

Lord God.

The wave crests, and plunges toward us. The earth shakes again. A drop of water flecks my cheek. Another and it's raining and this wave will have breached the walls of Moher. The cliffs of the island. This is it. All of us, together.

I walk into the street.

Gavin grabs my hand. My feet don't touch the ground. I am

flying through the street, back into the church. Flying like a ghost. The stained glass windows shatter and the stone of the castle groans and screams build like a wave outside on the street, pilot to the water flooding the west and I hear crying. Screams.

My heart, pounding so hard it hurts.

We run up the winding stairs of the bell tower, past the slow and the damned. I don't have the breath. I crawl into the organ chamber. Water spits through the burnished pipes of the organ, the wave made music through the flues and *Higher,* Gavin says. *Get higher.*

I keep on up into the bell tower. He keeps pushing me forward, his hand on my hip, past those crawling on their hands and knees. He pushes me forward, over others and my hand grips his. I don't want to go. I don't want to go on and this wallop goes through the church. The building shifts. Dust spits out of cracked stone. I look down, God help me, at dark, foul water rising up the stairs.

Water pushes Gavin into me. He shoves me ahead. His fingers slip from mine. The water crests at my heels, gurgling with all it has swallowed and as it recedes it leaves nothing. No one. He's gone. Gavin.

No.

I chase the water back down the stairs. Everything and everyone recedes with it. Another wave surges toward me and I scramble the rest of the way into the belfry. I close my eyes and hold against the screaming below, the people swept up and smashed against the stone and the columns and the bars of the organ and flushed out through the broken doors into the sea rising around us. This is it.

And then.

The floor soaked and mopped with the heaving, manic bodies of the people who made it up the stairs. Through the window, I watch the wave careen over the island, into the country beyond. All of Ireland west of us drifts past.

○

The light of fires reflect off the bellies of low, dark clouds of smoke. The skin of Limerick melting off into a glob of flaming flesh floating on the dark sea. Houses clump together in a kind of sculpture garden accessorized with useless cars, playground equipment and signs of buildings long shuttered.

O

I expect him to come back.

Like a God damned yo-yo, him. Comes and goes. Comes and goes. I don't know if I sleep. If I dream. If I do, it's of him coming up the stairs. Him lifting me off my feet and the both of us flying home. I soar through the smoke and fog and ash of the end and we glide over the sea back to the island. We touch down on the pier. Everyone is waiting for us. Colm. Aoife. Ma.

Where did you go? Ma says.

I'm after walking, I say. *We've just been walking, Gavin and I. Do you know we've walked so far, Ma.*

Do you know, do you know, do you know.

O

The water never recedes.

Eight of us up here in the tower. No room. No food. No heat. No hope. The pipes of the organ below hum like tuning forks, struck every so often with floating debris. Bodies. Knocks go through the church from the impact of drifting cars and scalped roofs. My lips bleed with his name. Gavin. I don't know how long I can wait. Strange sounds roll across the city, through the church, behind the door in odd harmony with tears. A clawing. Scraping. Scratching. The world scurrying with the flood of rats. Days of it.

Days of Hell.

O

Finally, a man goes out the parapet of the tower. He jumps. And then another. Another. They go one by one into the water like rocks, plunking the surface, and then.

I am the last.

○

The scratching never stops.

Like someone's at the door and they're not leaving until they're received. The room groans heavy as the church settles and sinks and crumbles insidiously into the sea. I go to the parapet. Fog shields the ruin of Ireland from sight. A last mercy.

Knock, knock, knock.

Just below, a fishing boat bobs against the stone. Empty but for a broken paddle. There's no point.

Is there?

Where could I get to? Not home. Not now. I climb the ledge, ignoring the steady drum of bodies. The knock, knock, knock of that little boat, slim as a casket below. The scratching at the door. The call of death familiar, like you're in a crowd and you think you've heard your name on the voice of someone you know.

But it's not you.

Not yet. You keep on going, uncalled. You go back to your living. You must always go back to living.

ABOUT THE AUTHOR

DARBY HARN studied at Trinity College, in Dublin, Ireland, as part of the Irish Writing Program. He is the author of the sci-fi superhero novel EVER THE HERO. His short fiction appears in *Strange Horizons, Interzone, Shimmer, The Coffin Bell* and other venues.

Stay Up To Date At
darbyharn.com

 twitter.com/DarbyHarn

goodreads.com/darby_harn

amazon.com/author/darbyharn

ACKNOWLEDGMENTS

This book simply would have been impossible without the support and feedback of Gregory Janks, Shelly Campbell, Ben Kral, Sugu Althomsons, Lisa Hanneman, Polly Brewster, Wayne Santos, Jennifer Lane, Al Hess, Essa Hansen, and Sunyi Dean.

Thank you all so much.

- Darby

ALSO BY DARBY HARN

Ever The Hero

The Judgment of Valene

The Book Of Elizabeth